Mountain Men of Moonshine Ridge Volume 3

The Diazes

Rocklyn Ryder

Magpie Press

Copyright © 2024 Rocklyn Ryder

All rights reserved worldwide
No part of this book may be reproduced, uploaded to the Internet, or copied without permission from the author. The author respectfully asks that you please support artistic expression and help promote anti-piracy efforts by purchasing a copy of this book at the authorized online outlets.

This is a work of fiction intended for mature audiences only. Names, characters, places, and incidents either are the product of the author's imagination or are used fictitiously. Any resemblance to events, locales, business establishments, or actual persons, living or dead, events, or locales is purely coincidental.

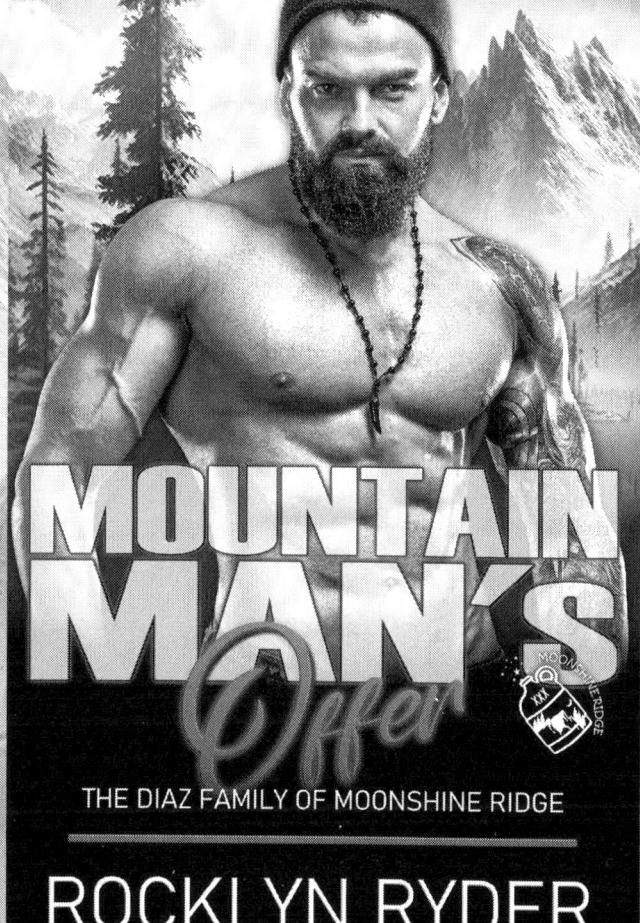

About
Vale Diaz

The pretty, young thing pouring my whiskey today is new around here. One look and immediately I'm a man obsessed. But Sparrow doesn't need a grumpy, ex-Marine hovering over her.

The corps left me with too many scars; both the kind that show and the kind that don't, for me to think this ray of sunshine would have anything to do with the likes of me.

Until some pencil-neck weasel comes into the bar one night while I'm nursing a drink I only ordered so I could see Sparrow.

He wants her back; orders her to walk off her job and come home with him this instant.

That's when I stand up, using all six foot, five inches of my wide frame to tell the nitwit to leave my fiancée alone.

Now Sparrow's stuck with me, pretending I'm the love of her life while we wait for her ex to give up and leave town without her.

But when our little charade crosses the line, I only have one chance to convince her that I'm not pretending.

Vale and Sparrow

Mountain Man's Offer

The Diaz Family of Moonshine Ridge
by
Rocklyn Ryder

Chapter One

Sparrow

Moonshine Ridge is about as far from Murfreesboro, Tennessee as I could get; just a tiny speck on the maps and a few thousand people in real life, at seven thousand feet above sea level, clear on the other side of the country from where I spent half my life.

My friend, Cami, and her husband run a bar and grill in this tiny community and I'm so glad I stayed in touch with Cam since we went our separate ways after the sixth grade when my family decided to move back east.

It's good to have someone in your corner when you need someplace to go, and Cam assures me Moonshine Ridge is a great place for starting over, or just hiding out.

Of course, she might be biased, since she came up here looking for a summer job and ended up landing herself a real-life, mountain man grump that thinks the sun rises out of her ass.

That's how I ended up behind the bar here at the Tavern, slinging drinks for the locals and envying the love my childhood bestie found for herself.

While I start filling a new pitcher of beer for Ozzie Lancaster and his buddies, I start daydreaming about finding my own mountain man happily ever after.

The first time Vale Diaz walked up to the bar and ordered a double rye on the rocks, I was done for: Black hair with just enough length that the curls can't be tamed, the full, thick beard, and dark eyes that have a way of making me feel like he can see my very soul.

The man is scorching hot. The kind of hot that could keep me a hell of a lot warmer on these long, dark, mountain winter nights than the pitiful wall heater in the room at the lodge that came with my job here.

He's also sixteen years older than me, with strands of silver running through his hair and beard, and lines at the corners of his eyes that crinkle when his eyes narrow with the scowl he always seems to wear.

Vale's been coming in nearly every afternoon, sitting on the last stool at the end of the bar, ignoring his drink while he watches me with his intense, dark gaze while I try to ignore my pounding pulse.

But no matter how I dream about this particular mountain man throwing me over his shoulder and carrying me off to his cabin to make me his own, he's never given even the slightest hint that he feels that way about me.

I guess I'll take what I can get and fill in the rest when I'm alone under the covers at night.

My thoughts are interrupted by the tavern's door opening; letting in the bright light of the January afternoon as well as a burst of the cold, mountain winter air, as a figure steps inside.

The man that steps inside isn't the one I've been waiting for.

Vale

I PROMISED MY FAMILY I WOULDN'T BE THE recluse vet-- staying holed up on the side of the mountain after retiring from my military career, never learning to live again-- so I started making a point to come into town once a week just to force myself to talk to someone I'm not related to.

That was a helluva lot harder before I discovered Sparrow behind the bar.

She's new to Moonshine Ridge; tells me she was friends with the owner's wife back when they were in elementary school, before her family moved to some place back east and gave her that sweet little accent that gets my blood churned up.

Sparrow's a ray of sunshine wrapped up in a curvy package that inspires a lot of inappropriate thoughts and I know a beat-up old man like me doesn't have a chance at getting a taste of her sweetness, but that hasn't stopped me from spending most every afternoon down here at Cedar McAllister's tavern to keep an eye on her like she was mine.

It's as usual a Tuesday afternoon as Tuesdays get here on the ridge as I pull the truck into the parking lot. I recognize Ozzie Lancaster's personal vehicle in the lot, along with Raine Hart's truck and a few other locals that don't have the kind of jobs to keep them from shooting pool over a couple pitchers of cheap beer on a weekday. A couple cars I don't recognize dot the parking lot as well, but that's getting more common this time of year since the ski lodge is open again.

I have my hand on the handle of the heavy, wooden door with my head full of ideas about the pretty, young bartender inside that remind me what a filthy bastard I really am, when I hear the shouting.

"Get your shit and let's get out of here, *now*, Spare!"

Inside the dark barroom, I can see Oz and Raine positioned between the bar and the shouting stranger while Sparrow has herself pressed against the wall behind them.

"I'm not going anywhere with you, Travis!"

"Dude, you heard the lady, you need to leave," Raine Hart tells the guy in a tone that's a lot calmer than I have patience for.

Sparrow's standing her ground but her body language and the quiver in her voice lets me know that this isn't just some drunk stranger acting up in the bar. She knows this asshole, and he's trouble.

Whatever the story is, I'll sort it later. Right now, it's pretty obvious that Sparrow's ex wants her back and she wants nothing to do with him...so I cross the room in a few long steps, grab the much smaller man by the collar, yanking him off his feet and backward while I shove him roughly.

At six five, I stand a good head taller than him and a quick guess says I outweigh him by a buck and a quarter.

"This is none of your business," he spits out at me when he sees the fury in my eyes.

God only knows what makes me say it, but the words are out of my mouth before I can think about them. I say the godawful thing I wish was true: "Anything you have to say to my fiancée is damn well too my business."

Chapter Two

Sparrow

This is probably not the most appropriate time for my panties to soak through, but ohmygosh do they ever.

Maybe it's the sheer power he exudes as he stands over the smaller man, maybe it's the protective stance as he makes it clear that no one is getting through him, maybe it's hearing Vale claim me as his in front of everyone standing around gawking at the intrusion into the sleepy community's usually calm afternoon.

Vale flexes slightly, his wide shoulders drawing back as his body gathers energy like a snake preparing to strike.

Travis's eyes widen, taking a good look at the mountain of man looming over him and staring down at him with murder in his eyes.

"You got fucking engaged, Spare?" Travis puts a solid two steps between himself and Vale.

"You've been gone for a month." He spits the words at me from his side of the bar and if anyone had missed the part where Vale called me his fiancée, they sure as hell heard Travis just now. "What did you do? Shack up with the first Neanderthal you could find up here?"

His eyes rake over Vale, who's still towering over him, his fists clenched at his side, steam virtually billowing out of his ears.

I'm so relieved that Vale is here. Without even thinking about it, I run straight for him and wrap my arms around him.

"You okay, Birdy?"

Vale's hand caresses the side of my face as he tips my head up to look him in the eyes.

He just called me his fiancée. Out loud, in front of the entire bar. And he already has a pet name for me?

"*Fiancée?* What the fuck, Sparrow, you've been out here a fucking month. What'd you do, give it up to the first Neanderthal you could find?"

Travis stares at Vale with open contempt as he goes back to his ranting. It's like he doesn't even notice that Vale's several inches taller than him and outweighs him by close to a hundred pounds. A hundred pounds that's all muscle, by the way, which I always suspected but now I know.

"Go stay behind the bar, Birdy," Vale tells me, giving me a gentle push away from him, "I'll be right back."

Reluctantly, I let go of Vale and go back behind the bar like he tells me to, where I find my cell phone already blowing up with messages from my friend, Cami. It's then that I realize how many of the locals have cell phones aimed at the scene and I realize that the entire town found out I'm engaged to Vale the same time I did!

Travis's feet are barely able to mimic steps as he dangles from Vale's grip while being unceremoniously pushed out the door and dropped in the mud and snow outside.

"Thank you," I whisper to Vale as soon as we're alone in the supply room where he dragged me away from the curious crowd that was gathering around us.

"Seemed pretty obvious you weren't interested in getting back together with him," Vale mutters, running a hand through the thick curls and pushing them off his forehead.

"Travis isn't my ex." I'm quick to clear up any misunderstanding there, taking a step closer to Vale before remembering that he only said what he said to get Travis to leave me alone.

"We worked together back home," I explain when Vale's eyebrows furrow, "he asked me out but I said no."

"I take it he didn't take that well?" Vale asks.

"He didn't really take it all," I admit, "he kinda built up a fantasy about us being a couple. I had to quit my job because he kept showing up and causing trouble. When I came to Moonshine Ridge, I thought he'd just give up."

For an answer, I get a grunt.

"I'm going to call Cedar and get someone down here to cover your shifts for a while," he tells me, pulling his phone out of his back pocket, "You're going to stay up at the springs with me till we can this asshole out of town for good."

"Look, Vale," I try to calm the hurricane inside my head and act reasonably, "I'd love to take you up on your offer and all but--"

"It's not an offer, Sparrow."

His tone is one hundred percent *"don't argue with me,"* and I would be lying if I said I don't want to hear him use that same tone with me in a totally different situation.

"An offer implies you can refuse."

Vale

My phone buzzes and I wince.

Steeling myself for what's coming, I accept the call, knowing better than to think the elderly woman smiling brightly from her photo on the screen is going to be sweetly asking if everything is all right in town.

Everyone on the Ridge knows who my grandmother is and the torrent of curse words punctuating the Spanish coming through the speaker of my phone is just a small reminder of how Marcia Diaz got her reputation.

There is no getting out of this now. My grandmother is still muttering when I end the call after promising that we'll stop by the house so everyone can meet my *fiancée.*

"I didn't know your grandmother spoke Spanish," Sparrows says once I've ended the call.

"Only when she's mad," I tell her.

"We're going to have to stop by my grandparents' place on the way up to the cabin," I tell Sparrow, not quite able to bring myself to meet her eyes. "I'm sorry I got you into this, but we can set the record straight about us when this is over."

Once I get her boss to send someone down to take over the rest of her shift, I walk with her back to the little studio she's been staying in at the lodge.

My grandmother's not the only one who wants to know why I hadn't mentioned being engaged-- or even dating. I've got messages coming in from all over the mountain. Hell, I didn't even know this many people had my phone number.

I kill the sound on my phone and slide it into my pocket.

Sparrow's foot slides out from under her on the icy asphalt and I catch her before she can hit the ground.

My words get stolen by Sparrow's sweet lips as they seal against mine.

I'm so fucking shocked; I don't even know what to do. I just stand there, still leaning down at her level, with my thoughts about getting her some decent fucking snow boots still whirling around in my head while her arms wrap around my neck and pull me against all those succulent curves like she fucking owns me.

It takes entirely too long to come to my senses and I'm sure I'm going to regret losing out on those precious seconds I could have been yielding to this beauty's kiss but I'm not about to waste any more of this opportunity.

My arm tightens around her, denting into the puffy coat she's wrapped in so that I can feel that curvy body properly.

I force my brain to give in and let this happen. Whatever reason Sparrow has for kissing me, it's a fucking gift from heaven. So I move my lips against hers, letting her set the pace and following her lead as she opens for me and slips her sweet tongue against mine like she's done it thousand times.

I'm wishing I'd trimmed my mustache before heading down to the bar this afternoon. No woman wants a mouth full of fur when she's kissing a man.

My cock is as stiff as the icicles hanging off the roof of the lodge and my hands instinctively reach for Sparrow's hips, digging my fingers into the plump curve of her ass and pulling her tight so she can feel my need for her.

Sparrow's arms move down my back. I can feel her small hands slipping under my coat as she settles even tighter against me and for one incredible moment, I'm lost in the heaven of feeling her body, supple and hungry against my own.

Of course, it's too good to be true.

"Sorry."

Her voice is breathless and shy as she breaks away from me, leaving me feeling a hell of a lot colder than the chilly winter air warrants.

"Travis is sitting in that car over there. He's

watching us," she tells me. Her mouth is still close to my ear, her arms still wrapped loosely around my waist, leaving space between us that I desperately want to close up again.

That makes sense. If we were a real couple, it'd stand to reason we might share a kiss or two. I guess she was just putting on a show, trying to convince this creep he came three thousand miles for nothing.

Chapter Three

Sparrow

"Half an hour," Vale tells me as the truck crunches over the recently plowed driveway of his grandparents' property. "I already told them we can't stay long."

It's hard not to laugh a little at the nervousness in his voice.

"You sure you're okay with this, Spare?" He pulls the truck up in front of four car garage and turns toward me before he even shuts the engine off. "I can tell them today's been too much for you. They'll understand."

"My high school Spanish didn't really cover most of the words I heard, but I'm pretty sure your grandmother is not going to be okay with us rescheduling." I let my hand rest lightly over the top of his where on the center console between us and I do my best not to think of how warm he is or how much bigger his hand is than mine and I definitely try not to think about what it would feel like between my legs.

I get a crooked smile from under the whiskers that I now know are much softer than they look.

Memory of my first real kiss comes flooding back and I'm glad the cab of the truck is dark enough that Vale can't see me blushing.

I didn't really expect him to kiss me back like that and I don't think I imagined the hardness pressing into my hip through my thick, winter coat.

"You're sure?" He asks, moving to engulf my hand in his.

"I've already met most of your family, Vale," I remind him.

Living in a community as small as Moonshine Ridge, you get to know just about everyone in town pretty fast.

"You haven't met my Abuela though." Vale's voice is wary with a hint of humor.

"But I've heard plenty about her," I point out, "Mable Hart's museum is just across the street from the tavern, remember."

"Don't believe anything that old woman says about my family," Vale gruffs, finally opening the door on his side to get out of the truck, "she's had it out for Abu and Alice since before I was born."

Vale comes around to open my door for me before I can get to it myself and I'm so lost in the sensation of his strong hand resting easily on my shoulder as he steers me around the side of the house to the door that leads direction to the kitchen from the back patio that for just a moment, I forget it's all fake.

Mountain Man's Offer

Vale

TWO HOURS INTO THE EVENING AND I'VE forgotten why I was so determined to get Sparrow out here in a hurry. It's obvious she loves my family and I knew they'd love her. The problem is that it's too easy to see her here forever. Too easy to watch her laughing with my baby sister, too easy to watch my brothers teasing her about her bad taste in men.

"Seriously, Sparrow," Glen jokes, "if we'd known you were into grumpy old mountain men, we'd have set you up with Howard Smalls."

The room roars with laughter at either my expense or Howard's, I'm not sure, but even I'm smiling. Because Sparrow is curled up beside me on the old love-seat sofa in the TV room where the wood stove is blazing hot enough that the French doors to the patio are cracked open a few inches, and she's got her free hand resting on my thigh just like we do this every night.

Her other hand is wrapped around a glass tumbler that my mother is currently refilling with a concoction she's calling a "horchata margarita" which I refuse to taste even though my little bird tells me it's pretty good.

"I can't believe you were going to put a ring on a woman's finger before you even brought her home to meet your family. I thought I raised you better than that, Vale Diaz." Mama tsks at me as she pats Sparrow's hand and carries the pitcher back to the kitchen.

Oh yeah, I'm in deep shit for that too-- bringing home a proper fiancée without a ring on her hand. Fortunately, that was an easy one to cover; as the oldest in the family, I get first dibs on my great, great, great grandmother Rebecca's ring which Abuela was eager to hand over to me in private as soon as she had a chance to give her approval to my choice in women.

Now the tiny box in my pocket is a harsh reminder of the situation I'm in, and thoughts of grandma Rebecca's original engagement ring, fashioned from gold that was mined from our own family claim here on the ridge back in the eighteen hundreds, sparkling on the same hand that Sparrow has resting over the denim across my thigh right now have me thinking crazy.

Of course, I'll keep the family heirloom safe and return it to Abu so she can hand it down to Mesa or Meadow or whichever one of us kids actually finds someone willing to marry into this crazy family.

"Las perras robaron las cabras!"

My grandmother bursts through the patio doors with what has to be the most impressive collection of curses that has ever been strung together in a single breath.

While Abu continues to swear, all eyes turn to my youngest sister, Terra, who had been out to the barn to help put the goats to bed for the night.

"They're gone," Terra explains, "all of them."

My grandfather already has Deputy Hawkins on

Mountain Man's Offer

the phone, Terra's yelling at Glen that the goats did not "just get out" of the barn, and in the background, I can hear my grandmother on the phone with her friend, Alice McAllister talking about some sort of revenge plot that might get them arrested-- again.

"We should escape while we can, Birdy," I stand up and give her hand a tug to pull her up after me. "This is going to get real ugly, real fast."

"Did Mable and Vera really steal your grandmother's goats?" She giggles as she lets me lead her through the mounting chaos toward the back door so we can sneak out before we get caught up in this mess.

"Probably," I mutter.

"They won't hurt them, will they?"

"The goats will be fine, Birdy. Not sure I'd make the same bet for Vera and Mable."

Sparrow looks back at the scene we're ducking out of with a smile on her face that makes my chest clench tight.

"Don't we need to talk to deputy Hawkins anyway?"

Is my girl really looking for an excuse to stick around and spend more time with my crazy relatives?

I chuckle deep and shake my head, thinking about what the new deputy on the ridge is about to get dragged into.

"I'll call Hawk tomorrow morning-- he's going to have enough keeping him busy tonight."

Chapter Four

Sparrow

It was so easy to get caught up in the energy of the family dynamic.

Everyone was so welcoming, and his parents were so immediately accepting; even though I'm so much younger than Vale, no one raised an eyebrow over our age difference or that we've known each other less than a month and are (supposedly) already engaged. The only issue the Diazes have is that the oldest son would dare to ask a woman to marry him before he'd brought her home to meet his family.

Their home is full of so much laughter, even Vale's usual stoic demeanor melted in the warmth of his family. It makes me see him in new light, what kind of father he would be, makes me wish this was real even more.

"So this was your great grandfather's cabin?" I ask as I follow Vale through the old house that was built large for its time, with three full bedrooms-- the modern bathrooms were added in the 1960s when his parents lived here as newlyweds, he explains.

"Great, great, *great*, grandfather. Martin Diaz, yeah. He built it for his fiancée, Rebecca Montgomery, as a wedding present."

I follow Vale into one of the big bedrooms that branch off one side of the house. Two queen size beds could easily fit in here, along with more than one dresser, but there's just one modest double bed to one side of the room, a dresser, and a comfy-looking arm chair, and a lot of empty space.

"Your grandfather was telling me some of the family history," I mention, stalling for time, desperately hoping for some sign that the affection he was openly showing in front of his family wasn't all a show.

"He said there are waterfalls near here that are named after your great, great, great grandfather?" I carefully tick off all three "greats."

"Yeah, Martin is the only person in history know to have survived going over them," Vale tells me, dropping my bag on the chair near the window. "The townspeople named it 'Diaz Drop' before anyone knew he was still alive though. Rebecca almost jumped off the falls too. Guess it's a good thing she didn't, or I wouldn't be here now."

Vale's brow furrows as he looks around the room like he disapproves.

"What happened?" I watch Vale straighten his shoulders and march over to the window and begin inspecting it as if it's somehow unsatisfactory.

Vale's grandfather, Alex, had been telling me some of how his great, great grandfather was one of the original founders of Moonshine Ridge back in the 1860s, and I definitely got the impression that there was a story behind it.

"This window needs new weather stripping," Vale mutters under his breath. Then he turns around and gives me a thoughtful look.

"I can take you down there on the snowmobile if you want," he tells me. "The old mule trail is a serious bitch of a Jeep trail in the summer months, but it's a beaut for the sled when there's this much snow on the ground to fill in the rocks and ruts. Maybe we'll go up there over the weekend."

Before I can enthusiastically agree to that plan, however, his dark eyes go hard again.

"I mean, if we haven't gotten things straightened out by then and you're still stuck up here with me."

How do I make sure I'm still stuck here with him?

Vale

I GIVE HER THE BEDROOM THAT'S RIGHT ACROSS the hall from mine. I like the idea of having her close and this is as close as I can put her without putting her in bed right next to me.

Much as I'd like that, I knew it's a damn bad idea. I've got no business even imagining Sparrow's soft curves pressed against me all night. Even if I could think of an innocent reason to share my bed with her, I know I'd never be able to resist touching her once she was there.

This old room would have been the nursery, and later, the girls' room, with the room on the other end of the hall for the boys; back when my ancestor built the house.

I always meant to remodel this room into a home gym. Someplace I could work out some frustration during these long, mountain winters when the storms close the road to town and I'm crawling the walls from loneliness.

Seein' Sparrow standing in here now has me thinking it'd still make a damn fine nursery again and suddenly my need her burns bright in my gut. I picture her, carrying our child on one hip, with her belly round with the next one and I'm overcome with the need to breed this woman. Plant my seed deep in her womb and watch it grow along with our love.

I have to put some space between us or I'll do something stupid, but Sparrow's still asking me about my family's history on the ridge. How did we end up with the hot springs, how did the Drop get named for us, how did my great, great, great grandfather survive his plunge over the falls and can we go see them.

I can't just run out of here while she's talking but I need some air. So I act like I'm checking on the cold draft coming through the window but really, I'm sucking in the fresh air and using every trick I can remember from my time back in the military to calm my breathing and keep my wits together.

Mountain Man's Offer

"Or you could wait till summer and have Hyacinth McAllister drive you up the trail in her Jeep," I back-walk my offer to take Sparrow up the trail this weekend quickly. I don't want her to think I'm expecting her to stick around once me and Hawk get her stalker run off the Ridge for good.

"She's the local expert on running the Devil's Driveway now that she's got that Jeep outfitted for the trail."

"Cami says that Hyacinth and Ash met up there on the river," Sparrow says, smiling at me and taking a step in my direction.

"Yeah, I'm sure she'd tell you all about how they met. They were quite the talk of the town for a while."

Sparrow's got me trapped between her and the edge of the bed and there's not a damn thing I can do to get out of here now unless I crawl over the bed. Believe me, I'm giving that some thought, because Sparrow's coming closer to me than is safe.

Shit. She probably just wants to pull down the bedcovers, fluff the pillows, whatever it takes for me to get the hint to get out of her space so she can get some sleep.

"I guess *we're* the talk of the town now, aren't we?"

Her laugh is musical as she comes up close and looks up at me.

The way she's looking at me has me going crazy. I know the way a woman looks at a man when she wants him and that's the look in Sparrow's pretty green eyes right now. Like she's begging for another rough kiss-- or maybe even more.

"Birdy," I lay my hands on her shoulders and I swear to God, I have every intention of stepping aside and heading for the door but her hands are on my chest, those delicate fingers toying with the buttons on my flannel shirt. "It's been a long day, maybe--"

But my feet are planted like they've rooted into the floorboards.

"I like it when you call me 'Birdy,'" she says, smiling while she pops a button undone.

Chapter Five

Sparrow

I was just going to hug him. Quick, light-hearted-- *friendly*. I was going to tell him thank you for rescuing me from Travis today and I wanted to say something about how much fun I had with his family tonight, but that's not what happens.

Vale stands there, right beside the bed I'm supposed to sleep in tonight-- all by myself-- like he's waiting for something. Like he wants to say something. It makes me think that maybe I'm not the only one who wants this to be real.

It makes me feel bold.

When I tell him I like his nickname for me, I don't even have to try to pull him down to my level, he's already there for me.

Vale's lips crush against mine, his arms lifting me like I weigh nothing and tossing me onto the bed beside us. Then he's over me, his mouth claiming mine again as I wrap my legs around him and revel in the feel of his hardness digging into my thigh.

Our tongues tangle and my hands are working to get under his shirt. I want to feel those hard muscles against my hands. Hell, I want to feel his hot skin against all of me.

I can't believe this is happening; that I'm in Vale's cabin with his weight pressing me into the mattress while his mouth burns hungry kisses down my throat.

His beard brushes against my neck, then between my breasts as he makes easy work of opening the button-front blouse I wore today.

"Fuck, Birdy." He breathes against a nipple and it has me arching my back and gasping for air. "Your tits are perfection, baby."

Those giant hands I've been eyeing for weeks wrap around my soft flesh and he sucks one nipple into his mouth and then the other, running a rough thumb over each one till I think I might come out of my skin.

"You like that, huh, Birdy?" His voice has gone even darker and now it has a rasp in it that makes him sound dangerous. Like he's feeling every bit as wound up as I am and like maybe if we don't stop now, there's not going to be an option to stop later.

"Mmmm, yes," I croon, arching my back to push my body closer to his.

Stopping is the last thing on my mind. All I want is for Vale to keep touching me, take that dangerous energy of his and use it to show me what a real man does with a woman.

"Good girl." He chuckles, gives one nipple another agonizing flick, and then his mouth is moving farther south and I feel my jeans undone as he tugs them off my hips.

Vale

MY LITTLE BIRD IS ALL SOFT MOANS AND squirming flesh under my hands and my mouth. It's like she can't get enough of my touch, like she's trying to feel me everywhere at once.

God knows I want to give her whatever she wants. If she wants my mouth on her, you can damn well believe, I'm gonna give her just that.

"Baby, what's wrong?"

But as soon as I get those skin-tight jeans of hers peeled down so I can spread her succulent thighs, I can feel the change in her; the eager woman who was yielding to my touch just seconds ago is suddenly shy in my hands.

"Nothing's wrong." It's little more than a yelp and when I raise my head to look up at her, Birdy's got her arm thrown over her eyes like's she hiding.

If I didn't know better, I'd think...

What the fuck am I doing? I'm a grown man almost twice this angel's age and I'm kneeling on the cold, wooden floorboards, practically drooling at the thought of getting a taste of Sparrow's sweet pussy.

I'm an asshole but I'm not a monster.

"We're getting carried away with ourselves." I press a chaste kiss against her knee and rock back on my heels. "I never should have let this get this far. I'm sorry, Birdy."

It's killing me; to get so close to heaven and have to turn away. But I'll be damned if I'm gonna take advantage of Sparrow. I'd rather die than have her regret a single moment she spends with me.

My shirt's off and I reach up beside her to grab for it when she sits up. Those pretty tits of her jiggle and sway, still on full, mouth-watering display, as her small hand does its best to go around my wrist.

"I don't want you to feel like you have to keep pretending you're in love with me when we're alone together, Sparrow. You don't have to take it this far; I don't want you to do something you'll regret. That's...that's not what this is about. I hope you know that."

It doesn't take much effort to pull my arm away from her, while I get to my feet and head back to my own damn room where I know I won't get a minute of sleep all night.

Chapter Six

Sparrow

Vale's barely through the doorway before I'm scrambling after him. He took his t-shirt with him, but his flannel is still in a puddle on the edge of the bed where I tossed it when I got it off him. Slipping it on, I leave my jeans on the floor where they fell and head to the big master bedroom across the hall.

"I'm not." I practically yell, pushing the door open without even bothering to knock first.

I'm kinda pissed off, to tell the truth.

Maybe I should be smart and take a hint but my body is still buzzing with need and the sudden loss of Vale's touch has me feeling achy and frustrated. I'm not thinking straight and maybe I'm not acting right either but I don't want him to think he did something wrong.

"Not what, Birdy?"

His deep voice comes from the side of the room near the big closet and the door to the master bath, it sounds pained and my heart clenches from thinking I fucked this up by getting embarrassed.

"Not pretending, Vale," I say softly. "I know I'm just a kid to you and that you're never going to want to really marry me and stuff, but I-I didn't want you to stop back there."

Light from inside the bathroom frames his large physique. The shower is running, but there's no steam billowing around him.

My mouth is suddenly dry, but that's about the only part of me that is. I can feel the course weave of the flannel against my nipples, sensitive from being so hard, and hot moisture pools between my thighs, soaking the panties that are the only thing I still have on under his shirt.

Vale's staring at me, naked to the waist, still wearing his jeans, his eyes dark and so intense I'm tempted to run back to my room, shut the door, and just give up.

"I know it's not real--" I swallow hard and brave a step across his threshold, my heart is pounding so hard it could be someone knocking on the door, "-- but I would never regret you being my...*first*."

My courage gives out on me and I barely manage to get the last word out at all.

When Vale's eyes flash fire and he moves toward me, I'm thinking I just put the last nail in my own coffin. He'll never see me as a woman after making that confession. He's going to order me back to my room and I'll be lucky if he even speaks to me after this.

"Your what?"

"Umm." He's right in front of me now. All those abs and that thick trail of hair running down his chest and into the waistband of his jeans on full display and making my hands itch to touch him again.

It's just-- I've never done that before," I say weakly.

"You've never had a man's face between your legs before, Birdy?"

There's heat in his voice that makes my clit come to life and throb at the very idea of Vale with his head between my legs.

His finger comes up under my chin and tilts my head up so it's a lot harder to avoid looking at him.

I shake my head and go for broke: "I've never had a man's anything between my legs."

I make my confession and wait for the world to end.

Vale

MY COCK SURGES PAINFULLY WITH THE NEED TO claim her. How can what she's saying be true?

Sparrow might be young, but she's a grown woman. She's gorgeous, with her curtain of dark hair, those emerald green eyes, all those curves, and those full lips that fit against mine like they were made just for me.

"Fuck, Birdy," I gasp when I finally let her up for air again, "how the hell can you still be a virgin?"

My shirt looks damn good on her, hanging open down to her waist with the hem skimming just above her knees. She's a goddamn vision in nothing but plaid and those skimpy little cotton panties I barely got a chance to appreciate before.

Let the shower water run. Fuck it. It's not like there's any hot water running with it that's gonna use up my propane anyway.

What I need right now is Sparrow's little pussy spread open on my mouth while I show her what she's been missing.

And you can believe I plan on doing a good enough job that she'll never let another man try it.

She giggles when I pick her up and carry her to my bed.

"I never met anyone that made me feel like I do when I'm around you."

She's all breathless, looking up at me with those pouty lips swollen from my kisses as she scrambles in the center of my king size bed to make space for me to crawl between her legs.

"Spread these pretty thighs for me and give me some room to work, baby."

This time she doesn't hesitate, her knees fall open and those thick thighs part like the pages of a good book, giving me an eyeful of the soaking wet center of her cute little panties.

"Let me take care of you, Birdy." I push between her legs, forcing her to lie back, and then I hook my thumbs under the elastic at her hips and slide that scrap of cotton away to reveal the prettiest sight I've ever seen.

Sparrow's virgin pussy glistens in the warm light of the bedside lamp and I'm not going to waste time sniffing her panties when the real thing is right in front of me and so obviously in need of my touch.

As soon as my mouth is on her, she whimpers, her hands threading through my hair as I part her folds with my fingers and lap up her sweet juices with my tongue.

While I work a single finger past her entrance, I tease her clit till the little pearl is slick and throbbing, loving every noise Sparrow makes as she gets closer and closer to her release.

"Tell me when you're going to come for me, baby," I mumble into her flesh, driving my finger deep inside her channel and stroking the sweet spot that has her going wild against my beard while I suck her clit harder and flick my tongue over the swollen bud.

"Now," she whines, "oh God, *now!*"

Sparrow's heels dig into my back with her thighs crushed tightly against my head while she rides my face to her release with my name echoing off the rafters while she floods my mouth with her sweetness.

"Good girl, Birdy." I lap at her seam and savor the taste of her, loving the way she quivers. "You're so perfect, baby."

My cock's so hard it hurts. I reach down and unzip my jeans to give it some space. I'm going to have to turn on the hot water in that shower and jack off twice to get the monster hard-on down enough to get any sleep tonight.

"Vale?" Sparrow's breathy voice wafts down to where my head rests over her stomach while I try not to think of what it would be like to have her completely. To fill her with my seed and have my child growing inside her.

"Yeah, Birdy," I turn and move up to kiss her lightly.

"I want more."

Sparrow's hand draws down my chest and doesn't stop till it's tracing agonizing circles around the swollen head of my cock.

"I want all of you, Vale," she whispers.

Chapter Seven

Sparrow

"Baby--"

His eyes are closed tight as I run my finger over the slippery tip of his erection where pre-cum is leaking out. His voice is full of warning.

"I want to be with you," I tell him, "all the way."

"Sparrow--" his hand covers mine, directing it around his girth and squeezing tight. It's like he wants me to touch him but also doesn't. It's so confusing.

I'm achy and needy still and I know it won't go away until I have him inside me but I'm afraid I'm asking too much. Maybe he doesn't want to be my first-- everything. Maybe he doesn't want a virgin.

He's so big, my hand barely wraps around him. Maybe he's worried he'll hurt me.

"You won't hurt me, I promise," I venture, tightening my grip on his thick cock and loving the way it pulses in my hand.

"I couldn't even get two fingers all the way in you," he tells me with a look in his eyes that's growing more feral by the moment, "it's gonna hurt, Baby. I'll split you open."

That should probably scare me. It should send me running out of here, but instead I feel all new heat flooding between my legs.

"I trust you," I tell him, "I know you'll make it feel good like what you just did. Please? I need to feel you inside me."

For a big man, Vale moves fast. His hips are between my thighs, forcing my legs wide as he pressed his length against my mound and lets out a deep growl.

"Birdy, tell me how you really feel about me. Now." His jeans have been shoved down on his hips with his movements, his cock still mostly trapped behind his boxer briefs but I can feel the naked head, slick and throbbing as it rubs into my seam.

"If we're doing this, we're not faking this engagement anymore," he growls, dipping his mouth to my neck and sucking a bruise into my flesh. "If I claim this pussy, it's mine, understand?"

Am I hearing this right? I moan when he thrusts against me again and even though I'd probably agree to anything right now to get him inside me, I'm desperately hoping he's saying what I think he is when I nod.

"Yours, Vale," I agree, "I'm all yours."

Vale

Mountain Man's Offer

I HOPE SHE UNDERSTANDS ME. THERE'S NO WAY I'll be able to let her go once I've been inside her. After tonight, Sparrow's going to be wearing my ring for real and the sooner I can get a baby inside her, the better.

Fuck. I don't have a condom anywhere on this whole damn mountain and I don't want one.

"I don't have any rubbers, Birdy," I grit through my teeth, forcing myself to keep some control, "I haven't been with anyone in a long damn time and the doc gave me a clean bill of health just last month. You okay with that?"

"Uh huh, I trust you." She nods, then whimpers when she feels me on her again.

It takes me three seconds to get the rest of my clothes off and those three seconds of losing contact with Sparrow are torture.

"I want to fuck you bare, Birdy," I tell her, my fingers sliding through her wetness and doing my best to prepare her for what's coming, "I want to feel that cherry splitting open on my raw cock."

Sparrow claws at my back, her little feet wrapped tight around the backs of my thighs like she's trying to climb me like a tree while I line up to her weeping hole and start to force my way past her innocence.

I can feel the place that has to tear open to allow me in and I know it hurts her because all her needy little cries go silent and her nails dig into my shoulders hard.

Maybe I'm a rough, filthy, bastard but I warned her. I figure the best thing is to just do it quick like ripping off a bandage. Sparrow's breath catches sharply but she doesn't cry out, and everything inside her opens up to take all of me.

It's more than I was prepared for, her tightness, her heat, the way she adjusts to me like she was made to take my cock. Because she was. I know it, I knew it the moment I saw her.

With some effort, I manage not to completely plunder her soft body and soon she's making those pretty little mewling noises again, meeting my thrusts, and begging me to make her come again.

I slip my hand between us and roll my thumb over her clit and make her come undone for me but I don't have much time to be proud of myself for managing to make Birdy's first time good for her. The feel of her tunnel spasming around my shaft as it clenches down and pulls me deeper into her interior causes me to go off like a fucking rocket, emptying my seed deep inside my woman's womb.

Chapter Eight

Sparrow

The jays aren't the only birds singing in the mountains this morning. I haven't been able to stop since I woke up.

After Vale made love to me last night, he told me he meant every word he'd said-- I'm really his now. I'm going to move into his cabin with him up here at the top of the mountain and have his babies and be his mountain wife.

Who would think that having that crazy stalker, Travis, show up on the Ridge would end up leading straight to my happily ever after?

I pull on my cheap snow boots without even pulling the laces tight and walk out on to the cabin's long, front porch.

It's a beautiful morning; the sun is shining on the pristine, white snow that blankets the land. It's hard to believe there are so many boulders and bushes under all that snow, but Vale was pointing out where everything is so I don't accidentally break an ankle out here.

Vale's cabin sits opposite the family's camp resort, with a wide clearing between us and the tiny office and general store that serves their guests through the summer months. From where I'm standing on the front porch now, I can see a row of small cabins fanned out along the shore of the lake, a big area for tents and campers. I can just imagine what it must be like up here in the summer time when it's full of happy people vacationing.

It's going to be a wonderful place to raise our kids.

My hand hovers over my belly, right where the cloth belt of Vale's humongous bathrobe is tied around my waist.

We're going to have babies together. I could already be pregnant with Vale's child right now, standing in the snow that's been trampled down at the base of the porch steps, wearing not a damn thing but my crappy snow boots, and Vale's bathrobe.

That's wishful thinking, but knowing how happy it would make Vale fills that hopeful space inside my tummy with butterflies.

I hear the sound of a snowmobile engine cutting the mountain's winter silence.

It's not coming from the direction of the large shed where Vale has been prepping his own sled for our day trip to the hot springs.

He said we can use the resort's man-made pools whenever we want but today, he's packing a lunch and some spare clothes onto the snowmobile and taking me farther up the trail that runs over the summit and into Paradise Point on the eastern side of the mountain range. He wants to show me his favorite hot spring pool, one of the original ones that was dug out by his own ancestor over a hundred years ago.

That's what I'm doing out here in the crisp mountain morning, wrapped up in the thick, terrycloth bathrobe that fits like wearing a blanket and smells like Vale. Waiting for him to bring the snowmobile around to the front of the house and taking full advantage of every minute I have left before I have to pull on the pair of his sister's old snow bibs that Vale found for me to wear for the short ride.

My coffee's gone cold in the mug and my feet have too, since these boots aren't exactly waterproof. But the sun is out and between that and just feeling like I'm going to burst with happiness-- I don't mind either.

The sound of the engine splits my thoughts, as a bright green sled slides up in front of me. Something isn't right, it came from the far side of the property, the figure obscured in snow gear that's racing toward me isn't right for Vale's size and height, and the gloved hand that grabs my wrist and pulls me from the porch is definitely not here to ask if the resort is open.

"Dammit, Sparrow, you always were too stupid to live. I don't know what you'd do with me, I swear."

The coffee mug flies from my hand as Travis yanks my wrist toward the back of the rented snowmobile's seat. I'm doing my best to gather up the bathrobe tightly against me, too desperate to keep my modesty to notice the thick cable tie till I feel it digging into my wrist and realize I'm bound to the passenger grab handle of the machine.

"Better get on." Travis sneers from behind his visor as he pushes my shoulder in an attempt to force me onto the seat. "Just swing your leg over it-- apparently you've gotten really good at putting things between your legs since you left me."

"I didn't leave you, Travis, we were never together!" I pull against the tie but my wrist is at an awkward angle that doesn't give me a chance to break free.

He's got my other wrist in his hands now, forcing me to comply with his attempts to get me on the machine while I scream for Vale.

It's no use, the engine is too loud and Vale's all the way in back of the house. I'm lucky I don't get bumped off and dragged when Travis jumps back in the pilot seat and opens the throttle up.

Vale

SPARROW'S SWEET SINGING HAS BEEN KEEPING me smiling all morning. Even while I'm packing down the snowmobile and checking the emergency kit to make sure we'll be prepared for anything that might go wrong, I can hear her humming happy little songs all the way from the front of the house.

It's too sweet a sound to tell her to get back inside, even though I know she's out there in nothing but my bathrobe and those slippers she calls snow boots.

First thing, we're getting her some good boots till her folks can ship the rest of her stuff from back east.

Mountain Man's Offer

The unmistakable sound of one of the newer snowmobiles on the market is headed up the mountain. From the sound of it, I'd guess it's a tourist on one of Howard Small's rented machines, taking advantage of the groomed snow on the Devil's Driveway and headed this way.

Sure enough, the mountains surrounding the resort property are reverberating with the noise soon enough. Probably someone checking the place out, wondering if the hot pools are open or if they can get a cup of hot cocoa before heading back down to return the sled.

We've been getting a lot more interest in winter hours since the ski lodge reopened. I'll be talking to my brothers about making some changes up here for next season, but for now, Sparrow and I have the mountain to ourselves and I plan on taking advantage of that.

Sure enough, I hear the engine of our uninvited guest's machine idle for a few minutes before speeding off back down the trail.

Firing up my own sled, I pull it around the front of the house, right up to the porch and jump off. Sparrow's nowhere to be seen outside, so that means she got her sexy little ass back in the house to change into some riding clothes before she gave some stranger a show, standing out here looking like heaven and sin all at once, with my robe hanging off her shoulders the way it was.

Good girl.

It's still early, we've got plenty of time left for a

soak in the hot springs, and my cock is already hard, just thinking about catching her half-dressed in my bedroom.

"Birdy?"

I don't hear her singing and when I complete a check of every room, I realize the house is as empty as it is quiet.

Confusion grips me, as I head back out front, wondering if she went out to the shed looking for me and we just missed each other. My confusion turns to panic, however, when I notice the pieces of a smashed coffee mug scattered over the stone walk where I'd shoveled snow away early.

My phone goes off in my pocket and I fumble to answer it with my gloves on, hoping it's Birdy. That would mean she's still within the Wi-Fi range on the resort property.

"Vale."

Hawk's voice cuts through the eerie silence that's settled over the mountain. He's using his sheriff voice. The one that says he's a man who's used to issuing orders that don't get questioned, not the voice of the easy-going buddy he quickly became when he took over the post in Moonshine Ridge.

My gut twists and I feel sick, looking at where Birdy's boot-prints go messy in the snow beside the tracks of a snowmobile that isn't mine.

"Look, Mable Hart just called to tell me she had a guy in the museum earlier that took an interest in your family history with the Drop. Guy sounds like he's probably the same guy that came after Sparrow.

Mable wanted to make sure I called to let you know, said he gave her the creeps. So I ran his license info from the records on that rental car he's been seen in-- he rented a sled from Howard this morning. Howard says he insisted on a two-seater, even though he was alone."

Back in my military days in the Corps, I survived by learning to think fast and act faster and that's what I'm doing while Hawk fills me in the best he can.

I don't have time to grab all the gear, but the 1911 and a couple extra magazines fit real well in my coat pocket and I know I can get to it in a hurry if it comes to it.

"Don't know man, but Mable was on her way to your grandmother's place while she was on the phone with me, said she's gonna bring Marcia up to your place."

"Mable's bringing my grandmother up the mountain?"

For a split second, my steps falter as that registers in my head. If I Mable Hart is headed toward my grandmother for anything other than a fight, she's really worried.

"I'm gonna head down the Driveway," I bark into my phone, "he's got Birdy and I got a bad feeling about where he's headed."

"Meet you there."

The call goes dead and I don't waste any more time. Hawk knows where to meet up with me, men like us speak the same language.

Chapter Nine

Sparrow

It'd be a pretty ride if it wasn't with Travis and if I wasn't tied to the damn handles. The trail wide, over well-groomed snow that's been compacted into a smooth road for nearly anything on skis to travel along the back-country route.

The sun can't compete with the windchill factor though. I'm glad I tied the belt on the robe tight before I went outside. Of course, now I wish I'd put on the borrowed snow gear. Nah, strike that, now I wish I hadn't been outside at all. At least, not without Vale right beside me.

Every fiber of my being is sure that Vale is on his way. He's probably got half the mountain waiting the other end of this trail, ready to make sure Travis never sets foot up here again-- possible to make sure he *can't* set foot up here again.

I could kick Travis. Probably hard enough to knock him off the seat in front of me, but going over the cliff, cuffed to a thousand pounds of snowmobile doesn't strike me as solution to the problem, so I concentrate on breaking through the nylon ties and freeing my hands.

Travis makes an awkward maneuver, nearly sending me off the back of the seat behind him, as he turns the snowmobile off the easy-to-follow track just before we cross the river.

I stop struggling against my bonds to try to process where I am. The river is running to one side of us; up ahead, the towering granite mountains part in a wide valley and there's nothing but blue skies and the sound of traffic.

Traffic? That can't be right.

Mentally I try to picture Moonshine Ridge on a map. There highway that twists up the mountain to Serenity Springs-- the Diaz resort-- is far behind us, on the other side of another row of rugged peaks. I think. Maybe I'm all mixed up and the trail curved back toward the main road without me noticing.

Still-- there's not a road with that much traffic on it till you get to the interstate corridor on the other side of Slow River Valley. Where the fuck are we?

And that's when Travis stops the sled.

"Did you know there is the cutest little museum of local history right across from that bar you work in?"

Travis stands next to the machine and casually takes off his visor and gloves while he tells me about the little museum that Mable Hart runs in town-- I keep twisting at the cord on my wrist, feeling hopeful when I notice a break in the edge.

"The old lady that runs the place was telling me all

Mountain Man's Offer

about how these waterfalls up here are named after your boyfriend's family."

The falls?

Now I realize that what sounds like busy highway traffic up ahead is actually the river plunging down the seventy-eight-foot cliff to the valley below.

"Travis," I almost have one hand free, even though I can feel the cable tie biting into my wrist as I twist to break through the strong, nylon plastic. I can't worry about that, or how my feet have gone so cold I can't feel my toes, or how the wind from the ride went straight through the thick robe and I'm feeling chaffed and freezer burnt.

"Yeah sweetie?" Travis uses a pocket knife and easily cuts through the tie holding down my arm on the side closest to him.

"Why would you bring me out to see some stupid waterfall?"

I was going to try for the *convince him I want to go home with him* approach, but the band on my other wrist snaps and my hand comes free with momentum that I use to knock Travis off balance with a surprise fist to the side of his face.

Pain blooms through my hand as it connects but inertia is on my side, sending me off the seat and into the snow beside the skimobile.

Unfortunately, my frozen numb feet aren't ready to catch me, and I fall on my knees right beside an incredibly pissed off Travis.

"Get the fuck up," he seethes between clenched

teeth as he hauls me off the ground, "I wanted to tell you this story I heard."

He's shoving me closer to the edge of the river and telling me about some woman who threw herself off the falls because her lover died going over them.

"That's not what happened!" I pull out of his grip and manage a few steps away from both Travis and the steep drop to the icy cold river below us. "Rebecca didn't jump and Martin Diaz survived his fall. God, Travis, you should have stayed and listened to the rest of Mable's story."

Off in the distance, I can head engine noise. I can't tell if it's another snowmobile coming up the trail or if it's Vale coming down from the cabin, but I know that as long as I can keep Travis from getting a grip on me again, I'll be safe.

"I like my version better, Sparrow." Travis sneers and lunges for me just as my ankle rolls as I misstep on a rock under the snow. "I think we can give these falls a better story; star-crossed lovers, plunging to their death in tandem so they can spend eternity together when the world was against them."

"The fuck?!" Travis's arms wrap around my waist from behind me, and pain blooms through my ankle as I do everything I can to avoid being dragged any closer to that river. "No one's going to believe I jumped with you, you asshole!"

I've never been so grateful for my curvy figure as I am right now. Travis is a skinny guy who's never seen the inside of a gym. Dragging me fighting and screaming isn't easy on him and now I can tell that the engine noise I hear is coming from both directions on the trail.

"Vale!" I see the dark shape of an older sled coming down the trail from the direction of the cabin. The machine catches air as it hits a small hill at high speed and then hits the ground again with enough force to send snow and ice exploding out from under its weight.

There is no mistaking the dark figure standing up and leaning forward over the handlebars as he steers in our direction.

Travis mutters as I grab a fistful of his hair and yank, but it's not enough to make him let go of me.

Vale

THIS MIGHT BE THE SLED'S LAST TRIP, GOD knows I'm pushing it beyond its limits as I open up the throttle and jump every hill, but there's no way I'm going to let anything-- *anything*-- happen to my little Bird.

I can hear the sound of a newer four-stroke up ahead and I don't know if I'm catching up with that asshole that took Sparrow or if Hawk's already on his way up the mountain.

As I hit the next snow bank and steer for the falls, I silently thank my brother for removing the governor on this thing years ago.

Up ahead, I spot a neon green snowmobile parked

closer to the river than is safe, considering how much snow is built up over the bank.

Then I see them and my blood boils. Red hot fury blurs my vision when I see that idiot with his arms around my woman, struggling to drag her toward the river while she fights like a hell cat.

Truth is, it's a damn good thing that the sled drops through a drift of rotten snow and the chain crunches on the rocks hidden beneath the deceptive white landscape. I might have kept driving, taking that bastard out and going over the edge with him.

"Vale!"

My name doesn't sound nearly as sweet on her lips when she's screaming in terror as it did last night when she was coming on my cock.

"Birdy!" I reach in my pocket, smoothly disengaging the safety lock as I pull the pistol free.

"Get the fuck away from her, asshole!"

At the sound of my voice, Travis's head snaps up to see me galloping toward them, the gun clutched close to my side.

Years of training drive my muscle memory now and my steps slow to a stalk that has me placing my feet much more carefully in the deep snow.

"She belongs with *me!*" The kid yells, his face near purple with rage and the frustration of realizing he doesn't have a chance of winning this fight.

I can't get a clear shot at him while he's so close to Sparrow though.

Now the sound of another sled is getting closer,

echoing up the trail where the canyon narrows just downhill from the river crossing.

Hawk is almost here, but I don't have time to wait on him. Travis has Sparrow too close to that bank. I can see the ice ledge that's holding the kid's weight, making it look like the cliff runs out farther over the river than it really does.

Do I run for them and hope to get Sparrow away from him and safely on solid ground? Or do I take the shot from here?

Sparrow makes that call for me.

"Fuck you!" She sounds like a damn warrior in battle, "I said *'no!'*"

With one hell of a good aim, I watch her hand fly toward Travis's crotch. It's not till just before she makes contact that I see the rock she must have pulled out from under the snow.

Travis goes down, reflexively doubled over with no choice but to let go of Sparrow. She immediately scrambles away from him, but one of her feet isn't holding her weight and she doesn't make good distance before she's slipping in the snow, giving that jerk a chance to grab for her.

His *last* chance.

The forty-five-millimeter rounds crack off with a series of sharp sounds that fill the canyon.

I might never know for sure if I hit him or not: Travis's eyes go wide and land directly on me, he takes a step backward, whether out of surprise or recoil, who knows? The ice under his feet cracks and the ledge gives way, dropping him off the sheer cliff and into the river just twenty feet or so before the bend where it plunges over the drop that shares its name with mine.

Hawk is coming up behind me and I hear him asking questions but the deputy's gonna have to wait.

"Shit, Birdy," I scoop her up in both arms easily and carry her toward my broken snowmobile. Her ankle is purple under the loose cuff of the soaking wet boot, and there are angry, red gouges in the skin around her wrists. "We need to get you into some dry clothes and back to the cabin for a hot bath and a fire."

"I knew you'd save me." Sparrow's head drops to my shoulder, her arms circling my neck. She's exhausted, but it's over now. She safe. She'll always be safe now that I have her.

"Looked to me like you did a damn fine job of saving yourself, Birdy."

Chapter Ten

Sparrow

"Hmm, so his plan to force you over the falls with him in a murder/suicide move then?"

Deputy Hawkins takes notes as I tell him my story and I curl deeper into Vale's lap where he sits with me next to the fireplace.

"I just wanted to make sure the girl was safe," Mable Hart's voice rises in the kitchen, where she's been stationed along with Vale's grandmother Marcia, Alice McAllister, and Vera Jones.

All four of them were already at the cabin when we got back, courtesy of Deputy Hawkins' country sheriff SUV that he'd left at the trailhead.

"If you're that scared to drive back down this mountain with me, then you can have Alice take you."

"Give me my fucking keys, Mable." Alice says again. "Next time you break into my store, I want you in jail for it."

Hawk looks up at me and Vale with a sheepish grin. Apparently, he couldn't arrest Mable and her friend for the goat-napping because Mable has a set of keys to Alice's general store-- leaving everyone wondering how the heck *that* came about.

"Fine, but don't call me when you lock yourself out of that damn shop."

There's a sound of keys being dropped on a counter and some more bickering that we can't make out from where we're sitting in the cabin's long living room.

"Yes," I tell Hawk, getting back to the report, "he said we were star-crossed lovers and that we were meant to be together in eternity if not on earth."

I shudder at the memory and Vale's hands slide up my arms and then wrap around me.

"Looks to me like the only stars crossed on this mountain today are ready for me to wrap up this report so they can have some well-deserved alone time.

"Congratulations, by the way, I had no idea you two had been dating all this time."

"I don't know why I even bothered to tell *you*," Mable spits at Marcia as she marches over to us.

"Because you wanted to rub it in my face that you knew something about my family before I did!" Marcia shoots back at her.

"Sweetie, I'm so glad you're okay," Mable leans in and presses a dry kiss against my cheek without a trace of the venom in her voice she was just spitting at Marcia. "You come see me at the museum and I'll fill you in on the parts of the story *they* don't even know."

Vale glares at the spot where Mable's lips touched my cheek and I can't help but laugh when his fingers come away with a smudge of bright pink where he wiped her lipstick off me.

"How are *you*, Deputy?" Mable's voice is downright conspiratorial as she looks at Hawk.

"Fine, Mrs. Hart," he mumbles, "thank you for giving us the very valuable tip today, you may have saved Sparrow's life."

Mable swats the air in Hawk's direction with feigned modesty, "Oh, I don't know if I'd go that far," she says coyly.

We all know she'd go that far.

It's interesting to see Moonshine Ridges most notorious all together in one room. There's definitely a lot of back story between those old women and I am dying to know more about them, but not tonight.

"Thank you, Mable," I tell her genuinely.

Some more grumbling and bickering and Mable and Vera take off.

Marcia fusses over me and Vale a bit longer and insists we come to dinner over the weekend when I've had a chance to recover from my ordeal.

Then she and Alice also say their goodbyes, with Deputy Hawkins following close behind them.

"He's worried they're going after Mable and Vee," Vale tells me as he locks the door after everyone has left.

"Why did Mable have a key to Alice's store?" I laugh as I wonder aloud.

"Who knows with those characters?"

Vale comes back to my chair by the fire and scoops me up in his arms. Doc Jones made it clear that I'm not to put weight on my ankle for at least two weeks and Vale's making sure I follow doctor's orders.

"Is there anything I can do for you, Birdy?"

"You can take me to bed," I tell him.

Vale

AS IF THE DAY HADN'T BEEN HARD ENOUGH ON Sparrow as it was-- having to relive her ordeal for Hawk's report while listening to Abu and her cronies squawking like hens over who did what to who and who started it all, I'm surprised my birdy has enough energy for what she's doing.

"Baby, you don't have to--"

Sparrow's hand is on me, under the waistband of my pants, and stroking my dick. I can tell she's liking the way it wakes up in her hand, filling her grip as it hardens.

"But I want to." She gives me a smile that's more sinner than saint as she props herself up on one elbow so she can work my cock. "We got cheated today; I was looking forward to trying some things."

She's got more than just my dick's attention now.

"Like what kinda things?" I go ahead and finish the question but by the time the words are out, I already know what she's planning.

Her hot little mouth wraps over the head of my cock and sucks my length farther down her throat than I'd have thought possible.

"Twist that ass around so I can eat your pussy while you're doing that," I manage to bark out between my clenched jaws. "Be careful with that ankle, Baby."

She swings a knee over my head and straddles my beard without hesitation and I'm careful not to bump the bandaged ankle that Doc Jones says is just a bad sprain. With both hands gripping her hips, I pull that round ass down and do my best to return the favor while she sucks me off with those pouty lips of hers sealed tight on my shaft that she follows with firm strokes her hand till I'm dizzy with the need to come down her hungry little throat.

"Ride me." My hand smacks her bare ass with a hard crack and the way it makes Sparrow jump and wiggle while I work her clit with my tongue has me making a mental note. But right now, I need her riding my cock instead of my beard. I want my seed in her womb.

Birdy doesn't argue, she skitters around so fast you'd think she been stung.

"Easy baby." It takes all my will power, but I figure her sweet pussy's gotta be sore from last night still. "Go slow and let me feel that tight little tunnel squeezing my dick."

With my hands gripping her thick thighs, Sparrow lets me guide her body down on my rock-hard rod and I do my damnedest not to rush it.

"Damn baby, you were fucking made to take my cock, weren't you?"

She gives me a happy little noise that makes me

lose my patience. "Baby I need you to move now," I say, but she doesn't need instructions.

Sparrow grinds down against the root of my dick, making me see stars.

"Vale," she moans my name and from the way her insides are already fluttering and milking me for my seed, I know she's as close as I am.

With one hand gripping her ass and the other pressing between us so I can thumb her clit, I look at those bouncing tits and the look of pure pleasure on my woman's face and watch her lose control while I pump my spend deep inside her and hope it takes root there.

Epilogue 1

Two Weeks Later
Vale

Birdy's ankle is still wrapped up. Doc says it's probably gonna take a few more weeks till she can safely put weight on it again. That means I'm still doing a lot more carrying her around, which suits me just fine. It keeps my hands on her so every one of the single assholes on the Ridge knows she belongs to me, and it keeps her in my sight too. So I know she's safe.

"Keep fussing over her like that and she's likely to run off the Ridge as soon as she can walk again."

Meadow's home from college after finishing her degree a semester early. She hits me with a hard shove over her shoulder and I let my sister push me sideways even though she's no match for my size. She steals my place on the short sofa next to Birdy and I grumble.

"Birdy's not running off," I tell Meadow while I

make sure Sparrow's foot is propped up comfortably on the ottoman.

Both my little sisters took to Sparrow in a hurry, but she and Meadow are practically besties since they met. Most of the time I love watching my girl fitting in with my family so well but tonight I was hoping to keep Sparrow's attention on me.

"I like his fussing." Sparrow reaches for my hand and gives it a squeeze with a wink and one of her special smiles that she saves just for me.

Meadow smiles at us but Terra rolls her eyes from her chair nearby.

"I don't know how you can put up with a man being so possessive," she tells Sparrow, "I'd punch a guy in the balls if he treated me like that."

"Well if you think wanting to take care of the woman I love is being possessive, you might want to leave now," I warn my baby sister as I reach into my pocket. "Because I'm planning on doing something to make sure this little birdie never flies away."

Somewhere between me flipping the little box in my hand open and the girls' shocked gasps when they see the ring, the rest of family has clued in that something important is happening and a crowd has gathered around to watch.

"Sparrow." I clear my throat and try to remember the short speech I practiced in the mirror earlier while I was trimming my mustache.

"Yes!"

Sparrow's eyes are shining like stars as she spreads

her fingers out so I can slip the ring on for her. It's loose, but we'll get it sized to fit.

"You didn't even let me finish, Birdy." I laugh and let her tell me *yes* again.

"Marry me, Birdy," I ask when she's done kissing me. I can tell her all the sappy shit I wanted to say when we're alone back at the cabin, but I feel like it's important to at least ask the actual question.

"Of course, Vale, of course I'll marry you."

Somewhere in the distance I hear Terra's disgusted *"that wasn't even a question,"* and I feel Sparrow's lips curve in a smile against mine.

Of course, as far as everyone in this room-- and on the whole ridge, for that matter-- knows, we're already engaged, but tonight, I have my grandma Rebecca's heirloom ring on Birdy's hand and a house full of witnesses-- there won't be anything fake about our engagement after this.

Epilogue 2

Ten Years Later

Sparrow

"Where's daddy?"

Wren squeals and lets go of my finger, heading off in a series of unsteady steps as soon as she sees Vale.

"How's daddy's little princess?" Vale scoops her up before she has a chance to take a tumble in the sparse grass sprouting now that the last of the snow has melted off for good.

Wren chatters her eleven-month-old chatter and Vale listens intently, nodding where ever he deems appropriate.

"You're pretty good at this dad thing, you know," I tell him as our paths unite on the footpath that's been worn through our property between the house and the barnyard.

"I've had some practice, you know." He winks and bends to give me a kiss.

He was good at it from the beginning, which started just ten months after that first night. It didn't happen right away, but we didn't do anything to avoid it and, sure enough, I had to have my wedding dress altered to fit over my growing baby bump.

Ten years, and four babies later, we've moved out of the family cabin up at the springs so that the kids can have more space-- and so we could add the barn and the fenced pen for the goats.

"How's we end up with these things again?" Vale stands beside me with one arm wrapped around me and the other holding Wren while she coos baby talk at the goats that have gathered along the fence in hopes that we brought carrots or apples.

"One for our engagement present," I begin the count, "one for a wedding present, one for Playa, one for Cardinal, one for Montana, and one for baby Wren."

When I get to Wren's goat, I tickle the back of her chubby knee as she kicks in her daddy's arms and giggles.

"That's only six, where'd the rest come from?" Vale grumbles about the herd of goats we've acquired over the years, thanks to his grandmother's mischief-- and the fact that the family has had a harder and harder time having their goats butchered for meat with every passing year.

"Honey, if you don't know where babies come from by now, I think we need to have a little talk later." I tease my husband with a light hip check that bumps him mid-thigh.

"Maybe this talk should include some demonstration to go with it," Vale leans down to whisper suggestively against my ear. "I want to make sure I understand the process *thoroughly*."

My tummy flutters and a tingle runs through me from where Vale's hot breath hits my ear all the way through me to the heat between my legs.

"You know, auntie Terra was just asking if we wanted a babysitter for the night. I think I'll just text her back and tell her she can pick the kids up on her way home later."

We decided that Wren was going to be our last baby, but I'm never going to turn down the chance show my husband exactly how babies are made.

Next in Series

<u>The Diaz Family of Moonshine Ridge</u>
Osprey "Oz" Lancaster

When it comes to Meadow Diaz, I can't do a damn thing right, including convincing her that she's mine.

Meadow Diaz's combination of feminine curves and take-no-prisoners attitude had me too wound up to remember my own name back when were teenagers. I might not have handled my crush very well.

In fact, I might have handled it by being a total jerk to her.

She was my best buddy's little sister and then, one day, my best buddy was beating the shit out of me and telling me to never look at her again. Suddenly I didn't have a best buddy or a chance in hell with the girl of my dreams.

We're all grown up now and Meadow's back from

college, working her first year as a back-country ranger, stationed right here in her hometown of Moonshine Ridge-- and partnered with the local wildland inspector-- the guy she sees as the asshole from high school that she still hates even though I'm even crazier about her than ever.

And that protective big brother of hers? His plan is to kill first and ask questions later when the guy that his sister once begged him to protect her from gets caught inspecting more than the wilderness fire protection plan.

How am I supposed to convince a group of Bigfoot hunters that the viral video that was filmed up here is a fake, convince Meadow to marry me, convince her brother not to murder me, and get all of us off this summit before the advancing wildfire traps us up here together?

About
Osprey "Ozzie" Lancaster

When it comes to Meadow Diaz, I can't seem to do a damn thing right, including convincing her that she's mine.

Meadow Diaz's combination of feminine curves and take-no-prisoners attitude had me too wound up to remember my own name back when we were teenagers. I might not have handled my crush very well.

In fact, I might have handled it by being a total jerk to her.

She was my best buddy's little sister and then, one day, my best buddy was beating the shit out of me and telling me to never look at her again. Suddenly I didn't have a best buddy anymore, or a chance in hell with the girl of my dreams.

We're all grown up now and Meadow's back from college, working her first year as a back-country ranger, stationed right here in her hometown of Moonshine Ridge-- and partnered with the local wildland inspector-- the guy she sees as the same asshole from high school that she still hates even though I'm even crazier about her than ever.

And that protective big brother of hers? His plan is to kill first and ask questions later when the guy that his sister once begged him to protect her from gets caught inspecting more than the wilderness fire protection plan.

How am I supposed to convince a group of Bigfoot hunters that the viral video that was filmed up here is a fake, convince Meadow to marry me, convince her brother not to murder me, and get all of us off this summit before the advancing wildfire traps us up here together?

Osprey and Meadow

Mountain Man's Treasure

The Diaz Family of Moonshine Ridge
by
Rocklyn Ryder

Chapter One

Meadow

The twelve-by-twelve footprint of the tower's cabin has to serve as both fire lookout and living space for the ranger stationed to the remote location on the seven thousand, nine hundred, eleven-foot summit of Benson Peak.

I push a bin full of personal items under the cot that's not even as wide as a twin-size bed and look around.

Three-hundred, sixty-degree views of raw wilderness spread out around me, visible from the cab's stormproof, acrylic windows that run from ceiling to mid-way down all four walls.

As a forestry ranger, I'll get to cover nearly every square mile of that land on foot, horseback, and snowshoes and Benson Tower is just the first of many remote cabins, towers, and yurts that are scattered through the back-country that I'll be calling home while I'm stationed here.

Landing the job in the Hart Wildland Management

Area was a dream come true; I'm back in Moonshine Ridge, close to family, friends, and the hometown that I've already been away from for six years while I completed my degree in forestry service and put in my initial internship and training back east.

A plume of dark gray smoke rises up from the other side of the mountain range through the west windows, billowing in the wind before dissipating into a sky that's usually a much clearer blue than it has been for the last few days.

The Placer Canyon fire got here the same time I did but, fortunately, local crews have it under control.

Grabbing a seat on one of the office chairs, I set up my vigil at the long counter that runs the length of the wall. And watch the smoke.

Lightning struck on the lower end of the canyon a few days before I took over the tower, and the fire's been burning since.

My peace and quiet is broken by the heavy idle of a diesel pick-up on the ground below.

What are the chances that it's just a hiker pulling into the trail-head parking area below the tower?

After the engine dies and the door of the truck slams, heavy footsteps start up the grated metal steps, causing the entire tower to shake under the impact.

Of course I couldn't get lucky enough to have a day of peace.

The biggest downside of being stationed in the fire tower has definitely been having to work with the local Wildland Fire Protection Inspector.

I straighten my back and steel my nerves for what I know is coming.

"Hey Red."

Osprey Lancaster's voice is like someone taking a vegetable peeler to my eardrums.

All my siblings inherited the sleek, black curls of my father's Latino heritage, but not me. No such luck, I managed to get cursed with some recessive gene bullshit that gave me a nightmare of rust-colored frizz.

I've always hated my hair; almost as much as I hate Oz.

"Thought you could use some reading material while you're stuck on the mountain all summer."

The sharp sound of a heavy box being dropped on the floor fills the small cabin and even though I'm doing my best to ignore the intrusion into my solitude-- that sounded really heavy.

"What the fuck is all this," I ask tersely, rummaging through a box crammed full of tattered old romance novels.

From the amount of Fabio pictures on the covers, I'm guessing they're from the eighties.

"Mom's had 'em boxed up in the garage for years, figured maybe they'd keep you warm up here while you're all alone at night."

Without giving him the satisfaction of a response, I head back to my desk and pick up the binoculars.

Is that a sexual innuendo? Can I get the jerk reassigned for sexual harassment?

Technically, we don't work for the same boss. And,

technically, I'm the higher authority in this jurisdiction.

The fact that I haven't talked to Ozzie Lancaster since my freshman year of high school is not an accident.

I've got my dream assignment at my dream job, but it came with my nightmare co-worker.

Osprey

Meadow Diaz still hates my guts and apparently there's nothing I can do to change that.

Which is a damn shame because even with nearly ten years between now and the day she had my best friend beat the shit out of me, she's still the most beautiful woman I've ever seen.

Mom's old romance novels were supposed to be a peace offering. I thought I was doing Red a favor. After all, *I'm* not the one stuck up here in this tower for the next few months.

Those steps are steep, more ladder than stairs. Sixty feet in the air and no, there ain't no fucking elevator. I sure as hell wouldn't have lugged a box of paperbacks up here for anyone else.

"Don't you have something to go inspect, *Inspector?*"

There's something I'd like to inspect, all right; the forestry ranger with the wild red hair pulled into a pony tail and the mouth-watering curves that make

Mountain Man's Treasure

that uniform look downright X-rated while she stares at me like she wants to throw me off the tower.

"Checked on Placer Canyon on my way up," I mutter, grabbing a seat at the desk that's not as close to her as I'd like and probably not as far from her as she'd like.

I was lucky to get into the wildland inspector position that covers the wilderness right outside of my hometown of Moonshine Ridge, without having to get a fancy, four-year degree. All I needed was a couple classes at the community college in Slow River Valley, my experience with the Moonshine Ridge volunteer fire crew-- and a good word to the right people from Mrs. Hart.

"Mesa says they've got it almost completely contained now."

Red's voice is civil, but her eyes are glued to the smoke rising over the mountain range in the near distance.

Her brother's name brings back memories. Memories of us all being kids together, back when Mesa was my best buddy and his little sister was just a bossy whirl-wind of wild red curls that didn't confuse the hell of me when she walked into the room.

By the time she got into high school with us she'd filled out in ways most of the other girls never would-- had my dick so hard my whole senior year, it's a wonder I never passed out from lack of blood to my brain.

She was too young and having all those feeling for

her bubbling all of a sudden was weird as hell for me after knowing her practically our whole lives.

I did what any self-respecting bone-headed teenage boy in love with his best friend's sister would do-- I treated her like dirt.

"That's not going to last."

Breaking myself out of those thoughts, I grab at the chance to have a polite conversation with her.

"All it's going to take is the slightest shift in the wind and they're gonna lose it. It'll go ripping up the canyon and then all we'll be able to do is hope we can keep it from jumping to the next ridge before we get more rain."

I've been arguing with headquarters for years over their fire management strategy. Hell, everybody on the mountain has been telling them we need to clear more of the dead trees out after the bark beetle problem we had a few years. We have too much dry timber standing in these narrow canyons and once flames get past the service roads, the hotshot crews are the only ones that can get on the ground up there.

"What the heck?"

Red grabs a pair of binoculars off the counter and trains them on a van that's heading up the old forest road toward the tower.

We both watch the van as it rolls right past the clearing next to the base of the tower and past the sign that clearly says it's the trail-head. As in, no motor vehicles beyond that point.

They stop when the road narrows too much for the vehicle, throw it in reverse and pull in near my truck.

Both me and Red head out to the catwalk that runs the perimeter of the cab so we can see who's in the van.

The driver's and the passenger's doors open, as well as the big sliding door on the side. Five kids that don't look old enough to be out of high school yet climb out and start pulling back packs and some sort of cases out of the van.

"What is this? A band gig?" One case looks a lot like the case for the trumpet my mom wanted me to play for band when I was maybe ten. That did not last long.

"I gotta go talk to them," she mumbles, setting down the binoculars and pushing her regulation ranger hat over all those curls that still make me crazy.

Chapter Two

Meadow

"Influencers."

The single word is all that's needed as I hang my hat back on the peg by the door.

Oz grunts.

He's staring at me with his usual look; his sapphire blue eyes narrowed slightly, watching me like he's got something more important to say than--

"So what's in those cases?"

"Camera gear."

"Let me guess, Bigfoot?"

It feels good to share a laugh with him.

My stomach does a flip-flop thing that has me thinking back to the old days. Back when Ozzie was always out at the house, hanging out with my brothers. When his teasing made me feel ticklish inside and I liked the way it felt when he was up close to me.

Before he turned into an asshole and I had to tell Mesa to keep him away from me.

"Bigfoot," I confirm, forcing one more laugh that

comes out as nothing but air and has me feeling as awkward as I did when I was fifteen.

We get a lot of Bigfoot hunters up in these mountains. Plenty of other towns like to call themselves the Bigfoot capital of the world, but Moonshine Ridge gets more reported sightings of Sasquatch and other unidentified creatures than any other area in north America.

Every year our mountains fill up with amateur monster hunters and, sometimes, even legitimate cryptozoologists and research teams. When I was growing up, my siblings and I would hike out past our family's property up at the hot springs resort to camp under the stars and scare each other stupid.

My brother, Glen, was always the first one to want to go back home.

"You see that last video though?" Oz asks. He sits in the other office chair at the desk, too close for me to pay attention to my work. "They're saying it's faked but it sure looked convincing."

"Haven't seen it yet," I mumble, checking on the smoke from the fire again and pretending to work on the report in front of me.

"You eaten anything today, Red?"

The note of genuine concern in his voice bothers me even more than the nickname.

I don't like this nice version of Oz; the one who's concerned that I've been too busy with the paperwork part of this job to eat, or the one who calls over the radio every night to make sure I'm safely in the tower after making any rounds I might have done on the ground for the day...or the one who lugs a box of books up the steps because I might get bored up here all alone.

Nice Oz makes it even harder to ignore the confusing way my body responds to his presence and even harder to remember that I hate him.

Osprey

"I'll eat after my shift," Red grumbles into her computer screen.

Gettin' to work with Red is a damn dream for me. When I found out she was going to be the new ranger assigned to this neck of our local woods, I thought for sure this was going to be my second chance to show her how I really feel about her. I thought working together was going to let her see that I'm all grown up now. I'm not the asshole kid that put lizards down her shirt and made fun of all the things about her that I actually adored.

I'm a grown man now. I still adore her and if she'll just open up and let me in a little, I'd make sure she knew how much.

Instead, our first week got off to a damn awkward start.

It's pretty clear she hasn't forgotten the way I treated her back when I was too fucking stupid to tell her how I felt about her.

Maybe we'd have been high school sweethearts if I

hadn't been such a boneheaded bully to her. We could've gotten hitched right after graduation and started a family right away.

Of course, I guess it always was Meadow's dream to get one of the ranger jobs up here on the Ridge. There's no way I could have held her back from that.

I'm going to support whatever damn thing makes her happy.

Right now, I know that'd be something to eat. My girl gets hangry and I've spent enough time up here watching her work over the last few days to know that she's not good about making time for meal breaks.

"You need to eat."

It's not a suggestion.

"I'll make you a sandwich," I tell her, getting back on my feet and heading for the tiny fridge under the counter on the other wall.

There's not a lot of space in here. Too many desks and equipment, in addition to the tiny area set up to serve as living space several nights a week for the ranger on duty up here.

It doesn't leave much room for two people to work together, especially when they're trying to avoid bumping into each other all the time.

Case in point, the way Red's long hair brushes against the bare skin of my arm as I push past her on my way to see if there's enough food in stock up here to actually make her the sandwich I promised.

It's enough to send my whole system off balance, getting me riled up in every bit the same way she always did back when she was my best buddy's off-limits little sister.

My dick comes to life as those soft curls seem to cling and follow me and all I can think about is how bad I want to wrap them around my fist and plunge into Red's sweet pussy while I've got her bent over that damn desktop.

"You okay?"

Damn. I must have groaned out load.

"Fine. You're out of those cheese slices you like." I keep my back turned to her, acting like I'm just pissed off about the lack of food in her fridge while I try to adjust my dick in these fucking tight uniform pants that don't hide a damn thing.

Making a mental shopping list of all the shit she needs if she's going to be staying up here for days at a time before getting down to Alice's general store in town for supplies helps tame my raging hard-on, at least.

"Take a break and eat," I order, setting the plain white bread and ham sandwich down on the desk. "When's the next time you're due to get out of here?"

She leans back in her chair, looking at the sandwich I just made for her like it might bite her back before picking it up in one hand.

"Until that fire is declared one hundred percent contained, I can't leave."

Red bites into the sandwich and I've never been so fucking jealous of processed ham in my damn life.

Watching her eyes close with those thick, cinnamon-red lashes fluttering against her cheeks as she moans in satisfaction has my pants choking my cock all over again.

"I'm going to go check in with the fire crew," I jump to action, grabbing for the jacket I left hanging on the peg by the door and praying it's long enough that she doesn't notice the bulge behind my zipper.

"I'll back tomorrow with some damn groceries so you don't fucking starve up here all week."

Chapter Three

Meadow

Over the last few days, I have run into Oz's broad back twice, stumbled into that muscular ass once when I didn't notice he'd bent down to tie his boot, and we won't even discuss what's involved with trying to walk past each other on the narrow catwalk that runs the perimeter of the lookout.

This tower is too small for the both of us and I swear Ozzie gets in my way on purpose.

Or maybe I'm the one responsible for all our accidental collisions. I don't even know anymore.

What I do know is that every time I touch him, I want to do it again.

"I notice you haven't moved that box of books I hauled up all those steps."

Leaning back in his chair, he props his boots up on the desk and smirks at me with a suggestive glance over to the narrow bed against the far wall.

"I've never been into bodice-rippers."

That'd be my sister, Terra. I should take the box

Ozzie brought up here home to her. She's probably depleted the entire supply of what's available in the little free library box in town.

"What rippers?"

Explaining romance novel tropes to Oz should not have me feeling on edge like this. My nipples should not be pebbled under the starched shirt of my uniform, I should not have to press my thighs tightly together under the desk to keep myself from squirming against the tingle that's running through my body and making me buzz uncomfortably between my legs.

I should not be picturing Oz in Fabio's place on all those book covers in the box shoved under my bed.

Damn. Too late. An image of Oz in one of those loose-fitting shirts, open to the waist with that thick, manly beard brushing some heroine's heaving bosom with her bodice savagely unlaced as she clings to his muscled arms has me practically swooning...*a heroine who looks suspiciously like me, mind you.*

"I dunno, Red, kinda sounds like you're into them--what is it about these books that you don't like?"

"They just tend have some particular elements in common that aren't how I want my first time to go."

Immediately, I regret the whole conversation.

Ozzie's boots land with a thud on the floor hard enough to shake the whole tower.

"Holy shit, Red! Are you still a *virgin?!*"

Shit.

"My V-card status is none of your business, Osprey Lancaster!"

This is not a conversation I want to be having with Oz. Especially not this new, grown-up Oz; the six foot, four, built-like-a-Mac-truck, Oz; with the muscles that make Dwayne Johnson look like he skipped too many days at the gym; and the thick beard that grows in in that Viking marauder shade of red that makes a liar out of me for saying the idea of getting ravaged by a lust-crazed mountain man doesn't turn me on...just a little.

"Look, Red, you're the one who just outed yourself. I was just asking what you don't like about those books."

"And stop calling me 'Red!' You know I hate it when you call me that"

What the fuck is that noise?

A high-pitched buzzing sound like a giant mosquito punctuates my lecture.

One quick glance out the window and it's easy to see the high-tech drone hovering above the tree line not far in the distance.

"Dammit, those aren't legal here."

Slipping on my jacket and squishing my hat down over the hair that I am particularly self-conscious about right now, I head for the door. Secretly, I'm all too excited for an excuse to get out of here.

"I can't believe I was starting to think you'd grown up to be a decent human being," I shout at the stunned-looking Oz right before I start down the steps.

Rocklyn Ryder

Osprey

"SINCE WHEN DO YOU HATE BEING CALLED 'RED?'"

How did she get so far ahead of me so fast?

I call out to her as I slow my pace when I catch up to her.

"I didn't know you didn't like me calling you 'Red.'"

Thank God for that drone somebody's flying out there. Drones aren't allowed in the wilderness area and I've never been more grateful for someone breaking the rules.

Things were definitely getting out of control back in the tower.

If we'd kept having this conversation in those tight quarters, I was probably going to lose my mind and do something extraordinarily stupid. Like kiss her senseless.

"You know I hate my stupid hair, Oz."

"What? No! I didn't-- why would you hate your hair? It's fucking sexy."

Her steps slow for a minute but then she speeds up, taking on the narrow path that climbs up to the nearby camp with a determined pace that has me jogging to keep up with her.

Hiking alongside her, I admire the view in silence; the way her skin is all flushed and the hypnotic sway of her ample ass with each step over the uneven terrain.

Just when I think she's not going to give me a response, she stops and puts her hands on her hips, staring up at me with fire in her eyes while those perfect tits of hers heave with every deep breath she inhales in an effort to calm herself down.

I don't want Meadow to calm down, I want her riled up. I want her fire; I can't seem to get enough.

The drone zips across the sky, hovering above us on the trail before heading off again, making me have to wait for whatever it was she was about to say.

We both watch the tiny aircraft disappear over the trees.

"Hermit camp," I say for the sheer purpose of stating the obvious.

"Looks like it." Red drops her fists off her hips and heads off without another word.

Hermit's camp is the unofficial name of a small, back country campsite that's become particularly popular with mostly amateur Bigfoot hunters who's most common sightings of the area's most famous cryptid has more to do with what they smoke around the campfire than whether or not Sasquatch is real.

"Can't believe those kids lugged all that gear up this far." I give a low whistle as the camp comes into view up ahead of us.

"Maybe they're more serious than I thought." Meadow sounds like she's as impressed as I am by the collection of cameras set up around the camp in addition to the drone that's now laying on a camp table next to a tablet computer surrounded by a group of people that don't look old enough to be drinking those beers.

"Hi guys," Meadow calls out as soon as we break

clear of the forest into the camp's clearing. "I couldn't help but notice you've been flying that drone out here."

Hanging back, I watch the scene from a distance.

Red's all business out here, with an authority in her voice as she explains the regulations to clueless campers that makes her even attractive to me.

"Your FAA unmanned craft license doesn't give you authority to fly in the wilderness management area..."

She gives them a tough but fair lecture and makes sure they understand the fines involved if she catches the craft in the air again.

Red's sexy as hell when she's in ranger mode.

"Yes ma'am." A lanky dude with hipster glasses and a downright pitiful excuse for a beard, answers in his best ass-kissin' tone. "We didn't know that; we'll keep it grounded till we're out of the wilderness area."

"Hey, Ranger? Can you tell us where this was taken?"

I take a step closer, curious about the video that the girl who just stepped up is playing for Meadow.

"Look, I know you're out here looking for Sasquatch, but this video has been debunked already, it's faked."

I watch five faces stare back at Meadow in various combinations of disbelief and disappointment. It's pretty clear they plan to stay out here and keep trying, whether the video online is real or not.

"Pack your trash out and keep the drone down," Meadow says, switching to her friendly ranger voice.

"We've got a fire burning on the other side of this

range," she says, pointing to the mountain looming above us, "it's mostly contained and not currently considered a threat, but if you've got access to the internet, you should be monitoring the incident website for the area in case something changes."

A chorus of thank yous and promises to behave and stay safe follow us we get back on the trail.

Chapter Four

Meadow

"I don't get it; how do they make money off of monster hunting if they don't find any monsters?"

Oz's steps pick up pace to catch up with mine while he muddles over the mysteries of social media monetization.

"They get their money from the videos where they're just freaking out over every little twig noise in the dark. They aren't actually trying to find any monsters," I explain.

An email went out just the other day, preparing us for what the department expects to be a higher than usual number of inexperienced campers and hikers this season due to the recent viral video taken in the area.

"You know where that video was taken, doncha, Red?"

There he goes with that *"Red"* shit again. This time it hits different.

Oz thinks my hair is sexy? My steps might slow

down a little-- but just a little-- to give him a chance to catch up with me.

"Doesn't matter where it was shot, the university has already declared the creature was deep faked with AI."

And whoever did it did a damn good job, too.

"Looked pretty real to me," Ozzie mumbles more to himself than to me. "That was new video too, not the one I saw a few days back."

Yeah, I know where the new video was taken: Clawson Crossing, where the stream runs through the alpine meadow only a couple of miles further into the wilderness from where we are now. And I didn't need Oz to point out that that was new video, I could see the date stamp on it just fine while I was watching it.

"You think they're real?" I ask.

You can't grow up in the mountains without seeing a few weird things, and there's no avoiding the local legends that date back way before gold was discovered up here.

I've never had anything happen that convinced me that the stories were more than stories, but I know a lot of people who have some interesting tales to tell; including my own brothers.

The mountains around us have gone suspiciously quiet. My shoulders shiver lightly under my jacket, and I give the surrounding forest a hard stare.

"You nervous?" Oz chides. "How are you going to be the big, bad, back-country ranger stationed out here on your own if you're scared of a little Bigfoot?"

"Dammit Oz! I was just starting to like you again

and you just have to be an ass and remind me why I hate you."

"You were starting to like me?"

A branch breaks somewhere beyond the tree line off the trail.

"Stay behind me," Ozzie orders.

Moving faster than a man his size should be able to, he jumps in front of me, positioning his massive body between me and whatever is crashing through the woods in our general direction.

"You got your firearm?" His arms are spread wide, like he's going to make sure nothing gets to me.

"I'm not that kind of ranger," I hiss.

"Shit, Red, what if you have a bad bear encounter?"

"I'll use my bear spray."

Our voices have dropped to whispers. Whatever it is, is big and it sounds like it's on the run in our direction.

"Great, gimme your bear spray." The fingers on his right hand twitch in anticipation of being handed something.

"I didn't bring my bear spray."

Osprey

IF WE MAKE IT BACK TO THE TOWER SAFELY, I'LL be giving Red a serious talking to about staying safe when she's out in the field.

When--When we make it back to the tower safely. I

do my best to kill the negative thought. Meadow will make it back; any other option is unacceptable.

More sounds of something running at full speed through the forest have me reaching back, making sure Red stays safe.

My heart is pumping double time, adrenaline running higher than the river in spring as foliage cracks and crunches beyond my line of sight.

About the only thing I can think of that would make this much noise would be a bear, but I'd be lying if all this Sasquatch talk hasn't got me on edge. I don't know what's about to come crashing out of that forest, but I know I won't let it hurt Red.

A mule deer darts through the trees, coming to a sudden stop a few feet in front of us, looking every bit as shocked as me before taking off at a dead run into the trees on the other side of the trail.

"Oh my gosh." Meadow gives a nervous little laugh and collapses willingly against my chest when I turn around to pull her into my arms.

Her ranger hat goes crashing to the ground and I get a chance to slide my hand over those wild, red curls.

Damn, her hair's soft.

And it smells good too; some fruity/floral scent that combines with soft curves crushed against my body to remind me of her femininity.

My heart is beating double time and holding her like this has my dick hardening, screaming its need to claim my woman.

Silently, I remind us both that Red's not my woman to claim.

She may have been laughing, but the way Red's arms are tight around my waist with her head laid against my chest makes me think she was a lot more scared than she's letting on.

"You're okay, baby girl," I whisper into those curls against the top of her head, stroking her back gently and waiting for the tension to leave her body. "I won't let anything happen to you."

Meadow's arms tighten around me and I hope like hell she can't feel the steel rod in my pants, but damn is it tough trying to keep enough distance between us to avoid embarrassing myself.

She feels just like I always knew she would-- *perfect*-- and I want to cherish every second she lets me hold her like this.

Before I go say something stupid again and remind her how much she hates me.

It's been a while, with us just standing together on the trail like this, but Meadow's body is still tense in my arms. I think I can feel her heartbeat, heavy and fast with those luscious tits of her pressed firm against my chest. When she tilts her head back to look up at me, I get it in my dumb head that this might be my chance.

Maybe I'm *not* imagining the softness in those caramel eyes, the pink flush darkening her cheeks, or the way those full lips part slightly as she looks up at me...

Chapter Five

Meadow

It's not the thought that Oz is about to kiss me that has me even more scared than when I thought we were about to be Sasquatch dinner-- it's that I want him to.

Dropping my arms, I step away from his hard, warm body. It's not exactly what I want to do, but suddenly I'm feeling all kinds of confused.

Sure, Oz is hot-- and maybe teenager me would have swooned over at the idea that one day he might look at me the way he was just now, but teenager me didn't have the best taste in guys.

Case in point, that time Oz dumped an entire blackberry milkshake over my head just to make the guys he was hanging out with laugh.

"We should get back," I mumble, straightening my uniform shirt and hoping the padding in my bra is thick enough to hide my hard nipples.

Oz clears his throat and nods once.

"Yup, better get back," he parrots.

"You good?" He asks, looking at me too seriously for a second, like he actually cares about me. It makes me feel some kind of way; my stomach flutters and something low inside me tightens. It's got me confused and I don't like it.

"All good," I assure him.

"'K then."

He stands there, just looking at me like he's waiting for me to say something else but all I do is point up the trail to indicate he should get moving.

Ozzie was going to fight a Sasquatch for me back there. Or a bear. Or anything else that came crashing out of the woods at us.

Remembering the way he moved in front of me to stand between me and whatever that noise turned out to be has me feeling decidedly less annoyed at the big man walking just ahead of me on the narrow track of trail that descends the hill down to the base of the tower.

Well, remembering him being willing to get killed by Bigfoot for me-- and that ass.

Ozzie's ass is the kind of work of art that goes a long way to making it hard to stay mad at him. He must do like, a thousand squats a day or something. It's so...perfect. Especially in those khakis he wears for work.

"You really think my hair is sexy?" I blurt out suddenly.

Oz turns to look back over his shoulder at me with a raised eyebrow.

It makes my stomach feel fluttery. I don't like it.

"I always thought you knew how sexy you are." He turns around again to look where he's going, and keeps talking in a tone far more serious than I'm used to from him.

"Those curls make you look like some kind of fire spirit, you know? And you've got those curves that make it impossible not to notice that you're a woman. Shit, Red, women like you drive men crazy...*Meadow*. Sorry."

I drive men crazy? That's news to me. In fact, I almost snort-laugh out loud. But the way Oz's voice goes strained and distant when he says it makes me feel powerful. Like maybe there's more behind the way he teases me than I've been noticing.

"Ladies first," he gestures to the steep, metal stairs that lead to the top of the tower as he stands to one side.

I move past him and start the climb, fully aware that he's got a better view of my ass now than I did his back on the trail. For the first time I can think of, I'm not feeling self-conscious about that. Or even about the fact that it's Osprey behind me. I might even put a little extra swing into my hips with each step I take.

Osprey

I SWEAR SHE'S SHAKING THAT ASS IN MY FACE on purpose, but I manage to climb a hundred stairs behind her without passing out from lack of oxygen due to my hard-on.

Back in the tower, it's back to business. Meadow checks the status of the fire while I respond to messages that came in while we were in the field.

Everything seems stable, with the local fire crews still keeping things under control.

This is about the time of day I head out of here. Usually in a hurry to put space between me and my fiery co-worker that makes my dick so hard I can't think straight most of the time.

Today feels different; Meadow's starting to act like maybe she doesn't hate me as much as she lets on. She's not trying to throw me out of her space, figuratively or literally, for once, and I want to soak up all that I can get.

Grabbing a seat near the little cot, I find myself picking through the box of mom's old books so I don't stare at Meadow.

The book in my hand has a picture of some dude looking like a pirate with long hair blowing in the wind and his shirt only halfway on. The woman in his arms is looking at up at him and her corset is halfway unlaced and her boobs look like they're about to pop out of her blouse.

Books like this were all over the house before Mom got her e-reader. I never read any of 'em. Now Meadow's got me curious.

Flipping through the pages, I skim the interior in search of what it is Meadow doesn't like about these books.

After reading a few passages, I guess I get what she's talking about.

"What *do* you want your first time be like?" I blurt out, out of the blue.

There I go again, saying something stupid. I wince and wait for her to start yelling and kick me out.

Much to my surprise, that doesn't happen.

Meadow's hat is laying on the long desktop that stretches along the cab's west side.

She's got her boots off too, with her small feet tucked up under that sweet ass of hers and she's sitting unusually close, on the cot beside me.

If I wasn't still here, she'd probably have changed out of the uniform already too. Maybe put on the cute little flannel pajamas with the tents and the bears on them that I saw folded on her personal shelf earlier.

Reaching over, she grabs the book out of my hand and studies me hard for a long moment.

Then, with a deep sigh, she surprises the fuck out of me by actually answering.

"Consensual, for starters," she says, staring at the book cover thoughtfully before setting it aside. "With someone I know and trust. Somebody that thinks my body is sexy and genuinely wants to be with me--not some drunk frat boy that's willing to "do me a favor."

Jealousy flares up hot and fierce in me at the idea of another man touching my Red. Especially some asshole that doesn't appreciate her the way I do.

How could any man look at this woman and not realize what a fucking treasure she is?

"You deserve better than that," I grumble.

"I know."

Red pauses and runs her fingers over the cover of the book, "I *do* kinda like the idea of giving myself to the man I love and only being with one guy ever though. Till death do us part."

Chapter Six

Meadow

"Didn't know you were so old fashioned." Oz is teasing but his voice isn't mocking and he's looking at me strangely.

Something changed between us out there on the trail this afternoon and I'm not sure if it's got me excited or scared.

"Yeah, well some people still believe in that shit, Oz, not everyone wants their bedpost all notched up."

"I don't have any *notches* on my bedpost."

Oz's face goes bright red to match his whiskers and suddenly he seems very interested in anything on the other side of the cabin that can give him an excuse to look away from me.

It doesn't take a genius to catch on to what he means.

"Osprey...are you--"

His jaw tightens, giving his profile an even more chiseled edge than usual.

"How is that even possible, Oz? I mean you're...but

you're--" I can't bring myself to tell him how hot he is so I just wave my hand at him from head to toe and keep stuttering in disbelief.

"Some guys believe in that shit too, you know," he tells me, his voice going low like he's sharing a secret.

"So why haven't you found your forever girl and put a ring on her finger then?"

Oz turns toward me, giving me an intense look. "There's only ever been one woman I wanted, Red-- sorry. *Meadow*."

"You can call me Red," I whisper. My voice shakes and I lick my lips to wet them because they've suddenly gone very dry. All the moisture in my body has pooled between my legs. "I mean...if it's really because you think my hair is sexy, I guess..."

"Fuck! Meadow, are you kidding me? I think *you're* sexy! You're the sexiest fucking woman I've ever seen."

"Since when?"

Everything inside me goes hot and liquid. It's too hot in here. My uniform is way too tight. It's a good thing I'm already sitting on my bed, or I'd probably melt into a puddle of need on the floor.

"Since high school, shit, why do you think I was such an ass to you? You were still just a kid-- Hell! We were both just kids. And I'd never had a crush on a girl before and suddenly my best friend's little sister is looking way too much like a woman than she had a right to.

"I wanted to kill every guy in school just to make sure none of them looked at you the way I did. I couldn't handle the way I felt about you all of a sudden and there was sure as hell no way you were ever going to think of me as boyfriend material...you did me a favor having Mesa beat the shit out of me."

"I didn't tell him to beat you up," I say, indignantly. "You were being an ass. I just wanted him to make you leave me alone."

Oz unbuttons the starched shirt of his own Forestry Service uniform, making my heart thump wildly in anticipation. Of course, he's wearing a dumb t-shirt underneath and any hope I had of catching a glimpse of his bare chest is lost.

"This scar, right here--" He pulls the short sleeve of the tee over the huge bicep that I think might be strong enough to lift me like I weigh nothing, and rolls it up over the top of his rounded shoulder. "--that's where my shoulder hit the concrete when he tackled me."

Leaning forward, I run my fingertip over the satiny strip of lighter skin that runs about an inch along the top of his arm.

"I'm sorry, Oz," I whisper without looking him in the eye.

Is it my imagination or is he leaning closer to me than he was before?

"It was only four stitches," he says, a glint of humor in the shy smile I see when I dare to look up at him. "I always figured I was just lucky Vale was deployed at the time. If you'd gone to him, they'd probably still be looking for me."

A light laugh escapes me but it's mostly nerves.

Oz is definitely closer to me now than before. His

head turned toward me, watching my fingers stroking lightly over his arm, the scar long forgotten already. I just want to touch him.

Osprey

"Do you have any idea what you do to me, Red?"

Fighting a Bigfoot out in the woods would be easy compared to the courage it takes to whisper those words aloud with Meadow's lips only a few inches from mine.

When her caramel eyes lift up to mine and I see her pupils blown wide and the way her full lips are parted softly-- hell, I couldn't stop myself if I tried.

My mouth is sealed to hers and the feel of her yielding to my kiss ignites something feral inside me.

We both go tumbling onto the small cot in a frenzy of hands and mouths, completely oblivious to the three hundred, sixty degree view the tower's thick, Plexiglas sides give to anyone in a mile radius.

Fortunately, there's not a damn soul in a mile radius to see what's going on up here.

My hands slide over Meadow's full breasts, filling my palms with all that softness that I've been fantasizing about since I knew what fantasies were made of.

Buttons are popping and shirts are tossed aside. Red's got my t-shirt off and when she runs her hands down my chest, I think it might be enough to kill me.

Then I've got her bra off and those perfect tits are in my mouth, sucking one nipple at a time till the tips are long and hardened while Meadow squirms underneath me making needy little gasping noises.

"Fuck, I want you, Red," growl, yanking that damn little band out of her hair so I can run her wild, rusty curls through my fingers while I nip the soft flesh of her throat between my teeth.

Meadow bucks her hips up, pushing her hot mound against the throbbing pole that's still trapped behind my zipper.

"So take me," she gasps. Her voice is throaty and deep and I don't need more experience with women to know how turned on she is.

Meadow's undoing the fly on my pants and feeling her hands on my cock has me seeing stars.

This is all I've ever wanted, Meadow's soft curves pressed against me while she begs me to make her mine.

"You don't know what you're asking, Baby," I mumble into rise of her stomach as I trail my mouth down her body.

Fuck. How far can I take this and still have the strength to turn back before it's too late?

My hands push at her pants, cursing the damned, double-thick polyester fabric that doesn't yield easily to giving me the access to her sweetness that I need to taste.

"I know what I want." she wiggles free of the pants, giving me a view of the sweetest sight of her soaking wet pussy covered by a pair of simple, white, cotton panties.

The scent of her is intoxicating. I know I've lost my damn mind as I bury my nose between her legs and inhale to remember this forever.

Just a taste, I lie to myself as I hook my fingers into the elastic of the little briefs and slide them down her curvy thighs.

Her curls down here are darker than the wild rusty sunset locks on her head.

I've never done this before; I'm just going on pure instinct as I draw my tongue through her slick folds and suction over the swollen pearl of her clit.

Meadow's back arches, her hands clutching my hair and I'm pretty sure I must be doing it right when those wide hips buck against my face and she coats my beard with her cream.

"Holy fuck. That was amazing, Baby. You taste like fucking heaven, Red."

"I still want you, Osprey."

Her ragged voice is so desperate, I don't know how I'm going to keep my control.

Chapter Seven

Meadow

On some level, I always knew it would be Oz.

"Red--"

The big man with his head still cradled between my thighs sounds like he might on the verge of tears. His voice is so strained, as he chokes on the nickname for me that only very recently became my favorite thing to be called.

A kiss to the inside of my thigh and he lifts himself up and comes back to me. When he kisses me, I can taste myself on him, his beard is wet with my juices and I'm entirely unprepared for how fucking hot it is.

My hips squirm and I push my knees up and spread my thighs so I can grind up against the hard ridge I can feel pressing against my sex.

"Meadow," his eye are a deep, cobalt blue, staring at me through dusty lashes with his brow furrowed, "this won't be enough for me, I know that. I want you, but I want all of you. Forever."

His fingers dance over my skin, skipping from the side of my breast, along my side, and down to my hip.

"You said you liked the idea of one man forever, Red. If I'm that man, I'll give you whatever you want. Always. But if this is just us blowing off steam, I need to leave now."

"I don't want you to leave," I admit. "I want it to be you...*forever*, Osprey. Make me yours."

Together, we're a flurry of movement, both of us working to get Oz as naked as I am till we're back on the narrow cot, with Osprey's large body pinning mine into the thin mattress. His hips settle between my thighs as his thick cock slides against my wetness.

Oz is a big guy; I probably shouldn't be surprised that the hard length of him rubbing against me is as massive as it is. Still, when I reach between us and take hold of him, I'm worried about how bad this is going to hurt.

"I don't exactly carry condoms around with me, Red," he says. He presses against my slit, the wide head of his dick teasing against my entrance. "I guess it's safe to assume we're both clean but--"

The possible consequences of what we're doing run through my mind but in every one of them, Osprey's by my side and I can't think of any future I'd rather have.

Nodding my understanding, I line the tip of him up against me and move my hand.

"I love you," Osprey whispers against my lips as he pushes inside me.

I want to say it back to him but I'm too lost in the sensation of feeling him sinking deep inside me.

There's a pinch when he tears through my innocence, but it doesn't hurt like I worried it would. It's over quick and he just feels so good-- pushing deeper and filling me completely till I can't help but move against him.

"Fuck Baby," Oz grunts, pulling back and slamming into me harder as we find our pace, "you feel so fucking good, Red. You do that again and you're going to make me come in this tight little pussy of yours."

His words are all it takes to send me crashing over the edge.

Osprey

MEADOW'S TIGHT LITTLE CHANNEL HAS ME fighting for breath already, but as soon as those walls clench down on my cock and start milking me for my seed, I've got no choice but to give it to her.

While Meadow's fingers grip my back with her body moving in time with mine, I let loose with everything I've been saving for this woman, filling her up with hopes of breeding her eager body with my child.

When there's nothing left for me to put inside her, I collapse heavily, doing my best not to crush her under my weight.

"You're mine now, Red."

I've never felt so possessive before, but something inside me has switched on like a fucking light bulb.

Meadow's my woman. I'm going to make her my wife and I'm going to make her the mother of my children-- in whatever order that comes in.

"If you hadn't been such an idiot back when we were younger, I'd have been yours already," Meadow says with a playful smack against my shoulder.

"I'm gonna make it up to you," I promise her, catching her lips with mine.

"Dammit," Meadow groans and so do I as the radio squawks a call signal from the desk across the tiny cabin.

"So much for personal time," she comments as we both pull ourselves off the cot and start looking for clothes.

"It's why you get paid the big money," I give her sweet ass a light smack before she can cover it with those cute little pajamas of hers.

"Yeah right," she laughs, "if I was in it for the money, I'd have taken a job at HQ."

Yanking my pants up, I follow her as she heads over to check on the call.

"Shit."

We both see it, the telltale orange glow above the ridge line just below us.

That fire has jumped their breaks and it's headed up the canyon walls. It's no surprise that the voice crackling over the two-way radio is telling us to evacuate the summit.

"OK, Yeah, we can do that...maybe forty-five

minutes. We've got some people up at Hermit's camp we need to round up...okay. Yeah, he's still here--"

Meadow's authoritative ranger voice gets soft momentarily and gives me a smirk. It's clear that the commander on the other the end of the line is wondering why I'm still hanging out up here with her.

"Actually, yeah, I see headlamps coming down the trail our way now, our campers might have seen the blaze...We will. Okay...got it."

She signs off and turns my way.

The fire jumped the road and now it's headed our way. The crews down there closed the road out of here and we are under orders not to allow any civilian traffic off the forestry road without an official escort.

"At least our Bigfoot hunters were smart enough to hike out," I say, pointing at the troop of hikers making their way off the trail in the dark.

"Guess we need to get down there and tell them not to try to drive off the mountain on their own."

Meadow sighs, and I'm feeling her pain. I'd have much rather stayed wrapped up with her soft body, squeezed together on the cot all night.

"Put some real clothes on, Red, I don't want those crypto-nerds gawking at my woman's tits--" Moving in close, so I can wrap my hands around those full orbs, I lower my mouth to her ear, "these are mine now, remember?"

"What. The. Fuck?!"

Chapter Eight

Meadow

Oz and I both jump at the angry voice booming from the door of the cab.

"Get your hands off her, motherfucker!"

Mesa crosses the floor in two swift strides, his fist already swinging for Oz's jaw before either of us have a chance to speak.

"Mesa!" I scream at my brother, distracting him just enough to give Oz a chance to step out of his reach.

If Mesa was inclined to take a breath and wait for an explanation, he changes his mind the minute he gets a good look at me.

"I fucking told you to leave her alone," Mesa growls, turning on Oz.

All my brothers are protective of me and our baby sister, but I've never seen any of them as mad as Mesa is right now.

Mesa crashes into Oz with a force that shakes the tower, but Oz is ready for the assault and catches him in a solid hold that at least keeps my brother from getting a shot at his face.

"I fucking work here, asshole," Oz seethes between gritted teeth as he fights to keep Mesa under control.

"Your job does not involve putting your hands on my sister!"

They're both huge guys. It's like having a couple of bison facing off inside a dressing room. The tower cabin is too small for this testosterone showdown and I'm worried they're going to break something important— like each other.

Sure enough, Mesa breaks free of Ozzie's grip and swings a fist. His blow glances off Oz's shoulder though and Oz comes back with a hit of his own that catches Mesa off balance.

Hastily throwing my jacket over my pajama shirt, I rush to put an end to this.

"Quit it, *now*!" I shove myself between the two hulking buffalo in the room and glare up at my brother. "If you hit him again, I swear I'll throw you off this fucking tower, Mesa Diaz!"

Mesa takes a step back, putting some distance between himself and me, looking stunned.

"Fucking hell, Meadow! What the hell is going on here?"

"Yeah, what the hell *is* going on, Mesa? What are you doing here?" Oz roars from behind me, and I have to put my hand out to calm him down.

His hands immediately land on my shoulders. Protectively. Possessively. Making it clear that I'm his and he'll destroy anyone that threatens me-- even if it's one of my loving-but-idiot brothers.

Mesa's eyes narrow into tight focus on Osprey's hands. If he had laser vision, I have no doubt that Oz would be incinerated by now-- but my brother doesn't move to get past me.

Probably because he knows I really will toss him over the railing if he tries.

"The fire jumped the fucking road. It's beyond our control at this point, and they're sending a hotshot crew in to take over. I came up here to make sure my *sister* was getting off the mountain safely and I find *you* up here with your *fucking hands* on her!"

This time Mesa does make a move, reaching over my head in half a lunge toward Oz. I shove my brother backwards, putting all my weight into it.

I grew up with three brothers that all ended up a foot taller than me before I hit puberty. I learned a long time ago how to win a fight with a guy twice my size.

Mesa takes two steps back and glowers-- this time, at me.

"You told me you didn't want him near you, Meadow. What the fuck is going on?"

Osprey

"THAT WAS *TEN YEARS AGO*, MESA! WE WERE

kids then and neither of us knew how to deal with what we were feeling."

Only one of the Diaz girls would be brave enough-- or stupid enough-- to put herself in front of one of the Diaz boys' fists, and damn if Red isn't doing a fine job of making her older brother cower like a scared pup.

I can't exactly blame her brother, if I had a sister, I'd do anything to keep her safe. If I'd walked in and seen Red with another man's hands on her, there'd have been no calming me down. Especially if the last I'd heard was that she hated that man.

That's different though. Mesa needs to shut up and hear what we have to say.

If he still needs to kill me, I won't make it easy on him. This time, I have something worth living for and I'm not giving Meadow up without a fight.

"You hated him two days ago! You were just down at the house telling us how much you hated having to work with him."

"I changed my mind." Meadow throws her hands in the air and shrugs like it's really that simple.

"I love Red," I tell Mesa, pulling her back against my chest and wrapping my arm across her chest-- more to keep her from trying to kill her brother, to be honest, but also because I want him to see the way she melts against me, letting me touch her like I own her, making it clear from the way her hands slide up over my arm that she owns me too.

"And I love Oz."

I guess we've said and done enough between the

two of us now that her words shouldn't catch me off guard, but they do.

My chest swells with pride and my heart is doing a happy tap dance while my dick attempts an ill-timed erection.

Mesa stares, his eyes moving from me to Meadow and back before his scrubs his hand down his face and tugs on his beard.

"And suddenly you're okay with the nickname, Med? You always hated that."

"*Oz* can call me 'Red,'" Meadow says, swiveling her head up to give me a wink. "If you try it, I will break your balls like egg shells."

Both Mesa and I reflexively tighten our thighs at the threat.

"Look, I get that it's big adjustment, but you're just going to have to get used to it. Oz and I are together and we're planning on staying that way."

"So you *don't* want me to kick his ass?" Mesa gives his sister a crooked eyebrow and a deep scowl but I might hear a hint of my old buddy under, his tone.

"No ass kicking," Meadow warns. "Now, if I can trust you two to act like grown-ups, I need to get those monster hunters down to the rendezvous point so the crew can get them past the fire area safely."

"And us too, for that matter," I point out, reluctantly loosening my hold on Red so she can gather her things for evacuation.

"Get changed, and meet us on the ground." I lean down to kiss her and give her bottom a light swat that earns me a giggle from my girl and a threatening growl from her brother.

"I'll go head off your monster hunters," Mesa grumbles on his way out the door. "Just hurry the fuck up."

Chapter Nine

Meadow

Mesa might not kill Oz, but I'm not so sure how safe I am from my grumpy big brother. I guess I'll cut him some slack, I really am throwing a lot on him all at once. When we get everyone safely off the summit, we'll have plenty of time to explain things to my family.

Once they see how good Oz is to me, they'll get behind us. My brothers will come around-- even hard-headed Mesa.

On the ground, I toss my stuff in the forestry service truck that's assigned to me and join the small group gathered together near the van that brought the influencers to the trailhead.

"So you need to follow us out of here and then the sheriff will escort you through the burn section, understand?"

Oz explains the plan to the girl that will apparently be driving them out of here while a couple of the guys pack away gear and video equipment into the van.

The campers are excitedly talking to Mesa about the footage they caught while my brother scowls at me and Oz.

"Hey, when do you think the area is going to be open again?" One of the monster hunters asks me. I can tell she's hopeful that the evacuation is precautionary and they'll be able to return in a day or two but I can't give her any assurances.

"Depends on if the hotshot crew coming in can keep the fire contained to the west side of the range," I tell her. "If it dies on its own when it hits the peak, then maybe a couple of weeks, if it decides to travel down the east slope-- could be years."

"Man, the 'squatches are going to lose a lot of habitat if that happens." One of the camera guys sounds genuinely concerned.

"Dude, I told you, they're inter-dimensional!" One of the other guys tells him. "They've been here for millennia, man, you got any idea how many forest fires they've survived and *still* never had to wander into human territory?"

"Because they can portal into the eleventh dimension and live inside the mountain, man."

Mesa's scowl turns on the guy giving the lecture on Bigfoot's ability to, apparently, travel into another dimension and I decide not to ask any of the questions running through my mind right now-- like, how does this guy know?

"You're gonna be right behind me, Red."

It's not a question. There's no mistaking Oz's directive, he wants me where he can see me in his rear-view mirrors.

"Mesa's going to run sweep, right behind our monster hunters. I'll meet up with you at the station in town."

After making sure I'm buckled in and have my door closed and locked, he leans through my open window for a kiss.

"Close up this window, babe," he tells me, "that fire is going to have all kinds of wildlife on the run, I don't want any frightened Sasquatches trying to climb into the truck with you."

He gives me a wink and a grin, and another kiss.

"Or bears," he adds more seriously, before stepping back so I can raise the window.

The silence of the night is suddenly split by a noise I've never heard in all my years of living in the mountains.

Something like the trumpet of an elephant crossed with a lion's roar echoes off the granite peaks surrounding us.

"What the fuck was that?" Mesa yells from the open window of his truck as he waits for the rest of us to pull out in front of him.

Before anyone can answer, a second bellow sounds from another direction, this one sounds more distant and higher pitched, whatever it is, there's two of them.

"Window," Oz's face is serious as he points at my half-up driver's side window. "Up. All the way. If you need me, I'm on channel four. Don't worry, just mountain lions, Red."

He jumps in his own work truck and leads us off the mountain.

I've heard mountain lions-- that was *not* what made that noise.

Osprey

RED'S TRUCK IS RIGHT BEHIND ME, WITH THE kids in the van behind her, and Mesa bringing up the rear to make sure no one stops or has trouble along the way.

It's a slow drive back down the service road in the dark, and the wildlife is definitely on the move. I have to stop three times to avoid scared raccoons and rabbits before we hit the paved road where Deputy Hawkins and his men are working with the local fire crew to escort us off the mountain and down to the main highway while the newly dispatched team of hotshots get to work cutting new lines and clearing brush.

All the while, telling myself that noise was just a couple of recently displaced mountain lions crying over new territory.

Everything has a perfectly reasonable explanation and that's what makes the most sense to me.

Even when then kids in the van are excitedly yammering about catching the 'squatch calls on audio.

Once everyone is past the burn and back on the main highway down to Moonshine Ridge, I might make a mental note to check in with Rapid Jones in the next few days. Not because I want to ask him about his Bigfoot stories or anything, I just haven't seen much of him since he married the Doc and stopped shooting pool down at the tavern with us.

That's what I tell myself as I keep track of Red's headlights in my rear view on the way down to the station in town.

I figure if Bigfoot's a thing, Red'll be safe up there on the job anyway. After all, damn near everyone in town's got a story about the hairy giants and not one of those stories has ever involved getting attacked.

Gotta make sure she doesn't leave base without her bear spray though.

Down at the station, we meet up, file our reports and check on how the closures affect our schedules from here on out, and swap work vehicles for personal ones.

"Follow me." It's not a question, I want Red on my tail all the way back to my place.

"Aren't you going home?" Meadow asks, her eyes twinkling in the parking lot light.

"Yeah, we are." I give her half a smile, running my hands down her arms and loving the way she shivers at my touch.

"I figure you should see where you live now."

Red's never been to my house, but I'm pretty sure she'll like it. If she doesn't, I'll tear it down and build her a new one. Either way, she's mine now and I'm not waiting another minute to move her in.

I'll have my ring on her hand as soon as we get

down to Slow River to shop for one, and if I have my way, I'll have my baby growing in her before we're back at work in the morning.

"Lead the way," she tells me with a grin that says she's thinking the same thing I am.

Epilogue 1

One Year Later
Meadow

My tenure as back-country ranger was short-lived, since we found out we were pregnant only a couple months after I moved in with Oz.

I was able to keep the job till I was about six months, after that, Osprey put his foot down and insisted I take a job down at the station in town.

Not that I minded. To be honest, Oz wasn't the only one who was a little freaked out about me being all alone up at the yurt during snow season with no way in or out that wasn't on skis or snow-shoes.

And now that Fields is here, I'm so glad that I never have to spend a day away from my family.

"How's my beautiful wife?"

Oz slides onto the sofa beside me, snuggling up against me while I gently rock our four-week-old son in my arms.

"Mmm," I coo as my hubby kisses me, "fabulous, just a little sad about going back to work in a couple of weeks."

"You don't have to; I've told you a million times we'll be just fine on one income if you want stay home."

Oz stretches greedy hands out to take Fields from me now that he's had his lunch and is sleeping it off.

Snuggling up against my hubby, I lay my head on Oz's shoulder and pet our son's shock of soft, red curls with my hand.

I'm determined he's going to grow up loving that hair.

"I know, but I really do love my job." Oz and I have talked a lot about this, and I'm still torn. Being a forest ranger was my dream job since I was little, but I had no idea how much I was going to want to be home with my babies once I started a family.

"Whatever makes you happy, Red. I'll support it. Just be warned that as soon as Doc Jones gives us the all clear in a couple of weeks, I have every intention of getting started on a sister for Fields to protect."

"Speaking of protective big brothers," I say, "I think Mesa might ask her at the wedding."

Osprey and I did the courthouse wedding just a couple weeks after we got together-- when you know, you know-- but since Fields came along so soon, we put off the big to-do until later this summer.

My brother's had a hell of a year, but Robin has been at his side the whole time. There's no doubt in my mind that I'm getting another sister-in-law soon.

"About damn time. Those two have been head over heels since first sight. Mesa should have married her a long time ago."

"He was kind of busy," I remind my hubby, getting up and gently taking our sleeping son from his arms so I can put him to bed.

Oz rolls his eyes and gets up when I beckon him to follow.

"He coulda at least proposed," he grumbles on about my brother as I put Fields down and take Oz by the hand back to our room.

"If I didn't know better, I'd think you had plans for me that are going to have the Doc cussing me out next time she sees us."

It's only been four weeks since Fields was born and we're not cleared to get back to the sex life we're used to, but I did ask Doctor Jones about other options and she gave me a few ideas that I've been dying to try.

"I promise not to get you in any trouble," I tell him, pulling him onto the bed with me with my fingers crossed not-quite-behind my back.

Epilogue 2

Ten Years Later
Osprey

"So, we're gonna have to sheer these every year?"

I look out at the fenced area where the kids are having a blast chasing the new kids. That'd be our children and the four Pygora goats that just joined the family.

"Yup, they're just like sheep," Red replies with a giggle, tucking her shoulder under my arm.

"Or Cypress and Violet's alpacas, I take it."

"The goats need less space," Red points out, "and they aren't nearly as obnoxious as those Spanish crosses that Abu pawned off on Vale and Sparrow."

I suppose it was inevitable that I was going to end up with a yard full of goats eventually, it seems to be the price you pay for marrying into the Diaz family.

But our eight-year-old daughter, Prairie, wanted "soft" goats like she'd seen at the fair, so here we are;

starting a new family tradition, raising fiber goats for fleece instead of the meat goats that Meadow's brother started with years ago.

Out front, the sound of a car coming up our driveway interrupts our conversation.

"Sounds like your brother's car?"

"They brought Heron out to see the new goats." Red stands on tip toe to collect a kiss and I add a swat to that sweet ass of hers as she heads off to meet up with Mesa and his family.

Ten years and three children-- and now four kids-- with that woman and I still can't get enough of her.

I watch my wife leading her brother and sister-in-law back toward me while my five-year-old nephew makes a mad dash to join the other children playing in the field.

As Mesa greets me with a one-armed hug, it's hard to believe this is the same man that tried to kill me-- twice.

"So you finally joined the goat club, eh, man?" Mesa jokes, standing beside me while our women disappear inside.

"Put it off as long as I could, though," I tell him.

"I wish I knew how you managed that." Mesa chuckles beside me and wraps his good arm around his wife as the girls join back up with us. "You two are the only ones who managed not to end up with a goat for every great grand-baby."

"Speaking of," Red slips her arm around my waist and I pull her against me, right where she belongs. "I hear you're finally going to be taking *your* goat off Glen's hands?"

Mesa and Robin exchange a glance between them that says plenty.

"Holy shit, man, congratulations! It's about damn time, brother."

I pull both Robin and Mesa in for hugs, happy as hell to hear their news.

Goats are social animals and with Heron being an only child for so long, his goat's been living with Uncle Glen's herd so it wouldn't be lonely.

Mesa and Robin building a pen means Heron's getting a little brother or sister-- and so will his goat.

Together, the four of us watch the kids and the goats playing in the field for a few more minutes before calling them to come in and clean up for dinner.

Later, when the kids are crashed out, and the guests have gone home, I snuggle up beside Red and slip my hand under her nightgown.

"You thinking what I've been thinking, Red?"

Her little pussy's already wet for me as she swings a leg over me to straddle my hips.

"Have you been thinking that there's going to be a new baby in the family with no one their own age to play with?"

Damn, my wife knows exactly how to get to me. She's got my cock hard as steel and she doesn't waste time getting it inside her.

"Maybe we could do something about that."

The thought of putting another baby in this beautiful woman is enough to make me lose my mind. Slipping my hand between us so I can thumb her clit, I watch Red ride me while she comes undone.

As we drift off to sleep, still tangled up with each other, the thought occurs to me that this is going to mean we'll be getting another goat.

Next in Series

The Diaz Family of Moonshine Ridge
Glen Diaz

These mountains are notorious for the mythical beasts reported to live here, but it's not Bigfoot that the curvy cryptozoologist needs to worry about.

The recent videos hitting the internet have a whole new crop of monster hunters crawling the mountains where I live.

When I come across Finch camped out alone with nothing to defend herself with but her camera, every protective instinct in my body surges to life.

There's more lurking in the woods than the legendary skunk ape, and I'll do whatever I have to keep this woman safe.

Because Finch isn't just another scientist looking for proof-- she's mine.

Thank you for Reading
Mountain Man's Treasure

For those who have been following the Moonshine Ridge Mountain Men series from the beginning, you probably recognize Osprey from a few very minor appearances in previous books.

When I first mentioned Ozzie, I had no clue that he would end up with a starring role as the hero of a future book.

That's what happens in small towns like Moonshine Ridge, though, everyone knows everyone and there's bound to be a couple or two who have been secretly crushing on each other for years.

I'm glad that Oz and Meadow were finally able to come clean with their feelings for one another-- and that Osprey had a chance to mature from the awkward teenage boy who dealt with his feelings all wrong.

I really expected to be writing Mesa's story next but the timeline didn't work out right-- and Mesa's kind of a hard-head with some issues to work out before he does something really stupid.

Fortunately, he's got a couple of equally hard-headed sisters and a grandmother who doesn't suffer fools lightly.

So Glen is next in line, with the curvy young, cryptozoology grad student who's hellbent on proving Bigfoot not only exists-- but that there's a thriving colony of the creatures right here in the mountains above Moonshine Ridge!

Glen's been hiking these mountains since he was a kid, he knows Bigfoot isn't the most dangerous thing lurking in these woods, and once he sets his eyes on Finch, he'll do anything to make sure nothing touches her but him.

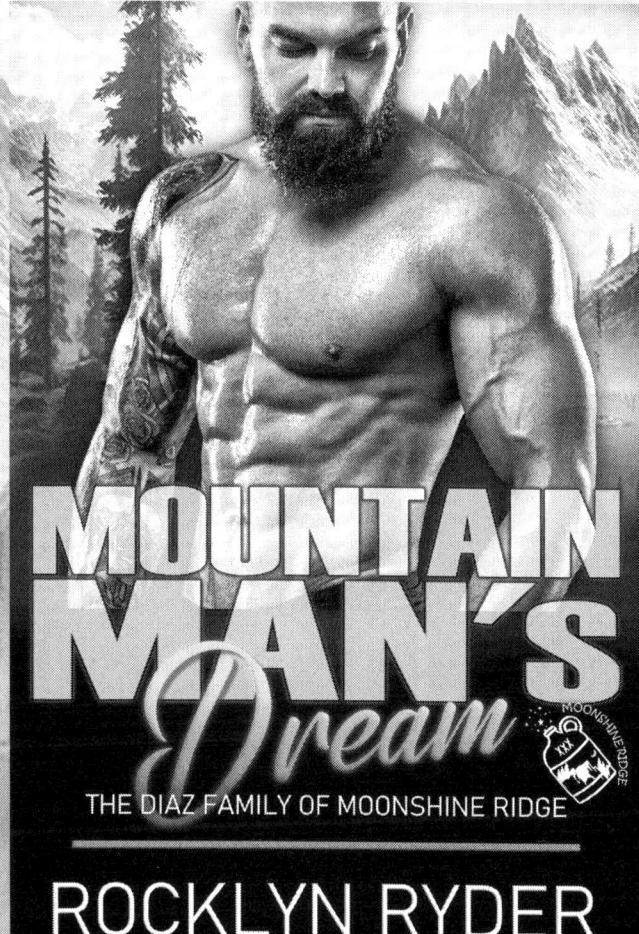

About
Glen Diaz

These mountains are notorious for the mythical beasts reported to live here, but it's not Bigfoot that the curvy cryptozoologist needs to worry about.

The recent videos hitting the internet have a whole new crop of monster hunters crawling the mountains where I live.

When I come across Finch camped out alone with nothing to defend herself with but her camera, every protective instinct in my body surges to life.

There's more lurking in the woods than the legendary skunk ape, and I'll do whatever I have to keep the beautiful, young grad student safe.

The only thing that's going to touch this woman is *me;* because Finch isn't just another scientist looking for proof-- she's mine.

Glen and Finch

Mountain Man's Dream

The Diaz Family of Moonshine Ridge
by
Rocklyn Ryder

Chapter One

Finch

Fake.

That's what the so-called "experts" at the university said about the videos.

Fake.

I seethe as I trudge up the steep mountainside terrain.

The official word on the best video evidence in history of North America's most famous cryptid is that it's a hoax. My own professor at the university, the one who oversees my graduate program in cryptozoology and the man currently considered to be the leading authority on Bigfoot in the world watched three videos and declared every one of them to be *fake*.

My disgust at the university's ignorance fuels my pace, giving me the strength I need to get up the side of this mountain.

The last videos were shot down by Clawson's Crossing, that area doesn't get a lot of traffic and the cameras were set up to record whatever came down to the water. Ultimately, they caught three clear images of two different creatures at different times of the day.

OK, the videos were poorly lit and the creatures both blended surprisingly well into the forest back drop. It took some careful editing to get the end results that so clearly showed what was on camera-- but once you saw it, you couldn't *un*see it, if you know what I mean.

I expected them to send a team out here. I thought we'd get a budget that would cover some high-end camera equipment and maybe a couple of photographers that know how to put it to good use.

I thought we'd finally be able to prove that Sasquatch exists. Not that there used to be a North American ape species living in these mountains that went extinct a long time ago, or that there's one or two lingering specimens that manage to elude modern humans despite us continually encroaching further into their territory, but that a genuine population of the creatures are thriving right here in these mountains surrounding the little town of Moonshine Ridge.

I thought I was going to be part of the most important scientific discovery of the millennium.

Instead-- the videos I had put so much hope into got dismissed out of hand as artificial intelligence-generated *fakes*.

So here I am, picking my way around boulders and trees, heading for an even more remote area where trails are few and far between and humans rarely travel-- thanks to rugged terrain and local superstition.

I've got five, motion-sensored, weatherproof, action

cameras with night vision nestled in my pack and I plan to set them up and let them record till the batteries go dead.

Hopefully, being in an area that gets little to no human traffic will give me a better chance at catching whatever lives in this rugged mountain terrain on camera.

As I push myself up the steep mountainside, following the barely-visible remnants of what hasn't been a maintained trail in decades, I decide not to think about the fact that I'll have to come back up here in a few weeks to retrieve the memory cards from the cameras.

Don't get me wrong, I'm in damn good shape for a plus-size girl-- but I never planned to go into field research and I always thought that any time I might have to, I'd be traveling with a team.

I'm going to do what it takes to get evidence that they can't debunk, even if it means hiking solo into the desolate stretch of forest that the locals call the "weeping wilderness."

Glen

It's hard to believe I used to be scared shitless of these mountains back when I was a kid.

My siblings and I grew up in these mountains. Not the way most folks in Moonshine Ridge grew up in the mountains-- we grew up *in the mountains.*

Rocklyn Ryder

Our parents run the camping resort that's been in my family for the last hundred and some years now, and we spent every summer up at the hot springs swimming, camping, running wild like only mountain kids can.

My older brothers, Vale and Mesa, they were always leading me and our sister, Meadow, off the property on overnight camp-outs.

Terra hadn't been born yet, so I was the youngest on those adventures.

My brothers would stay up late telling me and Meadow all the local ghost stories around the campfire, trying to scare us stupid.

Worked too. On me, at least.

Ironic that I'm the one that grew up doing all these solo hikes after all those nights hiding in my sleeping bag with my flashlight on till the batteries went dead and begging one of my brothers to take me home early.

When I hit my teens, I started pushing myself to wander a little farther, stay out a little longer. Got used to the sounds of the forest-- the angry chatter of squirrels and birds throughout the day, the rustles of skunks and raccoons investigating my camp at night.

I learned what to do when I find myself face to face with one of the massive black bears that own this territory, how to identify calls and tracks and scat, and which creatures are best avoided and how to make sure I avoid them.

The more time I spend out here, the more comfortable I get. My family can't believe that of all us kids,

I'm the one that grew up to be the hardcore hiker. The guy that throws his gear in a pack and heads out over the mountains for weeks at a time whenever time allows.

Which is exactly what has me out here for the next few days; making my way up the old road from the edge of our property where I plan to skirt the boundary of the weeping wilderness till I get over the saddle and down to Angel's Lake.

The old road isn't much of a road at all after being abandoned almost a hundred years ago. There's still a faint trail marking the old route that used to run over the pass but the road that originally connected us to the communities on the west side of the range was rerouted in the nineteen thirties, despite the cost and labor that went into cutting new trail into the mountainside to the south to create a viable path where nature never intended one to run.

That's what happens when a rich man's daughter joins the list of women gone missing on a road with a dark history.

Reaching the point where the old road used to run through the dense thatch of forest that stretches over the mountaintop, I stop to chug some water from my bottle and appreciate the views of the valley below.

Then I turn off what remains of the old trail to skirt the edge of the forest.

I might not be scared of what lurks in these mountains like I was as a kid, but you can fucking believe I'm smart enough to respect the boundaries of the local wildlife's established territory.

There's a reason that forest is called "weeping wilderness" and I might not be a woman, but I don't see any reason to push my luck.

Respect the mountains and they'll respect you-- that's how I see it-- and that means the mountains can have those woods.

I'm about a quarter mile from meeting up with the main trail to the lake when I hear something unusual coming from somewhere nearby.

It's not one of the sounds of the mountains. Not an animal or wind rustling through pine needles.

Stopping to give it my full attention, I realize it's coming from somewhere beyond the perimeter of the woods; the rather distinct sound of a woman's sweet voice singing

The sweet songbird singing the familiar tune-- and the fact that it's coming from far enough beyond the tree line that I can't see the source-- is enough to turn me off my route.

She shouldn't be in there.

Chapter Two

Finch

When I run out of lyrics that I remember to the older song, I switch to Taylor Swift. Not that my singing voice does her justice, but at least I know all the words.

Getting the cameras set up would be so much easier if I had help, or a ladder. Hauling a ladder up here was not an option; as for help?

Maybe once I get some video that the university doesn't immediately dismiss as fake, I'll find someone who doesn't think I'm a laughing stock. In the meantime, I'm on my own.

A rustle in the forest behind me has me suddenly feeling like I'm very much *not* on my own, however.

My first thought is that it's probably a deer. Moving slowly so I don't scare it, I turn to look in the direction the noise came from.

Not a deer, something bigger. Through the trees, hovering in the shadows, something massive stands perfectly still and watches me.

My pulse races and my lungs freeze as hope soars when I make out the outline of a large, human-like creature.

It's the right shape. It's the right size-- for a youth or a female, maybe-- at well over six feet tall with a massive shoulder span. It moves slightly, and I catch a glimpse of thick facial hair.

My nerves tingle in excitement. This is more than I could have hoped for.

"You shouldn't be here alone," His voice resonates through the thicket, carrying a note of concern.

My hopes crash. It's just a man.

Well, not *just* a man.

The man that steps out of the shadows and into full view is nothing less than a bona fide *mountain man*.

Jet black waves fall over chiseled features and dark eyes focus on me under brows that are drawn down as he scrutinizes me. The thick beard that covers the lower part of his face is long enough to brush the collar of a t-shirt that peeks out under a classic red plaid flannel shirt.

Maybe I should tell him my boyfriend is out gathering firewood or something but, honestly? My insides are screaming at me to make sure this guy knows I'm one hundred percent single.

"What's wrong with being out here alone?"

He shakes his head like he can't believe what he's hearing and shrugs the rucksack off his broad shoulders.

"This forest isn't safe for--"

Mountain Man's Dream

"Women. Yeah, I know the story."

Checking the camera I've been working to secure into the tree, I decide it's good and pull another of the small cameras out of my pocket, heading toward another tree.

"It's no joke. Women have been going missing in the weeping wilderness for as long humans have inhabited the area. Why the hell would you risk coming up here alone if you know the history of the area?"

There was a period in history when several people-- supposedly all women-- went missing from this section of forest. The area was eventually abandoned, and the mountain pass road rerouted, due to the disappearances. For nearly a hundred years now, there's been almost no human traffic through this area based entirely on superstition; making it a perfect location for my project.

I have to laugh, he looks so serious, like he actually buys into the myths.

He's does not laugh with me.

His eyes narrow and deep crease forms between his brows. Under the mustache, I can see full lips set in a grim scowl.

"It's just folklore," I assure him, but he looks anything but reassured.

Glen

Rocklyn Ryder

"What are you doing?"

The little songbird squawks when he sees me starting to set up my minimalist camp just a few feet from her own tent.

"If you're staying, so am I." I grumble at her while I string my camping hammock between a couple of trees.

My songbird turns out to be a curvy little siren, and she just might be calling me to my doom; because she's got me setting up camp in a place I swore I'd never stay another night in.

There's no way I'm going to let her stay here alone. I don't give a fuck if she believes in the legends surrounding these woods or not. Legends exist for a reason, and I've seen enough with my own eyes to know some of those reasons.

"How long are you going to stay?" She doesn't sound mad, exactly, but there's definitely a tone in her voice that suggests that having me camped so close to her is inconvenient.

Well, tough.

"As long as you are."

There's a good-sized rock that gives me a place to sit with a great view-- of the woods surrounding us, sure, but mostly of the luscious ass in the khaki cargo pants a few feet away from me as it flexes with her efforts to reach the lower branches of an old growth cedar.

"If you're staying, you're helping," she twists her torso so I get a look at those magnificent tits to go along with her round butt, not to mention the heart-shaped face with the pouty lips that have my mind full of obscene ideas.

I haven't even asked her what her name is, let alone why the hell she's stringing a bunch of cameras up in a haunted fucking forest, but I'm already obsessed.

"Sure thing," I stand up and yank at my pants, trying not make it obvious that what I'm really doing is relieving the pressure that's choking my dick since it insists on being ready to slip between those thick thighs of hers at a moment's notice.

"What am I helping you do, Sugar?"

Shit, what the fuck is wrong with me? I expect her to snap at me, give me a lecture about respect for giving her a pet name she didn't earn-- *yet.* She's just so fucking sweet, I can practically taste her already. I'll be happy to give her a chance to earn that pet name.

To my surprise, instead of shutting me down, her cheeks brighten with a rosy blush and she can't quite hide the twitch that fights to turn those pretty lips into a full smile.

Shit, if my dick was ready to claim her before, it's straining for the chance now.

"I need to get these cameras set up," she answers, "the least visible, the better, but with as much field of vision as possible."

She reaches into one of the pockets of her pants, the one that sits low on her right thigh, and pulls out a tiny camera. She points at a spot about a foot above her head where she wants the camera hung in the tree and my brain comes up with a list of ways I could help her out that all involve me getting my hands on her.

"No problem," I mutter, taking the camera from her hand and easily reaching up to affix it to a branch. No touching involved.

Why did I have to turn out to be the fucking gentleman in the family?

"So why are you setting up the cameras?" I ask, taking the next one she hands me and putting in the tree she directs me to.

"Have you seen the recent viral videos of Sasquatch?"

"Who hasn't?" I huff a short laugh. "You know they were faked though, right? The university looked 'em over and said they're all AI."

"They are absolutely *not* fake." Her voice is strong with certainty. The kind of confidence that says she knows what she's talking about.

Chapter Three

Finch

"What makes you so sure they aren't fake?"

Every time he speaks in that deep, rumbly voice I'm overcome with the urge to get naked and throw myself at him.

Why does this man have me so flustered?

"Because I shot them."

He stops what he's doing, turning to look at me.

Dark eyes lock with mine before dragging their way down my body slowly. The look is so heavy, so thorough, it might as well be his calloused hands making their way over every inch of my goose-pimpled flesh.

It's like my body is instinctively determined to respond to him. Heat blooms in my blood. Something in my lower belly pulls tight and tugs and moist heat soaks my panties.

"Thought you said the stories up here were just *folklore?*"

Grateful for a break in the tension, I swallow hard

and hope to hell my nipples don't look as hard as they feel.

"Sasquatch isn't responsible for all the people who've gone missing out here--"

"Women," he interjects. "*Women* who've gone missing. Single women. Every one of 'em."

They were all single women? That's something I didn't know. Still--

"Statistically speaking, it's likely that a lot more than just *single women* have gone missing, it's just that unaccompanied females are more likely to succumb to the dangers of a remote wilderness and far more likely to get talked about.

"It makes for great gossip," I point out. "But more importantly, those stories serve a purpose as cautionary tales to ensure that people who aren't prepared to survive the woods won't venture into them. Haven't you ever heard the story of Little Red Riding Hood?"

When he tears his eyes off me it feels like he has to put some effort into it.

He reaches back into the tree and finishes securing the last of the cameras where I'd indicated it should go.

"So, you're saying that you took those videos and that they're real? But four hundred years of legends about missing women in this forest are based on parents that didn't want their daughters to wander into the woods?"

"Sasquatch isn't stealing women," I repeat. "They're shy creatures that avoid humans."

"There are scarier things in these mountains than Bigfoot, Sugar."

Yup, there definitely are; like a mountain man that makes me feel more alive than I've ever felt in my life.

This man makes me feel things that I never thought were going to happen for me.

Glen

"Name's Glen," I tell her when we finally get around to the introductions.

It's getting late, the sun's already dropped behind the western range, leaving the forest drenched in the cool blue shadows of mountain twilight.

We spent too much damn time hanging her cameras up and not enough time preparing for the night.

"Finch."

Looking up from the fire that's just come to life, I give her another look. As much as I try not to stare, I can't help myself. I feel my eyes go hungry every time they catch sight of her: easily a foot shorter than my six foot, four inches; long blonde hair the same shade as the summer sun in the afternoon, hangs down her back in a single thick plait like a silken rope. I want to twist it around my fist and pull on it while I drive my cock into her from behind.

"So, you're a Bigfoot hunter, eh?"

I choke back my lust and stoke the fire.

If I keep staring into those storm gray eyes, I'll get lost forever. And maybe I'm already lost. God knows it's taking every ounce of will power I can scrape together not to pull her in for a hard kiss before laying her down right here by the fire and making her mine.

"Not exactly." Finch pulls a blanket out of her tent and spreads it down on the ground beside the fire.

"I'm a scientist."

Her voice is proud and I like hearing the sound of passion in it, but I want to hear it full of a different kind of passion.

"The asshole that debunked my videos is the professor that oversees my graduate program in cryptozoology."

I feed the fire one of the larger pieces of wood I was able to gather and watch the flames reach for the sky. Normally I wouldn't keep a campfire going longer than it takes to cook dinner and definitely not build it as high as I have this one, but I've camped in the weeping wilderness before and I'd have preferred not to do it again. I'm going to make sure that Finch is safe until I can talk her into getting out of these woods and into my bed.

"That fucking sucks," I mutter about her professor. Sounds like an asshole that probably doesn't want one of his students to steal his spotlight. "So, this is what you're gonna do with your life? Run around the world, looking for Bigfoot and the Loch Ness Monster?"

Her answer means more to me than it should.

Dammit, I just met the girl and, in my head, I put a ring on that a long time ago and we're already on baby number three. That's not fucking fair to Finch. She's a few years younger than me, still working on a graduate degree, about to start a crazy new career that'll take her all over the world looking for mythical beasts...settling down with a grumpy old man and making babies is probably the furthest thing from this girl's mind.

Her laugh is like music. She's moved over to give me room to sit beside her on the blanket and now I'm close enough to her to catch the scent of her. Warm, herbal and fruity, like rosemary and peaches.

My dick's hard again, determined to stake its claim on this beauty.

"No." It sounds like a confession, as she fiddles with the hem on the hoodie she's slipped on over a pair of soft, fleece camp pants. "My first love is entomology, actually. You know we find hundreds of previously uncatalogued species of insects every year? I'm particularly interested in lepidopterology. That's why I had those cameras set up at Clawson Crossing to begin with."

Those gray eyes look up to meet mine and there's that passion for what she does lighting up her voice again and it's the sexiest fucking thing I've ever heard-- my girl wants to chase butterflies in the mountains.

Chapter Four

Finch

There's no warning to prepare me for the feel of Glen's mouth on mine, the soft scratch of his beard, the hot, possessive invasion of his tongue into my mouth.

One minute he was sitting beside me on the camp blanket and I was telling him what I really want to do with my life, and then-- *holy shit*.

If I thought this man was scrambling my senses earlier, feeling his touch has me spinning into overdrive.

My back hits the ground as Glen's weight pushes me against the earth beneath us. The fire dances and crackles beside us. Glen's mouth ravages mine in a brutal kiss that has me clawing to get more of him.

The way his bulk covers me makes me feel downright tiny. It's not a feeling I have often and it makes me crave the feel of him even more.

His hands slide over my body and I position to give him access to whatever he wants, loving the heat from his large hand as it covers my breast over-- and then under-- the fabric of my sweatshirt.

Glen palms my flesh and then drags a calloused thumb over my pebbled nipple, causing me to moan into our kiss and arch my back to push closer to him.

When his hand keeps moving down, I think I might come out of my skin with the anticipation. His roughened skin scratches lightly against my ribs and then strong fingers knead into the flesh of my hip before slipping under the fleece of my camp pants.

"Fucking hell, baby." Glen's dark growl is barely audible where he curses against my throat. "These panties are fucking soaked, Sugar."

And then his eyes are on mine. The dilated pupils reflecting the fire make him look far more dangerous than anything that could be lurking in the woods around us but I've never felt safer-- or needier.

"Tell me that's because of me." His voice is thick with possession as he inches a blunt fingertip slowly between my folds and begins to slip it through my wetness.

Heat blooms where he touches and I move on the blanket beside him, raising a knee to give him better access.

When that thick digit presses to my entrance, I let out a moan but he hesitates, teasing, leaving me aching for him to touch me completely.

"Tell me, Sugar." Glen leans close and whispers against my ear. "Tell me you're wet for me, baby."

"For you," I manage to rasp out as his delves beyond the gate of my core. "I'm wet for you, Glen."

"You're fucking tight, Sugar." I can hear the strain in his voice as his single finger wiggles deeper inside me, filling me the way I've never felt before.

"Sorry," I pant heavily, tipping my hips to grind against the heel of his hand. "I've never done this before."

I'm shameless in my need for release, grasping Glen's wrist and pulling his hand harder to my throbbing core when suddenly he's moved over me again, pressing me firmly into the soft earth beneath the blanket.

"What do you mean, Sugar?" His voice is dark as the night outside the reach of the fire, pinning my hips to the ground beneath him with the hand that still has one finger pressed inside. "You mean you've never been finger-fucked by a campfire before?"

Half a grin perks up one corner of his full lips under his whiskers as he looks down at me with a predatory gaze that sends a new flood of need over his hand.

"Never been finger-fucked at all," I correct. "Please," I beg, "keep doing what you were doing."

"Better fucking believe it, Sugar." He begins that delicious stroking inside me again, moving in and out slowly this time, gathering my wetness and working me till my body is moving in time with his strokes.

I'm aching and needy, clutching the front of his t-shirt with one hand and the back of his neck with my other.

"Let's see if two fit." It's barely a whisper and I'm not sure he's even talking to me.

Glen's hand moves and a second finger slips between my lower lips, joining the first as they draw along my seam and circle my clit. Fuck! I'm so close, it hurts.

Then two of his thick fingers move together, pushing past my entrance. I feel my body being stretched deliciously as he pumps, holding his hand hard against my mound while I moan and buck against him.

"You ever been fucked at all, Sugar?"

Glen's voice is somewhere far away, it seems, hoarse and urgent.

I shake my head from side to side.

A strangled noise comes from somewhere near my ear.

"You want to get fucked tonight." It doesn't sound much like a question but the answer is absolutely yes.

"Yes," I'm nodding my head, feeling the blanket twisting under me, my braid undone as my hair tangles from my writhing. "Yes, Glen, I want you to fuck me tonight."

My body ignites. Muscles stop responding to brain signals, everything tenses, and I explode in spasms that wring a primal kind of cry out of me.

It's not my first orgasm-- but it's the first one I've shared with another person and it's definitely the first one that has me understanding what all the fuss is about.

I go limp until Glen begins slowly playing his fingers again. Slow, gentle strokes that make me jump when he gets close to my over-sensitized bud. It doesn't take long till I'm feeling that itch again, the need for him to give me more.

He pulls his hand off of me and I groan in protest.

When my eyes flutter open, he's hovering above me, propped on one elbow while he slides the two fingers that are coated with my juices into his mouth

"I knew you deserved that nickname, Sugar." His eyes shut, and he moans as he licks my flavor off his fingers. "You're so fucking sweet."

It's dirty and hot and I'm wetter than before, eager for what comes next.

Glen

"You're not done yet, Sugar, you still need to take care of this."

Taking her little hand from where it's resting against her stomach, I guide it down to the bulge in my jeans.

Sugar's eyes go wide when she feels how fucking hard I am for her. Or maybe it's realizing what she's gotten herself into.

This cock isn't exactly beginner sized.

But my girl licks her lips like she's starving suddenly. Then she pulls her other arm out from where it's been caged beneath me and scrambles to free my dick before I can do it myself.

The fire is still burning high and bright so I don't bother adding more wood to it.

Getting up on my knees, I move between Finch's thick thighs, stripping off my shirt now that she's got me so worked up I can't even feel the chill in the mountain air around us. Then I grab the waistband of those fleece tights I've been fighting with tonight, and yank 'em over her full hips, tossing them into the tent along with her panties.

Finch has my belt undone and my fly unbuttoned with her greedy little hands diving into my briefs.

I want this little goddess's hands all over me, dammit. I want that dirty little mouth of hers wrapped around my cock, drinking down my cum while I fuck her throat. I want to worship at that altar glistening between her legs for hours. But first, I need to get inside her, feel that virgin pussy clenching around my cock while I pump her full and make her mine.

"Down."

I order Finch back to the ground with a gentle push and add my jeans and briefs to the pile of clothes I've already tossed aside.

Taking my cock in one hand, I stroke it from base to tip, squeezing to relieve the pressure that's got me ready to rut like an animal while I get a good, full look at my girl all spread out underneath me, naked and waiting.

It's a sight so pretty I almost lose my load just looking at her. Her sunny blonde hair has come undone and lays in a tangled mess around her head; reflecting red in the flickering firelight. Her skin is pale and honey-kissed all over, and those feminine curves of hers are begging to be claimed.

Mountain Man's Dream

Out here in the summer night with the stars shining down on us and the fire dancing, I want to flip her over, pull her up on all fours and fuck her from behind. Wild and primal, till we're both howling in the moonlight.

But not now. I'm gonna take her face to face so I can watch her pretty features contort with all the feelings of knowing a man for the first time.

Possessiveness boils up in me. I'm the only man this beauty is ever going to know.

"You ready, Sugar?"

I crawl between her legs, pushing her knees wide with mine while I continue tugging my erection, distributing the pre-cum leaking out the tip till I've got this steel rod slicked up for getting past the tight ring of her virginity.

"I want to taste you." She whispers, her eyes locked on the throbbing monster in my hand.

Goddamn. She licks those pouty lips again and it's all I can do not to give her what she wants, but I know I'm not going to last long and I plan on coming in Finch's womb tonight.

I'm gonna breed this dirty little science girl and fill her with babies that we can raise in the mountains together.

"Sugar, we'll do anything you want, any way you want, but first I need to make you mine. Understand?"

I get the cutest little nod from her while she gnaws on that puffy lower lip and pinches her own nipples.

Damn. I almost lose it over that sight. I don't have

any more time to play around, I need to be inside my girl now.

Lining the tip of my dick up with the little slit of her entrance, we're both dripping for each other. That's a good thing, because when I was knuckle deep in her earlier, I could feel how tight she is and I'm sure this is going to hurt her.

"Finch--" I manage to grind out the words between gritted teeth, my self-restraint teetering on the brink. "This is forever, got it Sugar? I'm gonna fuck you raw so I can feel your little cherry pop on my dick. And then you're mine. Do you understand what I'm telling you?"

Finch's tits rise up and her stomach quivers with the sharp breath she takes but she doesn't protest. Not one fucking bit.

"Do it, Glen," she pants, her eyes trained between us where my cock pressed to her hole. "Do it, I want to belong to you."

It's fast. Faster than I mean to go but when she utters those words, I can't hold back any longer.

In one rough motion I'm inside her slick channel, feeling her tightness choking my shaft as she's split open around me.

"You feel so fucking good, Sugar. How are you doing?"

Finch's heart-shaped face twists, her eyes pinched closed tightly and her pretty little lips parted while she gasps a few times. But she nods her head even though it looks like she's hurting.

"Relax Sugar, try to relax and let it feel good." I

catch her lips in a kiss, trying to stay still till she gets used to my invasion. "Remember when had my fingers in you?"

Her eyes stay scrunched but she nods.

"Remember how good that felt?"

Another nod.

"This is gonna be better, Sugar, I fucking promise."

Chapter Five

Finch

Glen coos softly into my ear, telling me to relax and reminding me about how good he made me feel earlier. As I concentrate on his words, I'm aware that he's starting to move. Gentle. Slow. Almost imperceptibly. Until he feels me relaxing, and then he starts to move more.

Still slow, but long strokes that take him almost all the way out of me till I miss the fullness and beg for him to bring it back. Then slow pushes back till he's buried to the hilt inside me and both of us are breathing hard and gulping for air.

Finally, he's right. It is better than his fingers. I'm stretched tight and filled in the most amazing way and suddenly desperate for him to move faster.

"More," I tell him, my fingers scrabbling to get hold on the muscles of his back then clutching at his waist when they slip away through the sweat beading on his skin. "Glen, please, more."

His pace quickens, each thrust becoming more

forceful. Sweat covers us both and I hear myself making noises that should be embarrassing. But every cry and squeal that comes out of me seems to make Glen move faster, frantically, building friction between us till my clit is on a hair trigger and I'm grinding against the root of his cock in search of relief.

"You ready to come for me again, Sugar? Is that what you're telling me?"

"Please, Glen, oh God, yes, I need to come." My own voice sounds foreign and far away.

"That's my good girl, ready to come with her man." His voice is strangled, his forehead against mine as he slides one hand between us and finds my button with the pad of his thumb.

"Tell me you're mine, Finch. Tell me you want my cum claiming you as mine."

"I want it, Glen." I'm breaking out of my body now, setting sail on the night air, as I unravel on this mountain man's cock, but I know what I'm saying and God yes, do I mean it.

Within seconds, Glen's body stiffens and I swear I can feel him thicken inside me right before he comes. His huge body convulses with a series of hard shudders and I feel each spurt of his release until he finally collapses over me, rolling slightly to one side like he's afraid of crushing me.

We lay there for what seems like a long time, catching our breath and letting the cool night air dry the sweat from our bodies while the fire continues to crackle and flicker in the background.

Mountain Man's Dream

The fire is much lower now but not down to coals yet.

Somewhere not far off I hear a howl.

"That sounded like a wolf," I mention drowsily.

"Because it was," Glen pulls me into his arms, curling his big body around mine so that I'm less aware of the chill in the air now that I've cooled down.

"There aren't any wolves in these mountains," I inform him.

Glen chuckles, kissing my shoulder and drawing lazy circles on my belly.

"You tellin' me you're out here looking for Bigfoot, but you don't think a pack of wolves can exist without being tagged and tracked?"

Glen

THE WOLF SONG IS IN THE DISTANCE, PLENTY far enough away not to worry about.

I stoke the fire one more time anyway, memories of my last night in the weeping wilderness getting the better of me.

"Hang on a minute, Sugar."

When Finch starts reaching for her clothes, I beat her to it. Searching in the tent for where everything landed when I was eager to get it out of my way, but before I hand her night clothes back to her, I reach for my ruck and find the small toiletry kit I carry.

"Lie back, Sugar, let me take care of ya."

Taking the cloth I dampened with water from my drinking bottle, I take my time running it over Finch's body,

"Sorry Sugar, I should have warmed it up first." The water's cold and Finch jumps when the cloth touches her.

"It's OK, the fire's so warm. It's feels good."

She lets those pretty thighs fall open so I can wipe between them, cleaning up the mess we made even though I know I'll be making a mess of her again before the night is over.

The cloth comes away from between her legs pink, reminding me that I'm the first man she's ever had and my cock stirs at the thought of being the last.

"How are you feeling?"

"Good." In the firelight, I can see the blush in her cheeks and I don't miss the way her gaze falls to the monster rising again between my own legs.

The way she licks her lips has me completely hard in seconds.

"You still wanna taste me, Sugar?"

Finch's head bobs up and down enthusiastically, making me chuckle.

"Maybe we oughta move to the tent first."

She doesn't argue with me. My girl quickly scrambles into the tent she had no idea she'd be sharing when she set it up, giving me a view of her naked ass jiggling with her movements.

As soon as we're inside for the night, I lie back and let my girl explore my body every way she wants...by the time we fall asleep in a sweaty heap of exhaustion and satisfaction, I don't even care that the wolf song sounds like it's gotten closer.

Hours later, I find my eyelids springing open. At first, I'm not sure what it is.

The sky outside is a lighter blue, but only barely, letting me know it's early morning but still awhile before sunrise.

The forest around us is silent. Maybe that's the problem, birds should be beginning to sing by now.

Then I hear it. The smallest of twigs snapping, the softness of a careful footfall, what sounds like breathing; something is in camp and it sure as hell ain't Bigfoot.

My skin prickles and the hairs on my arms stand up.

I can hear it prowling outside the tent now.

Grabbing my clothes, I unwind myself from Finch's sleeping body, instantly pissed at being forced to leave her soft curves when I'd so much rather be sinking into her again.

Chapter Six

Finch

The absence of Glen's warmth against me pulls me out of a deep sleep. Outside the tent I hear something moving and Glen muttering low.

It's still pretty dark, but I can tell the sky is beginning to lighten. Still, it's hard to find clothes without turning on a light and something about the quiet movements outside have me wanting to keep my movements discreet.

After a little blind searching, I find something I can put on and then carefully creep toward the door of the tent that's still hanging open.

When I poke my head out, I see Glen's eye trained carefully on something outside of camp. He looks determined and on edge.

"Stay in the tent, Sugar"

He waves a hand behind his back, indicating I should stay put but it's too late. I've already climbed out of the tent, wrapped in nothing but his flannel that's somehow huge on me and hangs to my knees with my hiking boots slipped on over my bare feet.

The remnants of our fire are still burning, I can hear the glass-like tinkle of embers smoldering under the top layer of coals that have cooled to a deceptive gray in the cold air over night.

At first, I don't see what Glen's attention is focused on.

Coming up to him, he catches me with his hand and pushes me back, keeping me behind his wide body as if he's protecting me from something.

Then I see it.

"Is that..."

No. It can't be.

It's definitely canine, but much larger than any wolf species I'm familiar with. The fur is black as coal with eyes that reflect red in the smoldering remains of last night's fire-- giving off the eerie effect of glowing.

Last night, when Glen said that it really was wolf song that I heard, I didn't expect them to be so close. Now, seeing the creature that watches us from the edge of the forest, feelings of both panic and awe war inside me.

It wasn't my plan to make a career out of looking for the most legendary creatures that excite my colleagues in the cryptozoology field-- this Sasquatch lead was a fluke-- the wolf that takes a brazen step out of the shadows toward us now...

I tell myself I'm being ridiculous-- it's crazy enough to discover there really is an undocumented wolf population in these mountains-- this is just an ordinary wolf. It has to be. Anything else would be beyond cryptid, and edging into crazy.

Next thing you know, I'll be looking for unicorns.

Nope. Nope. Just a wolf. A really big, scary wolf that isn't even supposed to exist in these mountains and doesn't seem all that bothered by the huge man standing off against it with the short-handled hatchet in his hand that he used to cut up the firewood with last night.

Glen

THE THING AND I STARE EACH OTHER DOWN FOR what seems like ever but as soon as Finch climbs out of the tent, its focus zeroes in on her.

The last time I saw one of these things was the last time I ever set foot in this section of forest. One wolf encounter was more than enough to convince me there was a damn good reason the weeping wilderness earned its name and deserved to be left off limits to humans.

I don't know what I'll do if it attacks; wolves rarely hunt alone and that knowledge has my hackles up, worried we're about to get ambushed from behind.

One thing is certain, I'll die fighting if it means keeping Finch safe. There's no way I'm going to let anything touch her but me.

Thing is, this guy doesn't act like he's hunting.

The beast shifts its eyes back on me and takes a step closer, watching to see if I'm going to threaten it.

"Don't move, Sugar," I warn, "not a muscle."

"You know I have an undergrad in zoology, right?" Finch whispers, standing statue still behind me. "I know a wolf's prey instinct is triggered by movement."

The dog looks back at Finch and the uncanny feeling that it understands our words sends a creeping feeling tingling up my spinal column as it tilts its head just a bit.

Another step toward us, and it's easy to tell that its coat is as dark as the shadows it's stepped out of. At least the eyes don't have that eerie red glowing effect to them now. Must have been a trick of the dying fire and the predawn light.

It's still fucking huge though, and it sure as hell doesn't seem scared of me.

"I didn't think they usually approached humans like this?" I hiss at my science girl.

"They don't," she confirms. "This is really unusual behavior."

"This fucker better not be rabid."

At that, it turns its attention back on me and narrows its eyes. Pulling its upper lip into a menacing curl like I just insulted the thing.

"Yeah? You think you understand me then?" My own voice is as lethal as the growl that comes from the animal's throat when it hears me talking to it.

"Don't even think about it, buddy. She's *mine*. Go find your own woman."

Still staying behind me, Finch stifles a giggle. "I don't think that's what he's after, Glen."

Both Finch and I stand perfectly still. I'm ready to split the thing open and hang its hide on my wall if it so much as hints at making a move closer to Sugar, but it just stands there, staring at me.

Then it lifts its massive head and sniffs as if it's caught a new scent. The thing wrinkles its nose and shakes its head like it's sorry for inhaling. Then, with a disgusted look in my direction, it turns and runs off.

Both Finch and I stay frozen for long seconds. Maybe in shock, maybe just waiting for a surprise attack from more of the things hiding in the shadows beyond the tree line.

"Fuck baby, you OK?"

When my muscles relax, I spin on my heel and pull Finch into my arms.

The first rays of sunlight are breaking over the horizon now, and I'm not gonna act like I'm not damn glad to see the light of day.

"Yeah, good," Finch assures me, nodding vehemently against my chest. "That was crazy."

"I told you this forest wasn't safe, Sugar. Get your clothes on, we're getting the fuck out of here."

In fifteen minutes flat, we're both dressed and packed, the coals from the fire are drowned and smothered, and I'm leading Finch down the trail that skirts that godforsaken wilderness in the bright morning light.

"How have they gone undocumented all this time?" Finch wonders, "I mean, with as many Sasquatch sightings that get reported up here, you'd think a wolf pack would have been discovered long ago."

"I don't know, Sugar, but I get a feeling they don't want to be discovered."

"They're just wolves, Glen," she tells me. "That guy didn't seem shy about approaching humans. They can't stay hidden forever."

"You gonna prove they exist just like Bigfoot, Sugar?"

Finch stops to look back up toward the stand of trees we left behind us and gives the forest a thoughtful look.

"Not me," she tells me as we make our way back onto the level road that leads back to my truck. "Someone else can have that honor. I'm done chasing monsters."

Chapter Seven

Finch

Glen's place is more house than cabin, a pretty two story with log siding outside and modern drywall inside.

"It was built in the late eighties." He explains while he gives me a brief tour. "It was my parents' first house. Mom and Dad built a bigger place closer to town when we outgrew this."

"How do you outgrow a place like this?"

"Two bedrooms, five kids. You do the math." He laughs as he finishes the tour at the master suite. "And then I started raising goats, so it's a good thing they got the bigger place before then."

"You raised goats?" I try to imagine my hulking mountain man as an awkward boy, showing goats in the county fair.

Glen nods his head slowly, a grin widening across his face as he reaches into a cabinet and pulls out a few towels.

"Yup, the goats are all my fault. My grandparents still have a few."

The way he says it makes me think there's a story that I'll need to hear.

The subject of goats and grandparents gets dropped, along with our dirty camp clothes and I discover that the shower in the en suite is big enough for both of us to shower in, but not quite big enough for both of us to do much else in.

"We'll be getting that remodeled first," Glen grumbles in regards to the shower's limitations when we realize I can't kneel between his legs without flooding the bathroom floor.

"First?" I have to ask, laughing as we towel ourselves off and do our best to mop the floor with the towels when we're done.

"First," Glen affirms, grabbing me up in his and carrying me, bridal style, into the big bedroom where he drops me on the soft, king size bed.

"We're gonna need more bedrooms," he says, as he starts kissing a trail up the inside of my thigh, "and more bathrooms if we have girls. I've got two sisters-- there are never enough bathrooms in a house with girls."

"Can confirm." I giggle, but mostly because Glen's hot breath is tickling my thigh, "I have two sisters too."

"Then it's decided, we'll build each girl their own bathroom."

It's silly talk about a future that's still in the future, of course, but knowing that he's already thinking about the important things just further convinces me that Glen really is the right man for me.

"Now let me take care of this pussy, sugar," he says softly, speaking into the apex of my thighs. "I didn't get to give it nearly enough attention while we were on the mountain last night."

Glen's king size bed is a lot more comfortable than the hard earth of the mountain with nothing but a thin camp blanket for cushioning and there's plenty of room for me to lie back while he pushes my thighs wide and drags his tongue along my seam.

Glen

FINCH'S SKIN IS SOFT AND WARM FROM THE shower and the campfire and dust have been replaced with the scents of my body wash and shampoo, but when I dip my face into the hot, wet, center of her, I'm still greeted by the same earthy musk of Finch's natural scent.

The one that has my mouth watering immediately, hungry to taste her again. This time when I slip a finger inside her silky channel, I already know just how to measure my strokes while I flick the tip of my tongue over her swollen little pearl till she comes undone for me.

Damn, I am looking forward to figuring out every way she likes to be licked and stroked and touched, and especially, how Sugar likes my getting my cock.

Speaking of which, he's aching for his turn now, hard as rock and weeping pre-cum in anticipation of getting inside Finch's tight little pussy.

"Sugar," I rasp, lifting my head from between her pretty thighs and wiping her cream off my beard, "you're so fucking sweet, I could eat you all damn day."

"Maybe someday I'll let you," she purrs as her arms go around my neck.

She moans into my kiss, and rocks those full hips up against my hard cock but before I can slip inside her, Finch surprises the fuck out of me with a sudden roll that has me on my back looking up at the goddess straddling my groin.

"You look pretty fucking good up there, Sugar," I tell her, pushing against her with my hips while my hands grip her thighs. "What are you thinking you're gonna do now?"

Fuck me, I'm hoping. Ride me like a fucking Valkyrie with all that blonde hair of hers still damp from our shower, sticking to her skin while I get her worked up nice and sweaty so we can take another one together.

"There wasn't room in the tent last night." Finch looks down at me, her little hands pressing against my chest for balance as she raises up and positions herself before sliding onto me completely.

Her eyes go wide and she catches that full bottom lip between her teeth.

My whole body tenses up, trying to keep control of my urge to thrust into that velvet sheath that's choking my dick but I can feel Finch's muscles fighting to relax and I know she's still getting used to taking all of me. So I behave myself and let her have the reins, no matter how hard it is to fight my need to slam all the way up to the hilt.

"That's it, Sugar," I coax her down a few inches more with a gentle tug on her hips. "You're so fucking wet now baby. You're such a good girl, taking my cock all the way like that."

A soft little noise makes its way out of Finch's throat as she slips down to the root of my cock. Her fingertips dig into my sides, her eyes flutter closed, and she bites back the next sound that tries to escape those pretty lips of hers.

I need to hear that sound. I need to hear every sound Finch can make when I'm inside her like this.

My will power is out the goddamn window now and I'm moving like a man possessed, desperate to thrust into her heat until she's fucking screaming for me while I pump her full of cum.

Fuck, she's gorgeous, bouncing on my cock and rocking those sweet hips of hers, looking for just the right pressure to find her release.

"Come for me, Sugar," I command her roughly, settling my thumb over her clit when I can't take anymore. "Let it all out, baby, let me hear you screaming for me while I fill you up."

My girl does what I tell her, throwing her head back and letting her pretty screams bounce off the walls around us while her thighs shake and her sweet little tunnel clenches down on my cock like it needs me even deeper inside her.

I give her my best effort to answer that call, grabbing hold and pulling her down so there's not a bit of space separating us while I unload jets of hot seed deep inside her womb.

When Finch lays beside me, I hold her till her trembling stops and her breathing is steady and deep.

"I think you'd better get serious about adding those extra bathrooms at this rate."

Finch snuggles under my arm with her head on my chest and soon I'm dozing beside her, dreaming about all the years I'm going to spend wrapped up in those soft curves.

Epilogue 1

1 year later

Finch

"Your grandmother and her friend look like they're plotting again," I whisper to my husband, pointing toward the two old ladies huddled together at one of the tables on the patio.

Glen was smart enough to talk me into marrying him before I was fully caught up on the trouble his grandmother and her friends are known for around the small town of Moonshine Ridge.

If I'd known...well: I look at the family gathered around us up at the hot springs resort that the Diaz's own and I know I'd have jumped in with both feet just as fast.

"I'll give Hawk a heads up," he whispers back. "The last time they were left unsupervised, they set off an avalanche that had the Jones's socked in for weeks."

I bite my tongue, not reminding him that Vera Jones and her crony, Mable Hart, had deserved last winter's avalanche that closed the road to the Jones family estate when they stole the goats from Marcia and Alex's barn.

The great goat-napping escapade happened before I joined the family, but it's one of the bigger undertakings that the four old women have pulled off, so it's become the stuff of legend on the small-town gossip chain.

Besides, it wasn't even an avalanche that Glen's grandmother, Marcia, and her friend, Alice, pulled off. But they did manage to pile a staggering amount of snow on the private road to the Jones's River Bend property last winter and no one's figured out exactly how two women in their eighties managed to pull off such a caper.

Just part of the fun of living in a small town that's as isolated as Moonshine Ridge.

In addition to Marcia and Alice cooking up whatever trouble they're planning next, the rest of my in-laws mill around the resort along with the Lancasters and most of the other residents of town.

Glen's older sister, Meadow and her fiancé move through the practice routine for the wedding we'll be back here for in a few days.

Meadow and Ozzie got together just a couple of months before I met Glen, but they decided to do a more traditional wedding while Glen and I rushed down to the county courthouse in Slow River Valley within a week of knowing each other.

"You sorry we skipped this, Sugar?"

My husband's deep voice whispers against my ear, sending shivers down my spine like it always has.

"Not really." I shake my head and accept the glass of water he hands me. "It seems like a lot of trouble to go through just to get cake."

I never really liked being the center of attention. I think putting on a fancy dress and walking down an aisle would have taken all the fun out of my wedding day, to be honest.

"Are you saying my girls need cake?"

"We don't know it's a girl, yet! But yes-- we need cake."

My hand has already made a habit of settling over my belly, just where the little flutters are starting to become more and more noticeable even though I don't have a proper baby bump yet.

Glen's convinced we're having a girl just to make the new bathroom useful. Work on the addition of two new bedrooms and two new bathrooms was finished just in time for my positive pregnancy test.

We couldn't be happier.

I finished up my masters degree in May, but my Bigfoot hunting days are long behind me.

When Glen and I went back to retrieve my cameras-- with a few of his most intimidating mountain man buddies and a couple of fire arms, I might add-- they were missing. Not smashed or fallen or with dead batteries-- missing.

Each camera and its mounts had been carefully removed from the trees and had simply vanished without a trace.

It was enough to convince me that whatever has managed to stay hidden out there in the rugged wilderness surrounding my new home has done so intentionally and that should be respected.

So now I listen to the stories that float around among locals and tourists alike, sharing the sightings and occasional encounters that continue to occur.

And sometimes, when nights are quiet, I can hear the distant howl of a wolf pack that's not supposed to exist in these mountains.

Turns out, Sasquatch is just one of the local folktales clinging to the traditions of Moonshine Ridge and now that I have a much better appreciation of why folktales get started, I'm a lot less likely to disregard them.

We stay out of that forbidden stretch of wilderness when we hike and we've never had another run in of any sort or heard anyone else talk about one. And that's just fine by me.

Epilogue 2

five years later

Glen

My wife has that look in her eye, the one that says there's no point in slipping into my clothes and I better get my ass back in bed if I know what's good for me.

Finch is the best thing in the world for me, so I drop the towel from around my waist and head straight toward the curvy woman beckoning me toward her with a crooked finger and a grin that tells me she has plans for how to spend our day without the kids.

"I thought we were going downstairs to make breakfast?" I tease, already making my way between her legs, eager to start my breakfast right here.

Finch gives me a giggle because she knows as well as I do that anytime my sister takes the kids for the day; we don't make it out of bed till noon.

"Tell me what you need this morning, Sugar." I slip

my fingers through her folds, so hot and wet, already needy for attention. "You want me to eat this pretty little pussy? Slide my fingers into you and fuck you with my hand while you come all over my beard?"

"That sounds like a good place to start," she answers. Her voice is all throaty and deep and she's already on the edge, with her own fingers dipping down to circle her clit until I win the brief battle and suction my mouth over her. My fingers push deeper and stroke firmly till Finch's fingers tangle through my wet hair and she comes on my face so fucking hard I almost lose my breath for a second.

Before I even get a chance to enjoy licking her cream up, she's tugging at my shoulders.

"Come up here and fuck me properly now. I want your cock."

"Fuck, baby, already?"

Shit, she's still quivering from her first orgasm. Not that I'm about to put up a fight. Anytime my girl is greedy for my cock, I'm more than happy to give it to her.

"Yes, Glen. Please, now, I need you."

Without any argument, I give my wife what she's begging for, letting her control our rhythm until she's crying out on another orgasm that has her tight little walls clamped down on me so hard I don't any choice but to fill her up with my cum.

Collapsing beside her on the rumpled bed covers, I pull her into my arms and pepper her neck and shoulders with kisses.

"Damn Sugar, the last time you wrung me this dry

was right before we found out you were pregnant with Starling."

Our girls are four and three now, and I'm already glad I built the add-on to the house with the extra bathrooms.

"Yeah, about that."

Finch turns in my arms and looks at up me. Her pretty yellow hair is a tangled mess on our pillows and her fair skin is flushed bright from the romp.

For a second, she just stares at me, waiting for me to catch on.

"Really?"

My hand flies down to her belly, loving the feel of her curves under my palm and eager to feel her swollen with my child again.

"I had Doctor Jones confirm it yesterday while I dropped off the girls with Terra."

"This one had better be a boy, Sugar," I warn her sternly, "because we're out of bathrooms."

Next in Series:

Mountain Man's Hope
Mesa Diaz

Thank God Robin's all right. That's the last thing I remember thinking before I lost consciousness.

The headstrong young rookie joining the crew for the summer fire season is everything I could hope for in a woman. She's as tough as any of the guys on my team, with mouthwatering curves that beg to be claimed.

I have every intention of making Robin mine, until a chance accident puts me in a hospital bed for months.

Robin's by my side through it all; the air lift to the burn ward in Seattle, recovery, rehab, coming back to Moonshine Ridge less than the man I was before.

I'd be a fool to let her go.

Until I see what a life with me really means for her.

That's when I know the ring in my pocket can never go on Robin's finger.

I almost died to save her; I can't ask her to do the same for me.

Thanks for Reading
Mountain Man's Dream

In real life, I'm a sucker for most things folklore and mythology and one of the things I love best is discovering all the local legends, lore, and ghost stories that persist in small towns and remote areas.

Moonshine Ridge is jam-packed with these types of stories and I wish I could tell them all.

I had a lot of fun lending some more weight to the local Sasquatch sightings as well as getting to explore some other legends of the mountains around Moonshine Ridge.

I know Glen and Finch's story was a short one and quickly told, but sometimes you just want to get there quick and have a good time doing it.

As for Bigfoot-- they're up there. Probably. Along with an undocumented wolf pack that sticks to its own territory and guards it fiercely.

Someday, I hope to write that story too.

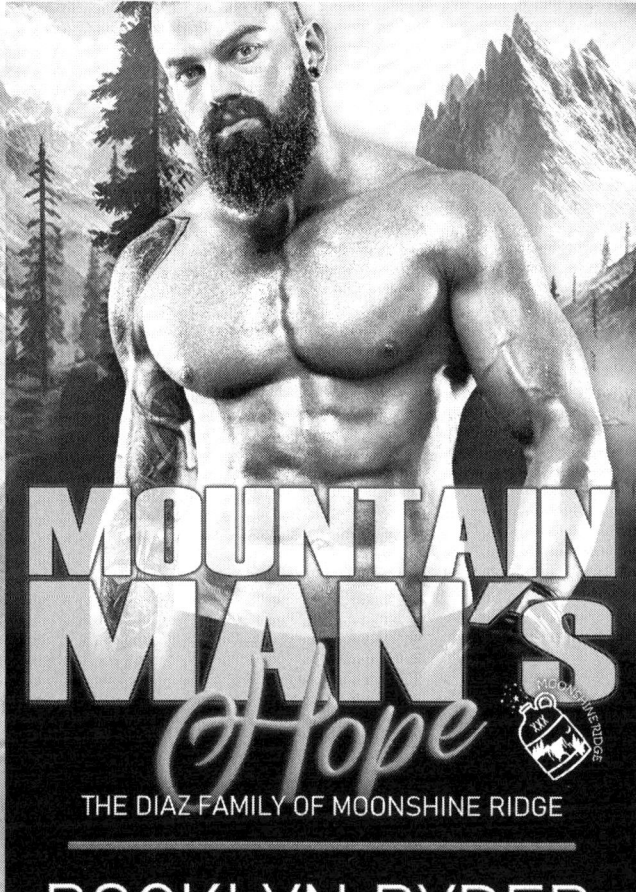

About
Mesa Diaz

Thank God Robin's all right. That's the last thing I remember thinking before I lost consciousness.

The headstrong young rookie joining the crew for the summer fire season is everything I could hope for in a woman. She's as tough as any of the guys on my team, with mouthwatering curves that beg to be claimed.

I have every intention of making Robin mine, until a chance accident puts me in a hospital bed for months.

Robin's by my side through it all; the air lift to the burn ward in Seattle, recovery, rehab, coming back to Moonshine Ridge less than the man I was before.

I'd be a fool to let her go.

Until I see what a life with me really means for her.

That's when I know the ring in my pocket can never go on Robin's finger.

I almost died to save her; I can't ask her to do the same for me.

WELCOME TO MOONSHINE RIDGE AND THE rugged wilderness surrounding the remote mountain community where the history is long, the local lore is deep, and the men are as wild as the mountains they come from.

Protective, possessive, totally obsessed; the men of Moonshine Ridge will do anything necessary to claim the women they love and give her the happily ever after she deserves.

The Moonshine Ridge books contain a lot of insta-love, some swearing, some steamy scenes, zero cheating, and a lot of swoon-worthy happy endings. They're interconnected with recurring characters but can be read as stand-alones in any order.

Mesa and Robin

Mountain Man's Hope
The Diaz Family of Moonshine Ridge
by
Rocklyn Ryder

Prologue
Mesa

Hot shot crews had come in to handle the worst of the blaze when it jumped the service road and ripped up Placer Canyon.

It took two months for Forestry to declare the incident one hundred percent contained. The specialty crews were sent home, and me and my local crew were left to handle the clean-up and any small patches that might reignite due to winds and the smoldering remains of what had been dense pine forest just weeks before the lightning strike.

It's probably the smell of forest fire lingering in the mountain air, even though it's been almost a year now. Or maybe it's catching a glimpse of the closed forestry service gates across the Benson Peak turn off-- the road we where we were clearing burned brush and cutting the downed trees that could be taken care of.

My hand tightens on Robin's and I clench my jaw, fighting the memories. The ones I have, at least.

She was a rookie assigned to my crew for the

summer season; she came up from Slow River to get some experience in the mountain terrain around Moonshine Ridge after doing a few years on a volunteer crew in the valley.

The moment I laid eyes on her, I knew she was mine.

Fuck the work dynamic. She was on loan from another station and she'd be out from under my command by September-- but not out from under me, if I had my way about it.

We'd spent the summer dancing around each other, grateful for the fire that kept us too busy and then too exhausted to act on the attraction. Otherwise, I'm sure things would have gotten out of hand long before she was due to leave my crew.

It was our last night; a new crew would be up to take over where we left off first thing in the morning.

Most of us were starting to relax, chugging bottled water, and cutting up while they made plans to invade the Brick and Porter in town to clean Ginger and Current out of pizza and beer as soon as we finishing slicing up one more of the trees that had come down over the back country access road.

I'd been busy staring at her ass when the wind kicked up: it was finally over, we were off the job and we'd waited long enough. I remember I was thinking that in twenty-four hours, she'd be mine.

In my mind, I hear the creak of the scorched trees moving in the wind all around us. My heart rate kicks up as if it were happening again right now. I remember the calm concern I felt then as I looked up for signs of danger. Years of experience assisting the forestry on these wildland blazes keeping my nerves in check.

Then the panic. That sick feeling when the sound of heavy wood giving way somewhere overhead split the air and everyone went silent.

I still see it in my nightmares; the heavy limb hanging suspended from the blackened trunk for a moment, as if it was giving everyone time to clear the area.

But Robin didn't have the experience the rest of us did, she didn't realize the branch that was about to come down was directly overhead.

The rest is just a blur for me. I remember pushing her out of the way, I remember her screaming, I remember the sounds of my crew members shouting orders around me, but mostly, I remember the intense sense of relief when I realized she was all right.

Everything else is blank.

"You okay?" She asks and I realize I'm probably in danger of crushing her fingers.

"Yeah," I mutter, leaning across the back seat of my parent's car to drop a chaste kiss on the pretty lips I haven't seen smiling nearly often enough this last year. "Fine. I'm fine."

My angel smiles at me, just a weary little quirk of those full lips of hers, letting me know she knows better. But she squeezes my hand back and lets me disappear into my thoughts again.

We both knew coming home was going to be an adjustment.

Chapter One

Robin

It wasn't supposed to be like this.

We were supposed to spend our first weekend off the Placer Fire in his cabin, drinking too much whiskey, eating too much red meat, and chasing each other naked.

I'd had a lot of expectations pinned on those plans.

From the moment I saw the captain of the fire crew I was assigned to for the summer wildland season last year, I'd been nothing but a horny school girl crushing on her boss. But who could blame me?

Mesa Diaz is six foot, four inches of bronze skin; corded muscle; wild, black curls cropped close to his head; and intense, dark eyes under a furrowed brow that had a way of making me feel like I was the one they needed to turn the hose on every time I caught him looking at me.

And I caught him looking at me a lot.

We were all of two weeks into the season when he made it clear he wanted me as badly as I wanted him.

Then the fire jumped the road and started spreading. Our crew was working one end of the road, volunteers came up from the Keller's Ferry station to help out, hot shots were called in to take care of the steep canyon terrain that none of our local firefighters were trained for.

Mesa and I were working round the clock on staggered shifts and when we did have time off, we spent it trying to catch up on four days of wildland fire fighting with too much smoke and too little sleep.

So when the blaze was contained and we got word our work was done, I was excited about more than the world's longest shower-- I had a date with the hottest man in Moonshine Ridge.

"Morning, angel."

Warm lips press against the top of my head and I smile into my coffee cup, happy to have my thoughts interrupted.

"Let me help." I jump up before Mesa can argue and he lets me carry the steaming mug of black coffee he just poured to the table.

"You want anything else right now?" I ask, waiting while he sets the cane to the side and takes a seat where I left his coffee. "I can make toast? I think we have some of that jam you like."

"I want you to stop fussing over me and let me put my hands on my woman," he pats the flannel pajamas pants that cover his thighs and gives me that look that turns my insides to goo.

"I missed you last night, angel. Was I keeping you up again?"

"Not too bad."

It's weird sitting on his lap after all this time, and I'm still not comfortable putting my weight on his bad leg even though he keeps saying it doesn't hurt.

I remember screams that will always make that hard to believe.

"Sorry, babe."

He cranes his neck upward for another kiss that I'm more than happy to deliver, but then I hop up and head for the toaster.

Mesa

ROBIN'S OFF MY LAP LIKE LIGHTNING, BUSYING herself making fucking toast when what I'd rather she was doing was crawling back in bed with me.

"Meadow texted earlier. She says they picked up your tux with Ozzie's, we just have to stop by their place to get it from them."

Watching my angel moving around the kitchen I've been microwaving leftovers in for years is one of my new favorite things. One of those dumb things that I never thought about any time I thought about what it'd be like to have a woman here, someone sharing my space and my future.

But here she is, all those curves wrapped in one of my old t-shirts that hangs down to her knees, with her thick, auburn hair pinned up in a messy bun and barefoot on the wood plank flooring, making my dick harder than those granite counter tops I custom ordered for the cabinets.

"I'll stop by and grab it when I go to the station later," I mutter, too distracted by the way my girl's braless tits jiggle and sway as she spreads butter and locally sourced, homemade black berry jam onto the wheat toast that just popped out of the toaster.

These last few days have been fucking killing me.

When I got the all-clear sign to come back home to Moonshine Ridge in time to watch my sister marry my dumb-ass buddy slash ex-buddy slash buddy-again-I-guess, I thought that was going to mean picking up where Robin and I left off before my injury put up a year-long cock-block.

Of course, things haven't been that simple: I'm still taking way more pain meds than I'd like and God knows I'm ready for the nightmares to piss off.

Robin hasn't spent an entire night next to me since we got home-- which means she's never spent an entire night beside me-- and I'm tired of waking up in the mornings to find her already down here with coffee made, staring out the windows like a zombie.

I want to wake up to her soft curves pressed against my throbbing dick so I can slip inside her and start our days off right. Not chase her out of bed because I'm talking in my sleep just to catch her down here lost in dark memories about why it started.

"You're going to the station later?" She asks, handing me a slice of the toast. "You want me to drive you?"

"Nah, I'm good," I promise. "Chief wants to meet up and talk about some stuff. He has a few ideas to get me back to work without putting me back on the line again. Why don't you stay home and take a nap while I'm not screaming in your ear?"

"You don't scream in my ear." She blushes a bit when she smiles and quickly finds something else in the kitchen to give her attention to.

"Well, whatever I say that's bad enough to wake you up."

"Mesa--" Whiskey-brown eyes turn to look at me and my gut churns.

"Don't worry, angel," I grab my cane and make quick work of crossing the small kitchen so I can wrap her up in my arms before she has a chance to apologize. "I get it. I'm not upset, I just miss you in the morning is all."

"They said it'll get better with time," she whispers, laying her head against my chest with her arms around my waist.

"Yeah, I know, Angel. I've just never been a patient man."

Robin's never told me what I say in my sleep. I know what kind of dreams I have-- images of burning trees falling on her, the sound of her screams as the flames melt away PPE and flesh. But it wasn't Robin under that branch, it was me, and I still have no memory of anything after someone saying everyone was clear. That Robin was out of danger.

I always wake up from those dreams with Robin's

sweet face hovering above me, her cool hands against my fevered skin, cooing softly to remind me that it was just a dream. She's fine. I'm fine now. Just a dream and that it's safe to go back to sleep.

So fuck if I know what it is that I must be going on about in my sleep that keeps her from getting any rest.

Chapter Two

Robin

After Mesa leaves to go meet with the fire chief in town, I take his advice, but it's not sleep I need to catch up on when I slip back between the sheets on Mesa's enormous, mountain man-sized bed.

It doesn't take long for me to get wrapped up in the smell of him with my fingers between my legs.

We never got our weekend together and then there were hospitals and surgeries, burn wards, rehab centers, and painful physical therapy while Mesa healed.

Even once he moved into the off-site rental with me for the last few months of his therapy, we never got a chance to be intimate beyond some a few hushed and awkward make out sessions.

There was always family in the apartment with us and, of course, Mesa's injuries: the femur that had been broken in a couple places and had to be pinned back together, the third degree burns that covered most of his right leg and hip, and a large section of fourth degree burns where our crew couldn't get the smoldering log off of him before it had melted away the wildland turnout gear, as well as flesh, nerves, and muscle beneath it.

There were weeks of not being able to sleep beside him because my slightest movement put him in agonizing pain. Then there were weeks of not being able to leave his side because of the nightmares that only I seemed to be able to soothe when he'd wake up screaming my name in terror.

The one time we tried was the night before his parents arrived to drive us back to Moonshine Ridge.

Mesa has the all-clear signal from all his doctors to attempt any physical activity he feels he can handle and there was only one thing he wanted to try.

We had the apartment to ourselves for a blissful twenty-four hours and we'd waited long enough.

Guilt still grips me when I remember that night. The determined grit of Mesa's jaw as he tried to pretend he was okay, until he couldn't deny it anymore and collapsed in a heap on the bed beside me, covered in sweat and shaking uncontrollably in pain.

Since we've been back home, he hasn't tried to touch me again.

He works out at the gym down at the fire station every day and I know the day will come when he's ready. Till then, I'm not going to pressure him.

I figure I've waited twenty-three years so far; I can wait however much longer it takes before the man I love is ready to make me his in all the ways a woman wants to belong to her man.

Mountain Man's Hope

But damn, if it's not hard as hell to wake up aching and needy every morning with him beside me, saying those filthy things while he's lost in some sex dream I can't wake him from.

That's the real reason I've been out of bed before him every day since we got back. The reason he finds me downstairs, staring out the windows, lost in my own fantasies.

That's what I think of now, while I have the house to myself and I can lose myself in Mesa's manly scent clinging to his pillow while I spread my legs wide and rub my throbbing clit while I picture the day I'll finally have him inside me.

I imagine his intense, dark eyes on me, that gaze that says he'll die if he has to wait another minute as he stalks toward me and captures my mouth in a rough kiss before forcing me back into the sheets...

Mesa

LEANING AGAINST THE SIDE OF THE TRUCK while I reach behind the seat for my cane, I take a deep breath of fresh mountain air.

Damn, am I glad to be back home. Another minute in the city, dealing with doctors and therapists and I'd have probably lost my mind.

Of course, the fact that Robin was with me the whole time made it a hell of a lot easier to get through. That woman is my rock-- my angel.

Once I get the cane in hand, I reach back in and grab the garment bag that has my tux for Meadow's wedding this weekend hanging inside. I pat down my pockets and make sure everything else is accounted for, and then I close up the truck and head for the house.

I've lost a lot of the swagger I used to have, that's for damn sure. Hard to walk like you own the world when you're hanging on to a fucking cane to keep from collapsing. But nothing can stop me from whistling the light tune as I make my way up the porch and toward my front door.

All things considered; things could be a hell of a lot worse. If the worst I end up with is a limp and a cane, I'll take that any day, as long as I've got Robin by my side.

Not many women would have stuck it out through the last year. My girl deserves the whole fucking world on a silver platter and all I can offer her is a life up here in the mountains with my bossy ass and my crazy family trying to pawn their goats off on us-- and she wants it.

Patting down my pocket again just to double check that the little box is still there, I let myself in through the front door. Yanking my boots off and leaving them on the mat in the mud-room, I grab the tux in its zippered bag back up in my free hand and the cane that's become damn near permanently attached to my right hand these days and head into the house.

Angel isn't downstairs and I don't see her out on the back porch through the big, picture windows running the length of the living room. She must have taken my advice and gone up for a nap after I left.

Climbing the stairs, I hook the cane over my wrist and use the hand rail, trying to keep my steps light so I won't wake her. Taking care of me can't be easy, she deserves the rest.

Not that I wouldn't love to disturb her.

My thoughts immediately go dirty and my dick starts to swell.

Claiming Robin's sweet little body with my cock has been just about the only thing I can think of lately. I sure as fuck never thought it was going to take an entire goddamn year to make that woman mine.

Between the fire, and the accident, the recovery, and family coming and going the whole time I was able to be at the apartment with Robin and not giving us a minute of privacy, it's a been a long fucking year.

Then there was our last night in the city, when we finally got the place to ourselves and I was cleared for whatever the fuck I felt I could do. Turns out, I couldn't do the one damn thing I've wanted most since I first laid eyes on my angel.

Stopping on the landing at the top of the stairs, I take a minute to breathe deep and try to shove that memory out of my mind. That night was a fucking disaster.

Robin hasn't tried to touch me since and I can't blame her. But since we've been back home, I've been working on building the muscle control in my leg so the cramps don't take me out like that again.

The cane is for balance, not for strength. There's

some severe nerve damage where the burns went through the muscle tissue. I've been working hard on managing the pain from that, but the docs say I might never be able to give up the cane.

Doesn't matter to me. Chief is working on finding a position that keeps me working down at the station, my sister is getting married this weekend and she's in on my plan to propose to Robin during the night, and come hell or high water, nothing is going to stop me from finally feeling Robin when she's coming all over my cock for the first time.

After I hang the tux up in the spare room, I make my way toward our bedroom door.

Soft moans and jagged breathing coming from the other side of the door make me pause before I push the door open.

Robin is spread out across my side of the bed, naked and squirming with her fingers between her legs, completely lost in her pleasure.

It's the hottest fucking thing I've ever seen and as much as I want to stand rooted here to the spot to watch her making herself come on her own hand, if I don't get a taste of her right fucking now, I will come unglued.

Chapter Three

Robin

By the time I realize I'm not alone, it's too late to hide what I'm doing. I don't even have the sheet over me anymore, for fuck's sake. The covers have gotten twisted and shoved back to my side of the bed, leaving my overheated body exposed; naked with my fingers working my clit furiously while I imagine Mesa doing it for me.

The sound from the doorway has my eyes fly open. Mesa stands there, his knuckles white from the tight grip on the hand of the cane at his side and heat burning hotter than any fire I've ever fought blazing in his dark eyes.

Before I can sit up or pull the covers across me, he's crossed the space between the door and the foot of the bed. The cane falls to the floor as his knees hit the mattress and then there's nothing I can do now.

"Let me help with this."

Mesa's voice is gravel and desire as he slides

between my legs, his rough hands gripping my thighs to spread me wider as his mouth finds my core.

For a second, I try to push him away, worry slamming into me for his injuries, but when his tongue connects with my clit, my mind goes blank to everything but the sensation of his heat and the wetness of his saliva as it mixes with my own liquid need.

I was so close on my own already but as soon as my fantasies turn real, I'm spinning out of control.

Mesa's fingers slip between my folds and sink inside me while his tongue flicks across my swollen bud before he suctions down and has me bucking my hips against his face, riding his beard till I'm coming harder than I've ever come before.

"You taste so fucking sweet, Angel," his voice is thick and deep between kisses along the inside of my thighs, "I want one more."

"Mes--" I start on a laugh but end on a moan.

Mesa's fingers are stroking my inner thigh and his tongue is drawing down my seam and spearing past my entrance and then back up to flick so lightly over my still-sensitive clit that my body arches up in search of more.

One thick digit slides inside me slowly then slips back out to trace the ring of my opening before delving deep inside again.

Mesa's tongue is doing something utterly torturous to me and when I feel him push a second finger into my aching channel, I'm lost in that sensation of being filled while he locks his mouth over my clit and pulls another orgasm from me that my body is all too eager to give him.

"Angel."

Damn, I love that tone in his voice. The way it's gone so deep and ragged, it makes everything he says to me sound like a plea for mercy.

Mesa kisses his way up my body, his hands following his mouth. His fingers trace through the beads of perspiration that are drying on my skin and I break out in goosebumps.

"It took too damn long for us to get here," he whispers to one pebbled nipple before taking it between his lips.

"Making you come is *my* job, Angel."

He pinches my nipple between his teeth just enough to make me gasp before raising his head to face me. His hand grasps my mound possessively, making me squirm against the pressure, already wanting more of him.

"And I'll be damned if I'm not going to do it from now on," he growls before kissing me hard. "How long have you been taking care of yourself like that, baby? Why didn't you let me know you were hurting like that?"

"Your leg," I answer. "I don't want to hurt you; I was waiting till it got better."

"Fuck my damn leg, my woman has needs and I've been neglecting them. We'll work around the fucking leg."

Rocklyn Ryder

Mesa

Robin's voice is full of concern but her body is responsive as fuck as I run my hand over her curves, taking my time to drag my fingers over every hill and valley, from the hollow of her throat to the flare of her wide hips.

Walking in on my angel lost in her own pleasure like that was a treat, but finding out that she's been hurting for my touch and afraid to ask for it slams guilt and frustration through me like I was hit by a fucking train.

It's true, the nerve damage in my thigh still sends pain shooting through my leg when I stress the muscles for too long, and the time I spent between Robin's soft thighs, drinking up her sweet nectar already has my leg throbbing almost as painfully as my dick.

I'll be damned if I'm going to let that stop me again.

"Come here, Angel."

It's easy enough to pull her body with me when I roll onto my back.

"I need to feel that sweet little pussy of yours on my cock. We're way overdue for this."

Robin straddles my hips and braces herself with her hands against my abs.

Looking up at her like this, I'm having second thoughts. There's no way I'm going to last with a view like that in front of me.

"Show me what to do." Her voice is so sweet, so

fucking *innocent*, as the tip of her little pink tongue darts out to wet her lips.

"You're doing just fine, Angel," I choke out.

Watching her give in to her instincts, has me ready to burst.

Robin slides her wet center along the length of my shaft, grinding against me, using me for her own pleasure while those pretty tits of hers rock and sway above me.

"Now. I need inside you now, baby." The words come out demanding, so gruff, I don't even recognize my own voice, but if I don't get my cock inside this woman, I'm going to be painting her skin like a Picasso.

And that's not good enough for me right now.

With a grip on her hips that's likely to show for days, I pull her up and position her dripping opening over the swollen head of my cock.

"Slide down, Angel. Go as slow as you need to."

One of Robin's small hands finds mine and holds on for dear life, squeezing my fingers as she lowers herself down my length.

This is her first time and I have to hold my breath if I hope to keep any sort of control as I watch my girl giving me her cherry.

"Good girl. Keep going," I encourage her, coaxing her past the point where she stops to take a deep breath.

I can feel her tight tunnel as it's stretched further than it ever has been before; the way her body fights my intrusion at first, the sudden give when her virginity gives way and allows me all the way in, the squeeze of her sucking me deeper when the wince of pain leaves her pretty face.

"Fuck, Angel, that's it, baby. Take the whole thing like a good girl, you can do it."

"Oh my God, you're so big."

Angel's words come out raspy and I can't help my grin.

"You're doing such a good job, baby, you're almost there."

Her grip on my fingers tightens again and when I look down between us to where our bodies are joined fully now, I have to fight the urge to thrust hard.

"Does it feel good yet, Angel? Are you proud of yourself for taking your man's cock all the way?"

She's breathing hard, her heavy tits rising and falling fast. The skin across her stomach ripples with a muscle spasm somewhere below the surface. I can feel her walls starting to flutter around my girth, the way those muscles deep inside her are beginning to milk me, demanding my seed.

Robin bobs her head a few times and when she opens her eyes and looks down at me, any control I was managing is lost.

"Angel, I'm going to fuck you now. I hope you're ready."

I pull my hand from her grasp so I can grip both her hips and then I get lost in the feel of thrusting up into her wet heat.

Looking up at my girl, she's lost in it. Her head tilted back, her thick curls bouncing wildly except for where they've caught on her sweat-slicked skin, her breasts bobbing to the rhythm of our movements.

I love everything about what I'm seeing, the way her mouth hangs slack as she breathes hard, and then the way she snaps her head back up, fixes those hazel eyes on me in a stare that goes right through me.

"That's it, Angel, come for me one more time. Come on my cock while I fill you up."

Moving my thumb to massage her clit, I ease her over the edge one more time before giving in to the need to pump my seed into her womb in thick, sticky ropes that seem to go one forever.

Chapter Four

Robin

When I finally stop shaking, it's suddenly as if all my bones have dissolved.

Collapsing against Mesa's chest, I listen to the hard beat of his heart against my ear while I catch my breath.

I had no idea orgasms could feel like that.

"How are you feeling?"

Mesa's fingers comb through my hair, pulling it off my face where it had stuck to my skin, then tracing around the shell of my ear and down the back of my neck till his hand flattens out over my bare shoulder.

"Better," I snuggle into him with a contented sigh. "Much better."

"I'm not saying I don't want to watch you touching yourself like that again, but I never want you to choose that over my cock, Angel. Understand?"

Smiling against his skin, I nod to let him know I'm on the same page.

My hand runs over the defined chest beneath my

head, over to trace along the thick arm draped heavily across our bodies, then over the rounded muscle of his shoulders and down the little dip between the deltoid and the bicep that remains impressive even when relaxed like this.

I like it when Mesa uses that bossy voice. The one that's all confidence, like he knows what he's talking about and expects people to listen. Turns out, I really like it when he's using that tone to say filthy, bossy things while he's fucking me.

Under my ear, I feel his chest move as he clears his throat and then that bossy tone is gone, replaced by something that makes my heart squeeze for the vulnerability in his next words.

"And stay, baby...in the mornings."

I hear him swallow hard, his fingers curling over my shoulder possessively, as I raise my head to meet the gaze from his intense, dark eyes.

"If I'm having bad dreams, they're better when you're with me. I hate that you're not with me when I wake up."

The corners of my lips curl up in a grin that I can't stop even though I'm trying to be serious.

"I don't think they're *bad* dreams," I confess.

He gives me a raised eye brow and a smirk lifts one corner of his mouth under his mustache.

"What kind of *not* bad dreams would make my woman leave me alone in bed every morning?"

It's my turn to clear my throat nervously and I feel my face burn hot with my blush.

"Oh really?" He laughs and squeezed me tight

against him. "Guess I shouldn't be surprised by that. I've been obsessed with making you mine for over a year now.

"But baby, why have you been getting out of bed instead of waking me up? You sure as hell weren't scared of my dick a little while ago."

"The last time we..." I let my voice trail off and curl into the warm, solidness of him, not wanting to think about it. "I didn't want you to do anything that would hurt like that again."

Mesa

FROM MY PERSPECTIVE, THE WHOLE DAMN YEAR has been a lesson in new ways to feel pain.

Thankfully, I don't remember the burns when they happened. I remember panicking about getting Robin out of harm's way, then I remember getting hit by something heavy and not being able to move. Next thing I knew, it was a week later.

I had medical staff to care for me and damn good pain killers pouring through my veins for months while I healed.

By the time they let me go stay at the apartment, I thought the worst of the pain was behind me. I was wrong. Those weeks were full of discovering that my limits were nowhere near what they'd been before and trying to push past them resulted in a kind of agony I couldn't just ignore.

I'm not good at the kind of words I need right now. I'm better at giving orders than I've ever been at taking them, and it's already been a fucking rough year of listening to doctors and therapists so I could do what needed to be done to heal and get back home. To get back to my girl.

I hadn't realized how hard it's probably been on Robin.

She's so strong, it's easy to forget that she's delicate too.

"How long were you planning on waiting, Angel?"

"As long as it took."

Her voice is sounding a little sleepy now and when she shrugs her answer, it's enough to move her so our bodies finally part.

I hate the feeling of slipping free from her warmth and the dampness of my spend leaking out of her has me thinking about filling her up again but my angel is lying heavy and relaxed against me, starting to give in to the nap she's overdue for.

"Hang on, baby." I kiss the top of her head and slide the rest of the way out from under her, "let me get you cleaned up."

"Oh." Robin's eyes pop open when she feels me move. "No, you stay, I'll do it." She starts to get up but I push her back into the pillows with a firm hand and a gentle kiss.

"The fuck you will." I growl at her but she just laughs at me. "I'll be right back."

As soon as I put weight on my leg, I know it's a

mistake, but I'll be damned if I'm going to let Robin see the pain I can feel etched on my face.

Keeping my back to her, I stand balanced on my left leg, letting blood circulate through my injured side and silently counting till the pins and needles pain of damaged nerve endings runs its course, before managing to retrieve the fucking cane from I dropped it when I lunged for the bed and the woman spread out on it when I came in.

When I come back from the bathroom with a soft washcloth soaked in warm water, Robin's fallen asleep. She doesn't see the frustration on my face with my dependence on this damn stick to even make it across the room when I sit beside her and gently wipe away the remnants of our love-making and the pink hints of blood that make me swell with pride knowing she's fully mine now.

Almost. I remind myself as I arrange the down comforter over her sleeping form. *Almost* fully mine.

There's one more thing left to do.

The ring's already in the pocket of the tuxedo jacket I'll be wearing for the wedding this weekend and Oz and Meadow are already on board with the plan.

Chapter Five

Robin

Weddings are a big event in this tiny community. Looking around me, I'm pretty sure everyone in Moonshine Ridge is somewhere on the hot springs camping resort property that's owned by Mesa's family.

Meadow arranged the ceremony so that the wedding party would be seated while she and Oz did their vows. It meant that Mesa was easily able to take his place between his brother, Vale, and Raine Hart, who looks nervous sitting with the two older Diaz men.

Apparently, there's some sort of ongoing feud between Mesa's grandmother and her best friend, Alice verses the other two older women who make up the founding members of Moonshine Ridge's historical society.

No one seems to know what's it's about, but I gather that the Harts have been on the other side of the line and apparently, their oldest brother turned out to be kind of a jerk. But it was Raine that became Oz's best friend after he and Mesa had a falling out.

Trying to keep track of all the small-town drama has me thinking I should start keeping notes.

After the newly married couple dashes between guests pelting them with birdseed, and the rest of the wedding party files back off the stage of the open-air amphitheater, the real party kicks off.

Alex, Mesa's grandfather, has been working over a huge, charcoal grill since early this morning to prepare a feast for what they estimate will be at least a few hundred people in and out through the rest of the afternoon.

"Do you need a plate for Mesa too?" Marcia asks as I pile one of the trays with a variety of grilled meats and vegetables that her husband just pulled off the grill.

She hands me a stack of tortillas that she's busy making on her own side of the grill.

"We're sharing," I tell her, raising the overloaded plate as if to explain that I couldn't possibly eat this much food by myself.

The older lady laughs. She's barely five feet tall, with a rounded figure, and the kind of face that looks like it's been laughing like that for all of her eighty-three years.

I adore Marcia and Alejandro. In fact, I adore all of Mesa's big-- and growing-- family.

"Have you seen Mom?" Terra, the youngest of the family, is holding a sleeping six-week-old baby Fields in her arms as she eyes the plate of food in my hand

Mountain Man's Hope

jealously. "I was hoping to hand him off and join the party."

Fields is Meadow and Oz's son, and Mesa's newest nephew. Mesa missed his sister's entire pregnancy, but I think that might have been a good thing. He got injured just a couple weeks after finding out his sister was with Oz and well-- he's still having a hard time accepting that his little sister is grown up enough to have a baby.

"I saw her over by their cabin," I say after Marcia shakes her head, pointing at the grill and the spread of food as if to make it clear that she doesn't have time to keep track of everyone.

"Don't get the avocado on Mesa's side, he won't eat anything that's touched it," she warns as she heads off in search of her parents.

"Good to know." I laugh at the new information; for all we've gone through so early in our relationship, it's strange that I'm just finding out the little things. Like, apparently, the fact that my man won't touch avocados.

The sound system crackles and the DJ starts the usual announcements and small talk about the bride and groom.

The reception is not an organized event; just a lot of tables set up around the periphery of a large, dirt parking lot that is currently being used as a dance floor, and people everywhere.

It reminds me of a lot of the country weddings I've gone to back home in Slow River.

"How's my sexy angel?" Mesa takes the plate from

me, giving the sliced avocado on one side of the carne asada a suspicious look as he sets it on the table beside him before grabbing me around my waist and pulling me onto his lap. "I missed you."

"You were stuck on stage, remember?"

Mesa draws his head back to look up at me.

"You should have been up there with me." His deep voice rumbles, smirking under his whiskers as he pulls me down to him for a kiss.

When he lets me up for air, I discretely move the hand that's crawled up my thigh beneath the hem of my dress to a more appropriate location just above my knee and laugh as I look toward the dance floor where Oz and Meadow are kicking things off with the first dance.

"You look good in the fancy suit, Diaz," I purr in his ear.

"Hmm. Maybe I'll have to think of a good reason to get dressed up again for you, Angel."

Mesa

SITTING THERE ON THE STAGE, WATCHING MY sister and my dumbass old buddy that finally managed to talk her into marrying him exchange their vows had me more choked up than I care to admit to. Especially when I was wedged between my older, ex-marine brother, Vale and that fucker, Raine Hart; having to pretend him and his brothers haven't been the utter shitheads they are since we were coming up together on the mountain.

Of course, I'll be giving Oz a hard time about all the sniffling he did through his own damn wedding. Wasn't even the real thing, either, he dragged my sister down to the courthouse in Slow River to make it legal as soon as they found out they were having my nephew.

I keep Robin on my lap as long as I can, she's not nearly as heavy as she worries she is and I don't care if it stresses my leg, it's worth it to have her curvy ass pressed against my crotch while we share our food.

This is also the first chance I've had to show her off and my chest swells with pride knowing all the single assholes in town can see that she's mine-- and by the end of this night, I plan on that being official.

The music kicks up with a pop song and I see my baby sister, Terra, and Vale's wife, Sparrow, out on the floor, beckoning Robin to come out and join them.

"Go, Angel," I give her a pat on her pretty ass, "have fun, baby."

I reach down and absently rub into the muscle of my thigh. All the weight training I've been doing has paid off; my strength is up and holding weight on my leg is almost as easy as it was before. It's the damn nerve damage that still keeps me tied to the fucking cane. I can barely take a couple of steps on my own without losing my balance like I'm half a bottle deep in whiskey.

Dancing was never my thing, but before the damn leg injury, I was able to hold my own in a two-step, and I never minded holding a pretty girl close and swaying slow.

Now it looks like that's just one more thing that's off the list for good.

Watching Robin dance with the girls has me smiling. It's good to see my girl laughing and having a good time after the year I just put her through.

She's a damn good woman to have stuck by me through it all. Even at my worst, no one could drag her away from my side.

I'm lost in big ideas about the future while I watch her and the girls jumping and spinning each other around while they dance in a circle to the upbeat music, but then the song ends and the next one is slow.

Hawkins shows up out of nowhere, asking Terra to dance.

I like our new sheriff's deputy-- a lot. With his military background, he fell in fast with our family when he took over the sub-station on the Ridge a few years back. But it's pretty obvious he's got a thing for my baby sister and I'm not sure how I feel about that.

Fortunately, I know Terra. She's got a rebel streak in her a mile wide and she does not take direction well-- she's never going to give our clean-cut lawman the time of day.

To prove my point, I chuckle as I watch her give him the stink-eye before she marches off the dance floor, making a beeline to anywhere that's away from him.

Vale shows up and catches Sparrow in his arms,

making me wonder just what kind of spell she's got him under that would get my hard-ass older brother to dance.

The dance floor is quickly filling up with couples wrapped up in each other's arms, swaying in time to the rhythm of the sentimental love song.

I feel the smile slide off my face as I watch Robin stand still for a beat; the way her shoulders sag and the sadness that creeps into her face as she looks around at the dancers before she squares back up and heads my way.

When I see the way her smile doesn't light up her eyes the way I'm used to, something inside me drops. I've been so busy thinking how lucky I am to have Robin, it hasn't crossed my mind that she's far from lucky to have me. I hadn't bothered to think of all the things she'll be giving up if she's stuck with me for the rest of her life.

So when I miss my cue a few minutes later, after Meadow, Ozzie and baby Fields all have wedding cake smeared across their faces and my sister shoots me a questioning look from across the way, I shake my head at her with a stern look that says I've changed my mind.

Chapter Six

Robin

Terra's eyes land on my left hand as I reach to take the baby off her hands so she can chase down a toddler.

The giddiness that she'd met me with when I stopped by her daycare center in town for a quick visit evaporates, quickly replaced with confusion.

"What?" I ask. It's not like Mesa's youngest sibling to keep her thoughts to herself.

Once she's got the young boy separated from the fist-full of magic markers he was running with, she gives me a thoughtful look as if she's deciding what kind of mood I'm in. Then she shrugs nonchalantly.

I feel like I missed a memo.

"Nothing, I just expected...." Her eyes drift toward my hand again. "Because Meadow and Oz had made plans for Mesa to....but then we thought maybe he wanted to do it in private instead but..."

Yeah, I am definitely not up to date on something here.

I follow Terra through the center, back to the main room where a few older children are watching a movie together.

For only being twenty years old, she's got a good head on her shoulders. She started baby-sitting when she was still in high school and, instead of spending her money on clothes or a car like most teenagers, she saved up to start a proper day care center when she graduated.

It took her a while after finishing school to find a space and get some certificates she needed, but now here she is, running her own business like the girl boss she was born to be.

Seriously, Mesa's baby sister is the kind of "down with the patriarchy," rebel, bad-ass I could only dream of being despite her absolute love for kids and her insistence that she's going to have at least as many as her own parents did.

If she ever finds a boyfriend who's secure enough to handle living in her shadow, that is.

"Tare, what are you talking about?"

After I hand off the baby off to Zephyr Hart-- Terra's bestie and part time help at the day care, I follow Terra into the kitchen area where I have her cornered.

"I mean, it's not like a surprise, right?" I don't know if I'm actually expected to answer that. "You knew my brother was going to propose, right? Like, that's something you guys already talked about, right?"

I can feel my face blanching, the edges of my vision

blurring slightly as I fight the tears that suddenly threaten to spring up.

"Oh shit." I hear Terra mumbling something about being an idiot but I'm too busy putting together bits and pieces of information from the last few days to pay attention to her.

"Robin? Are you okay? I didn't mean to ruin the surprise, I'm sorry."

Terra slides a glass of juice in front of me as I plop into one of the not-exactly-adult-size chairs at the table in the kitchen area.

We had been talking about marriage. For months, actually. It was never even a question of *if*, only a matter of *when*.

It's not so much that I'd been expecting him to propose at Meadow's wedding, but since that night, Mesa's mood has definitely changed.

He's been deep in his own head like he was when he was still in the hospital, pushing me away again, and he hasn't wanted to make love. He's been blaming the nerve damage and saying his leg is bothering him more and last night, he suggested that I might be more comfortable in the spare bedroom.

"I just thought it was his injuries," I explain. "He's had some ups and downs before; I figured it would pass. I understand there's more to his healing than just his body but...what if he changed his mind about us? What do I do then?"

Terra pulls another few tissues from the box and hands them over to me, her face a combination of sympathy and anger.

"My brother is fucking asshole," she mutters not-quite under her breath. "I'm sorry all I have is juice."

"It would be weird if a daycare had something stronger." I joke through the sudden tears.

"You should talk to him, Robin," she closes her hand over mine. "Mesa's always been an ass but he's a good guy. And once he sets his mind on something, he goes all in. He's been all-in with you since before he got hurt. Something weird is going on with him."

Mesa

IT'S BEEN THREE DAYS SINCE THE WEDDING, AND I know I've been acting like an asshole around Robin.

If I were any kind of man at all, I'd sit her down and come clean with her. I'd tell her what I decided and I'd help her pack her things and move back to the valley.

Instead, I've been moping around the house, making excuses not to get too close to her, blaming my fucking leg and hating myself while I lose sleep with her not beside me at night.

I've been doing a damn good job of avoiding her. Staying at the gym, spending time at the station, stopping by the homestead under the pretense of helping out my grandparents with the goats.

When I walk into Abu's kitchen, it smells like it always has-- the comforting smells of home cooked meals, fresh baked cookies, and three decades of love and happy memories...memories I'd been planning on making more of; making my own contribution to the next generation of rowdy kids that will be running through these rooms, stealing cookies and getting scolded for putting grimy hands on Abu's clean walls.

Abu finds me with my hand wrapped around two of the peanut butter cookies that were cooling on the rack.

"Why didn't you put that ring on Robin's finger, Mijo? You've been planning it for months; we were all waiting and then you chickened out."

"I didn't chicken out, Abu."

"You think you're going to find a better one? You're a damn fool. Give me back my cookies."

"I'll never find another woman like Robin. I know that. But I can't give her the life she deserves. This is for her own good."

Judging from the way she slams the back door behind her as she enters the kitchen, Terra must have expected to find me in here when she saw my truck outside.

"You are such a fucking idiot," she scolds as she takes the cookies from Abu that just got commandeered from my own hands. Obviously, she overheard what I just said.

Abu doesn't even flinch at my sister's profanity, instead she moves so she's shoulder to shoulder with Terra, creating a united front of disapproval scowling at me from across the kitchen island.

"So what now, brother? You're going to trash the

best thing that ever happened to you and break Robin's heart because you're feeling sorry for yourself?"

Terra grabs two more cookies off the rack while Abu pours her a glass of milk to go with them. She does not offer me one.

"You're just a kid, Tare. You've never even had a serious boyfriend. You're looking for a damn fairytale," I snap back at my little sister. "You have no idea what marriage is."

Somewhere in my brain I know I'm being just being a jerk, while somewhere much closer to my consciousness, I know I'm about to get my ass handed to me by my kid sister and, judging from the harsh glare and tsking noise my grandmother makes, probably her too.

"I grew up watching Mom and Dad work out their problems, I see how Abu and Pops are with each other, *I'm* not the one that doesn't know what it means to make a fucking commitment to someone, Mes."

"You aren't planning on breaking up with that sweet girl, are you?" Abu's pissed. "She sat in the hospital waiting room for seven hours while you were in surgery when you first got there-- she was straight off the fire, still in her gear. She didn't sleep for 39 hours-- just to make sure you were alive, Mijo.

"Your mother had to physically pull her away from your bedside and make her go to the hotel for a shower and sleep. She has been there with you through this whole ordeal...and you repay that by leaving her now?

"That's not love, Mijo, that's chicken-shit

cowardice...you think any of you would be here now if your grandfather had done something so stupid when he came back from the war with a bullet hole in his chest? When he kept me awake with night terrors for years after he returned? Because he thought he'd be doing me a favor?... this is *commitment* Mesa. This is *marriage*. This is *life*. This is the reason we fall in love and build our lives *together*, so we can stand beside our partner when they need strength and so we know we have their strength when it's us who are weak.

"What kind of man are you to decide for Robin? She's proven her loyalty and you repay her by running away like a frightened pup."

Abu follows up her lecture with a muttered string of Spanish words. None of them are something sweet little old ladies that bake cookies should say at all, let alone in front of their grand-children.

"At least you're showing your true colors now." Terra's voice has cooled to an icy sarcasm as she chews a bite of cookie. "Instead of leaving her high and dry with bills and babies to complicate her broken heart when you bail at the first hint of a challenge.

"I think *you're* the one who wants the fairy tale, brother. I expect a man to have a fucking clue what 'for better or worse' means. I need to know he's going to man up and handle things when shit gets real. Because no one knows what's going to happen. One of us could get hurt. We could lose a child or get really sick. We don't know how bad it could get, but I need to know that my partner is going to have my back and that we'll be facing it together...and I need him to let me have his back too.

"And *'I broke up with you for your own good'* Is. Not. That."

Terra wiggles her fingers in the air to make quotation marks when she mocks me.

"When you find your person, you don't make their decisions for them. That's how *I* expect it to work."

Terra pulls a few more cookies from the rack and gives me a look that matches the force of her lecture.

"But I'm just a kid. What do I know about being married?"

Abu and I watch in silence as Terra marches out of the room.

"Your sister is right, Mijo." Abu says softly, watching me head for the cookies before they're gone. "You're fucking up."

Chapter Seven

Robin

After my visit with Terra, I didn't have the energy left to go by Alice's general store to pick up the things I needed to make the dinner I'd planned.

I was hoping to cheer Mesa up with one of his favorites.

Instead, I went to the lake where I knew I wasn't likely to run into anyone who knows me and then I sat in my car and cried for an hour.

And still, even though I'm home late, Mesa's truck isn't in the driveway and the house is dark.

It's all the sign I need to confirm my fears: he's avoiding me, or rather, he's avoiding the conversation he's planning on having with me.

That hurts even worse, Mesa's not the avoiding type. It's one of the things I loved about him from the first time he told me plainly that I was his. Way back in the beginning, before the fire, before he got hurt...before whatever is going on in his head now that's obviously made him change his mind.

Letting myself in the house, I flick on lights. It doesn't look like he's been home at all since he left early this morning.

A glance at my phone reminds me he hasn't responded to the texts I've sent today either. Or left any messages letting me know he'd be late tonight.

Lost in my thoughts, I go upstairs and look at the things that have made it up the mountain since we've been back from Seattle. Not much, really. Most of my things are in a storage unit down in Slow River, waiting for me to go through them.

I took my name off the lease with my roommate when I found out Mesa wouldn't be coming home for at least six months-- there was no way I was going to be more than a quick drive from him when he went to the rehab center.

After a few quick texts to Mom, I gather the things I have here together, throwing them into my bag. Then I sit on the edge of Mesa's bed-- our bed-- and fight more tears.

I should not make this easy on him.

His own mother would tell me to call him out on the list of ways his behavior is unacceptable. His sisters would tell me to make it hurt.

That's just not me though. Maybe I'll get pissed off later, when it has time to sink in but right now, I still have hope. Maybe there's still a chance that things will work out once we have a chance to talk.

And I know we need to have that talk, but...not right now. I can't handle facing him right now. Having to hear him tell me he's changed his mind about me--

about us-- no matter what his reasoning is, isn't something I have in me right now. My poker face is good, but it's not that good.

With a deep sigh, I get up and grab the first load; a delivery box I found discarded in the back mudroom waiting to be broken down.

The new duvet set that we ordered when got back came in it. That was the first purchase we'd made together for the house when Mesa said we should start making it ours instead of just his.

Now it's full of my toiletries, and a couple of used paperbacks from when I needed something to distract me while I sat by his bed in the hospital.

After I set the box in the back seat of my car, I head back upstairs for the last of my things. Just a couple of gym bags with my shoes and clothes.

Even after I switch off the light in the spare bedroom where I've spent the last few nights, I can't help but linger in Mesa's room. Trying to imprint the manly scent of him into my memory forever. Trying to absorb the best of my memories from the short time we spent together here while I'm still calm and numb. Before reality sets in.

Mesa

MY GRANDMOTHER DIDN'T EXACTLY LET GO OF the subject after Terra had her mic drop moment. I didn't get out of the house with a cookie but I did leave with an earful of advice and enough guilt to carry back in a bucket.

I had no idea Papa D had had such a hard time after Vietnam. I knew he'd been in the war and I knew he had a Purple Heart for his trouble, but it's not something he talks about. The man I grew up with has always had a smile on his face-- and usually a set of bar-be-Que utensils in his hand.

Hearing Abu talk about years of night terrors and flashbacks gives me a new appreciation for the strength of their marriage.

Dad was in the first Gulf War, back in the early nineties, when he was fresh out of high school. It's the reason he didn't know Mom was pregnant with Vale for so long and why there's such a big gap between my older brother and me.

I didn't know he'd broken up with Mom before he deployed-- before they knew she was pregnant. That he'd thought he would save her from the stress and potential heartache of being a soldier's wife when she was barely eighteen.

Us kids grew up hearing a much different version of the family stories, ones that reflect the strength of the marriages we grew up with as models of what real love looks like.

Terra made a lot of good points. She's a smart kid-- who's not a kid anymore. My baby sister is all grown up and it's looking like she's a lot smarter than me.

Just when I'm thinking I owe her an apology, my phone lights up with a new text.

Speak of the devil: Aside from the texts from Robin

that I've been too fucking chicken shit (as Abu enjoyed pointing out) to even open today, there's a new one from Terra. The preview of her message says *Zephyr's going to set R up with Raine.* I don't open the text so if there's more, I don't see it.

Over my dead, fucking body is Raine Hart ever going to get a chance at my woman.

I'm still seething at the thought when I turn the truck into the gravel drive and pull in behind Robin's little cross-over hatchback.

The dome light is on in her car when I walk up to it, like the door hasn't been closed too long ago and the locks aren't engaged-- no one worries about people breaking into our cars up on the Ridge, but bears are another story. You keep your car locked up here.

As I approach her vehicle, I see a box on the backseat. It's full of girl stuff, hair dryer, makeup case, shampoo. It takes a minute to register as the dome light times out, but then I'm heading into the house as fast as the damn cane lets me.

Except for the living room light when I first walk in, the lower level is dark and obviously empty. I find her upstairs, standing by the foot of our bed looking around at the room we've shared for only a few weeks as if she's committing it to memory.

"You won't get to dance at your own wedding, Angel."

It's not like I was quiet about coming up the stairs, so when she jumps at the sound of my voice, I realize just how lost in her thoughts she must be.

"I won't be able to carry you over the threshold."

Damn. My voice is rough.

"I can't help you chase kids around the yard."

Robin's shoulders tense with each one of my statements before she finally turns around slowly to face me.

Her eyes are red and her face is swollen from tears that have already dried.

My breath hitches as my chest constricts at the sight. It's only the cool look in those hazel eyes that keeps me from closing the distance between us to take her in my arms.

"I'm not going to be able to dance with you, Angel."

Saying it out loud feels like shoving a knife into my own gut.

Chapter Eight

Robin

As much as I know it bothers him, I've seen tears in Mesa's eyes before. I saw tears in his eyes when he was barely conscious as they loaded him into the chopper. There were tears in his eyes when he woke up from the first surgery in agony from the broken bones and the burns-- before they got the pain medication dosages dialed in. There were tears in his eyes when he started rehab-- when the pain and frustration of not being able to hold his own weight on his leg sent him into a rage of frustration.

And now.

He's standing in the bedroom doorway, blocking my exit so all that's left for me to do is turn around and face him. Looks like we're having this conversation tonight, after all.

His words don't make any sense. Talking about dancing and chasing babies seems irrelevant. But when I see his dark eyes glistening with wetness, it hits me: what he's really talking about. What he's really afraid of.

"Mesa, we pulled a *burning tree* off of you. Your vital signs kept dropping during the flight to Seattle. You were in surgery for *seven hours* before I even knew how bad you were really hurt.

"They pinned your leg back together with metal brackets and screws." My voice is rising, taking on a hysterical tone but I can't stop talking even when I'm practically screaming at him.

"The muscle damage was so extensive that we didn't even know if you would be able to *walk* again! You think I give a single fuck about whether or not you can *dance* with me? I'm just so fucking glad you're *alive*, Mesa."

Whatever energy I had left leaves with my outburst and I sag back onto the foot of the mattress.

After the worst was over, when Mesa transferred to the rehab center, I did a few sessions with a therapist on the recommendation of the social worker assigned to Mesa's case.

She'd been worried that I might be prone to PTSD if I didn't get the appropriate treatment early on, making it clear that it wasn't just Mesa who was going to need time for healing.

It helped a lot, but now I realize this is the first time I've ever said these things to Mesa. I've been so busy being his cheerleader and his caretaker and his support; I never wanted him to know how fucking scared I was for those first few weeks.

I don't even know if he ever understood just how

uncertain his doctors were about what to expect of his recovery.

Judging by the look on his face now, I'm guessing he didn't.

I thought I'd cried myself out earlier but now all new tears spill from my eyes, dripping hot liquid down my cheeks in an uncontrollable torrent while I struggle to breathe steadily.

The bed dips beside me while I still have my face cradled in my palms, then Mesa's arm is around me, pulling me into his broad chest and holding me tightly against him.

I listen to his heart beating and the carefully controlled cadence of his breaths till the tears finally abate.

His shirt smells like him. Not like when he's freshly showered, with the spicy deodorant he wears and the herbal fragrance of the oil he sometimes runs through his beard, or the cologne he sometimes puts on that smells so good on him that it makes me weak in the knees.

The navy-blue Moonshine Ridge fire dept t-shirt stretched across his muscles now smells like Mesa. Like Mesa when he's asleep beside me, like Mesa when we're making love, like Mesa when he's been working out. It's just his natural scent, filled with those damn pheromones that make me forget that a few minutes ago I was reliving the panic I felt when he was in and out of consciousness in a hospital bed, or the ache I was feeling earlier when I was coming to terms with us breaking up.

Maybe we still are, even. I don't know. I just know that I need him right now. Whatever happens after, I need to remember he's alive and that those nightmare times are behind us both.

Mesa

WORDLESSLY, I HOLD ANGEL AGAINST ME TILL she stops shaking, not knowing what to say.

I feel worse than stupid, I feel helpless. I don't know how to fix this.

When I finally got to the point where I was maintaining consciousness after the first few weeks of surgeries and pain medication that kept me knocked out most of the time and pretty out of it when I was awake, I remember the surgeon talking to me.

There was a lot of doctor talk that was over my head but all I heard was that they *didn't know*. It didn't sound ominous, it sounded like it was going to be work. I've never been afraid of work.

Robin's never told me the things she just said. She's never mentioned being afraid I wasn't even going to pull through that first surgery.

Suddenly, I realize that Angel's been sticking by me through more than just my pain management and temper tantrums with rehab setbacks.

"Hey, Angel, it's okay." I stroke my fingers down her mahogany locks, rocking her gently as I hold her. "I'm okay, baby. We're okay."

Robin sniffs against my chest and raises her head, pulling back to look at me.

"Are we?"

It's not the hopeful voice of a woman who's asking for reassurance though. It's the voice of a woman who's reminding me that I made promises and she expected me to keep them.

"I can't dance with you, Angel."

"Why do you think that matters to me, Mesa?"

"Because I don't know what else I can't do. What if I never get any better than I am right now? What then, Angel? What if you need more than I can give you?"

There's a flicker of relief in her golden eyes and the corner of her pouty lips twitches like she's about to smile.

"You've already been giving me as much I can handle."

The twitch gives way to a full, wicked grin.

"Are you being naughty right now, Angel?"

"I'm just saying, Mesa, if this is as good as it ever gets, we're doing just fine. I'll dance with your Abuelo."

"Pops would love that." I chuckle.

"So are we okay?"

Robin leans so close to me that her lips brush mine when she asks, but there's still a trace of doubt in her eyes when she looks up to mine.

"I'm okay, Angel." I press forward softly, sealing my lips to hers. When she takes my kiss and gives it back with a tender little moan, my entire body is flooded in relief.

"I'm okay too, Mesa," she says so softly, I feel it more than hear the words.

Then her mouth is greedy against mine, angling toward me for more.

Bringing my hand up to brush the thick waves of her hair away from where they've fallen around her face, I wrap those soft locks in my fingers and hold her hostage to my kiss as I claim her mouth with mine.

A soft whimper makes it way out of her as I lay us down together, softly kissing my way down her throat and moving lower, till I'm sucking her hardened nipples through the material of her shirt.

Robin clutches at my shoulders, yanking my tee up and over my head while I fumble to get through her buttons without tearing the fabric that stands between me and the full breasts beneath it.

Her blouse gives way in my impatient hands with a tearing sound. My hands push under her bra while Robin twists to help me release her heavy tits while I knead the soft flesh in my palms.

What started as tender and slow has ignited into a burning need to claim this woman again. To have my cock encased in her wet heat while I lose myself inside her.

"Stop," I command when she begins to shimmy those thick hips in an effort to move higher toward the headboard. "Stay put."

Chapter Nine

Robin

Mesa slides further down till he's kneeling on the floor, between my knees where my legs are hanging over the edge of the bed.

"Lie down, Angel," he orders when I try to sit up. "Let me take care of you, baby."

He unzips my jeans and pulls them all the way off. Then he uses those big, callused hands to grip my body and pull me toward him, wedging his broad shoulders under my thighs to position himself close to my core.

"I love this," he whispers reverently as he draws finger against the gusset of my panties where I know the material is already soaked through with my desire.

He hooks his fingers into the elastic over my hips, but before he bares me completely, he presses his face to the wet fabric and inhales.

"Love the way you get so fucking wet for me before I even touch you, angel."

And then I'm exposed to him and his mouth is

working against my sex, drawing his tongue between my folds while he holds my hips in place so I'm at his mercy while he fucks me with his mouth like he's trying to prove a point.

If that point is to show me just how well he's learned to make me come, he makes it with several exclamation points when I'm suddenly breaking apart in a stuttering rush of stars and glitter with my ankles clasped behind his neck and the bed sheets fisted in my hands at my sides.

It seems like it takes forever before my body stops shuddering with the aftershocks of the orgasm. Or maybe it's because Mesa continues to swirl his tongue in soft circles around my sensitive clit, seeming to enjoy the way it makes me jump and squirm each time he does it.

"Up."

He slaps the side of my thigh with his hand, hard enough to make it clear that we aren't done.

"Spin around. Hands and knees for me, Angel."

Like he expects me to argue, Mesa pulls me onto my feet for a moment before spinning me by the waist and half lifting, half pushing me back onto the mattress.

A firm hand on the small of my back guides me onto all fours.

"Fuck, Angel." Mesa's hand runs down my spine, making me shiver, then over my ass, squeezing appreciatively before slapping at me lightly. It's still enough to make me whimper at the contact and if Mesa didn't look so fucking turned on when I glance back at him, I'd feel embarrassed.

"I can't believe I haven't gotten you in front of me like this before."

His voice is a dark growl, his eyes fixated on my body, bent over and presented to him like I'm begging for him to take me.

Maybe I am.

Heat courses through me and I feel it leak from my core, open where I know he can see.

Mesa presses his fingers there, coating them in my essence before sliding two thick digits past my weeping entrance.

He exhales on a harsh rattle and as watches his fingers disappear inside me.

My arms give way and I go down on my elbows, my head dropping against my forearms in front of me.

"Mesa." My voice is a muffled whine and I know I've got my ass in the air, shamelessly fucking his fingers while he stands behind me.

"What is it, Angel?" He works his fingers deeper, moving them so the pads rub something inside me that makes me pant with need.

"Tell me what you need, baby. I'll give you anything you want."

Mesa

I'VE ALREADY GOT ONE HAND ON MY BELT, pulling the buckle open and reaching for the button on my fly. Having my angel on all fours in front of me like this is the hottest thing I've ever seen. Watching her writhe on my hand while her juices cover my fingers and the soft, needy little mewling noises she's making, has my cock harder than I can remember it ever being.

My bad knee is braced up against the edge of the bed, keeping me planted firmly so I can enjoy teasing my girl while I appreciate the view, but if I don't get inside this wet little pussy quick, I'm going to be spraying her down.

The idea of my cum coating Robin's skin and dripping off her pretty ass makes my dick surge before I even get my zipper down. As tempting as that thought is-- and it is tempting as fuck-- I want my seed inside her.

I want my cock buried deep, feeling her tight little pussy clamped down and milking me for it. I want to feel her body begging to grow my child in her womb.

"I need *you*, Mesa."

Angel's voice is strained and I can feel her quivering. At this point I know neither one of us is going to last long, but damn if it doesn't feel good to stand behind her and watch while she begs me for my cock.

I still need to brace my leg for balance, but the strength training is paying off.

"Tell me, Angel, tell me what you want."

"I want you to fuck me, Mesa, I want to feel you inside me. Please."

Robin's not the only one who groans when she utters those words.

"Good girl," I praise as I make good on my promise.

Slipping my fingers out of her channel, I bring her ass back to me, lining her up perfectly to my height as I stand while she's on her knees on the bed in front of me.

My dick is leaking pre-cum in anticipation of being inside her. Lining up the thick head of my cock against her entrance, I give her ass a swat, liking the sound and the way her rounded butt shimmies from the impact, before sliding all the way to the hilt in one stroke.

Robin cries out beneath me, pushing back to meet my thrust, her body greedy for my length.

She's heaven. Fucking heaven, squeezing me in her vice grip as I rut inside her till we're both panting heavily.

Lifting my knee to the edge of the mattress, I use it to spread her legs wider, opening her up to take me deeper at the same time it takes my weight and I use my grip on Robin's hips for my balance.

I love the way her body gives me little warnings when she's close, the change in her breathing, the way her inner walls flutter and pulse, the way her fists clench, nails clawing at whatever's in reach.

This time that's one of the pillows, but I like it when it's my back or my shoulders.

Right now, Angel's body slams back on mine, demanding all of me and I'm more than happy to give it to her. Her pussy convulses around me, all of the muscles deep inside her tightening, clenching, pulling my seed from me whether I'm ready or not.

Robin cries out, a primal sound ripping from her throat that triggers a sense of pride inside me as I'm pulled into my own release, pumping cum in hot, heavy spurts that seem to go on forever till finally, there's nothing left of me to put inside her.

"That was..."

Her voice is distant and awed as she breathes hard beside me where we've collapsed together on the bed.

"Yeah," I agree, reaching out to pull her against me, despite still being over-heated from the exertion.

"Your leg okay?"

It's not. The muscles burn like I ran back-to-back marathons. It'll take more than aspirin to keep it from cramping up overnight, but I'm not about to mention that to Angel right now. It was worth it. Just like all the work I'll be doing in the future to keep improving so I can show her more ways I can make her come is going to be worth it.

"It'll be fine, Angel." I bring her closer, till her head is resting on my chest, loving the way her body feels as she wraps her arm over me.

"You sure you want to be stuck with a busted old man for the rest of your life?"

"I'm not the one freaking out about a dance."

My eyes drift up to the wood planks that line the peaked ceiling above us. My brain going back over all the ways I might never be whole again. So many little things that other people take for granted that I might never do again-- like dance at my own damn wedding.

Kissing the top of Robin's head, I find myself smiling in spite of my worries.

Thinking about what I learned from my grandmother tonight-- not to mention the hell I caught from my baby sister-- I reach up to the nightstand without letting go of Robin and grab the little box I almost locked away in the safe forever.

"You deserve better, Angel," I tell her as I open the thing with one hand. "You should have gotten the whole speech, all the people applauding for you-- hell, you deserve a man who can get down on one knee to do the asking but..."

Robin's hand is already in the air, fingers spread out, waiting impatiently.

"Just put the damn ring on my finger, Mesa," she says. "You know damn well I'm going to marry you."

Sliding the ring onto her finger, I meet her eager lips for the kiss she's offering me.

I'm going to spend the rest of my life making sure she doesn't regret this.

Epilogue 1

Six Months Later
Robin

We've been pronounced man and wife, our friends and family have doused us in bubbles-- which seemed a better option than birdseed for our mid-January, indoor wedding-- and Mesa's brothers have suffered through the formal photos in the tuxedos that were quickly changed out for jeans and flannels as soon as the reception started.

My husband, however, is still looking like the sexiest mountain man in Moonshine Ridge in his classic black and white tux that perfectly complements my contemporary gown.

He even trimmed his beard for the occasion; and by "trimmed," I mean he let the barber even-up the ends and ran a comb through it.

Not being able to go out on the line anymore means he's been able to grow his beard out much longer and fuller than when we were active on the crew.

Mesa's still working full time with the Moonshine Ridge fire department; he's training volunteers and even helping with the paperwork. We both thought he'd hate driving a desk, but it turns out that he enjoys the process of running the station from the other side of an ax and a shovel.

It was never my plan to be a full-time firefighter. I'd only come up to work on the Moonshine Ridge crew for the summer for the experience to help with my conservation degree.

I'll be graduating this spring and I'm excited to start working with the local wildland inspector-- AKA, my brother-in-law, Osprey-- later this summer.

"You ready?" I ask Mesa as we walk onto the dance floor together.

The hall goes silent around us while everyone waits for the music to begin.

Mesa uses his free hand to whirl me into position so that we're facing each other. He gives me a nod that's far more confident than the look in his eyes.

We both look toward Terra, who scurries up to us and takes the cane from Mesa when he hands it to her.

There's an audible ripple of gasps and sighs and a smattering of light applause through the hall as the first bars of our song come through the speakers.

Mesa wraps me in his arms and we dance.

It's not a waltz or anything with fancy choreography to wow the crowd, but we did practice it for months.

Just standing together and swaying gently while we shuffle our feet in no particular pattern at all.

Mesa still needs me for balance, but his strength is good enough that he can stand on his own for several minutes now before his leg gives out on him and he keeps working on it. His doctors think he'll probably be able to walk unassisted for short distances at some point, but he'll probably never completely be able to lose the cane.

That's okay with me, I got him a fancy, hand-carved one for Christmas and, frankly, I think he looks kinda sexy with it.

"What are you thinking about, Angel?" His voice is deep, whispered against my ear before the music gives way to the next dance.

"I was thinking I changed my mind." I give him a smirk.

"Well, it's too late now, baby. The license is all signed and witnessed and the preacner man took it to get recorded at the courthouse-- you're mine now."

"Not about marrying you."

There's a question in his eyes, waiting for me to explain.

"About waiting till after I start working."

The song ends. Guests cheer as the music gives way to a livelier beat-- we opted to skip all the other traditional dances, so guests begin to fill in around us but Mesa's eyes are burning hot on me.

His hand shoots out, fingers beckoning Terra to bring the cane back quickly. As soon as she does, Mesa catches me completely off guard.

Crouching into a squat, he wraps his good arm around the back of my thighs and tips me over his shoulder in-- appropriately enough-- a classic fireman's carry.

I giggle, swatting at his gorgeous ass as he hauls me out of our own wedding reception and down the hall of the ski lodge's resort hotel where we're holding the wedding.

We'd planned on waiting till after I'd been working for a while before we started trying to get pregnant, but once I was assured that it wouldn't be a problem if I was already pregnant when I started my new job this summer, I stopped taking my birth control.

I mean, it's only been a week, I doubt our efforts will be successful any time soon. But you can believe, we're going to try.

He doesn't put me down until he's carried me through the door to our suite and dropped me on the bed.

"And you said you wouldn't be able to carry me over the threshold," I tease as he begins unbuttoning my gown.

Epilogue 2

Eight Years Later
Mesa

Our oldest son, Heron, stands next to his baby brother and shows him how to hold the carrot for the goat with its head through the fence.

Glade's only two and a half and the goats are still a mystery, and a little bit scary, to the toddler but he worships his seven-year-old brother. I watch from a distance and try not to laugh at I watch our youngest hesitantly hold his hand out flat and snatch it away quickly as soon as the fluffy goat takes it from him.

"Good job, bro!" Heron holds his hand up and patiently waits for his brother's high five.

We didn't mean to have the boys five years apart, it's just the way it worked out.

Angel got pregnant with Heron almost immediately after she stopped her birth control but it was five more years before we got pregnant again.

Not for lack of trying.

"Morning, Angel."

I greet my wife with a kiss as she joins me on the back deck of the cabin where I'm keeping an eye on the boys.

Heron loves the goats. If we'd known how much he was going to love them, we'd have built the pen earlier and just gotten more than one.

Abu started a new tradition of giving goats to each of the great grandkids as they're born. I think it's just her way of getting rid of her own herd as her and Pops get too old to want to deal with them on their own anymore.

"He's going to want another kid next spring," I mention to Angel as we watch our oldest son putting out feed for the animals.

"Well, we'll get a new one anyway."

Robin says it casually, like she doesn't expect me to catch on right away but when I look over at her I see the way she's fighting to keep a straight face and I know.

I get up so fast, my coffee spills when I bump the table, but nothing's going to stop me from pulling my wife into my arms so I can kiss her crazy right now.

"When? How long? What is it? We need another name, Angel."

My hand is on her belly, already impatient to meet my son or daughter.

"Doc Jones thinks I'm about eight weeks along, so April." Robin laughs, pressing her hands over mine.

"You know we won't know for months yet, but I'm thinking Playa or Paloma."

I want to pick her up and spin her around but there's not enough room with the picnic table out here on the deck.

Robin gently walks me back to the chair I was sitting in and settles into my lap.

Yeah, there is still that too.

Almost a decade of time and hard work has gotten me to the point where I can walk short distances without the stick in my hand and I've found ways to compensate for most things but I can lift or I can walk unassisted, I can't do both.

So it's just as well that the table is in the way.

Having my angel sitting on my lap with my baby growing inside her while my sons play in the yard is better than knocking the patio furniture over anyway.

Next in Series

Mountain Man's Need
Deputy Justice Hawkins

She needs a man who will hold her *down*, not hold her *back*.

When I became the face of the law in the tiny mountain town of Moonshine Ridge, it was easy to resist Terra. She was my buddy's baby sister; far too young for me and about as off-limits as girls in my new jurisdiction can get.

I've done my best to be a man of honor, but Terra's sweet curves and fiery spirit have become too much temptation for me to resist.

Problem is, she hates my badge.

Terra's got a rebel streak in her that's wider than the mountains that split this state in half. She's not about to give her heart to a man in a uniform but my blood boils to claim this woman.

My little rebel says she doesn't like being bossed around, but it turns out that's not exactly true and now there's only one way I need Terra to lose control.

Thanks for Reading
Mountain Man's Hope

I suspect there are a fair number of readers who won't completely understand how something as trivial as realizing he wouldn't be able to dance at his wedding could possibly send Mesa into one of those classic "bonehead romance hero break up" moves where he was ready to throw everything he was so grateful for away in one panic-stricken moment.

It's not uncommon though, people often make it through the hardest times, only to fall apart over the tiniest details down the line. For Mesa, it was seeing his angel's sadness in a fleeting moment and being overcome by the panic of feeling like he'd never be able to make up to her everything she'd already done for him.

That dance was just a tiny, first domino falling in a line of sudden realizations of all the very small ways his life had changed and was totally out of his control.

Mesa doesn't really like being out of control. When I first "met" him, far back when I was writing the

McAllister brothers, I had no idea how his story was going to go.

Frankly, I'm really impressed with how well he handled the accident, but he's got an incredibly supportive family, and he's been working with the Moonshine Ridge fire department since he was old enough to work as a volunteer-- he knows the risks and he knows he was lucky. He's also determined, kinda stubborn, and willing to take on the pain if it meant Robin was okay.

Anyway, it was somewhere during Oz and Meadow's book (Mountain Man's Treasure) when I saw that moment through Mesa's eyes and knew he was going to try really hard to pull a really boneheaded move. Which is why Glen and Finch's story was told first-- I had to talk Mesa off the ledge. (Because I am one of those authors who is not entirely in control of my characters.)

These books were never supposed to get too emotionally stressful. I did my best to convince Mesa not to be too dramatic. Hopefully you enjoyed meeting him and Robin and watching them work it out.

About

Deputy Justice Hawkins

She needs a man who will hold her *down*, not hold her *back*.

When I became the face of the law in the tiny mountain town of Moonshine Ridge, it was easy to resist Terra. She was my buddy's baby sister; far too young for me and about as off-limits as girls in my new jurisdiction can get.

I've done my best to be a man of honor, but Terra's sweet curves and fiery spirit have become too much temptation for me to resist.

Problem is, she hates my badge.

Terra's got a rebel streak in her that's wider than the mountains that split this state in half. She's not about to give her heart to a man in a uniform but my blood boils to claim this woman.

Rocklyn Ryder

My little rebel says she doesn't like being bossed around, but it turns out that's not exactly true and now there's only one way I need Terra to lose control.

Terra and Hawkins

Mountain Man's Need
The Diaz Family of Moonshine Ridge
by
Rocklyn Ryder

Chapter One

Terra

The hall erupts in cheers when my brother throws his bride over his shoulder and carries her out through the doors that lead to the hall.

Mesa was injured while fighting the forest fire that torched Placer Canyon a couple seasons ago. For a long time, we didn't know if he was even going to be able to walk again. Seeing him dance at his wedding was pretty cool.

Mom's still wiping tears out of her eyes.

The music continues, people start dancing. It's pretty clear the newlyweds aren't planning on coming back to the reception any time soon. Everyone starts to go back to enjoying the party.

"Do me the honor?"

The deep voice comes from over my shoulder and when I turn around, I can't help the exasperated sigh.

Deputy Hawkins stands there, his hand held out politely, with that hopeful puppy dog look in his eyes.

I turn him down and make a quick getaway,

knowing he'll follow me if I head for the buffet table and God knows he'll throw a fit if he sees me sneaking a drink from the bar.

Technically, our state makes exceptions for underage drinking on private property with certain adult permission. With only a few more months till my twenty-first birthday, my folks are fine with me having a beer at my brother's wedding.

But Hawk is one of those by-the-rules types. Everything is black or white to guys like him, no room for bending rules, let alone actually breaking a few.

Just to fuck with him, I head for the bar anyway. Stopping to give my grandmother a hug on the way, I see Hawk out of the corner of my eye. Sure enough, he's watching me.

"Come sit with us, Mija," Abu's eyes shine with mischief and whiskey as she pats the seat of the chair beside her. "Alice and I were just--"

"Uh uh." I put my fingers in my ears to make it clear I don't want to know what she and Alice were *"just."* "Plausible deniability, 'lita,"

Alice barks a laugh and downs one of the shots of amber liquid that are lined up on the table between the old women.

"Smart girl," Abu coos at me, running a gnarled hand over my hair and giving me a loving-- but drunken-- smile. "Are you having fun?"

"A blast," I tell her, dropping a kiss against her forehead. "Please don't get in trouble tonight." I shoot a warning glare first at my grandmother and then at her notorious accomplice.

Mountain Man's Need

Abu picks up one of the shots and Alice gives me her best innocent old lady expression.

These two are anything but innocent and, if tradition holds, they will be on their absolute worst behavior tonight.

Anytime there's a wedding on this mountain, my abuela and her friends get into trouble.

We've had to drive down to the sheriff's substation in town and bail Abu out of jail more than once. Although Hawkins does seem to have a soft spot for Abu and her friends. Since he's been assigned to Moonshine Ridge, I don't think any of the Infamous Four have actually been arrested. He just takes them to the station and calls family to come pick them up.

My eyes dart over to the man in the sheriff's uniform hovering nearby.

Ugh-- and what's up with the uniform? I swear, he wears that uniform all the time. It's like it's his actual skin. I don't think the man even owns regular clothes.

Hawk took over the deputy position a couple of years ago. Moonshine Ridge is a small town, so everyone knew him inside of about a week but he's ex-military, he was in the Marines like my oldest brother, Vale. They bonded right away and now he always seems to be around. He's like part of the family now.

"Why don't you dance with the deputy, sweetheart? He likes you."

Alice snickers behind her hand and eyes another shot glass before getting to her feet.

"Abuela, ewww. He can't even grow a beard, he looks like a teenager." Scrunching up my nose at the thought, I give her another quick hug. "I love you 'lita. I'm serious, no trouble tonight."

"Got us a ride. Let's go." Alice calls to my grandmother and Abu jumps up eagerly to join her friend.

"Don't worry, I'll get 'em both home safe," Hawkins assures me with a polite nod of his head when I turn to see my grandmother and her friend practically pulling him out the door.

What the fuck? Weird.

Dad could have driven them both home. He's not drinking tonight for that exact reason. Why isn't Abu going home with Papa?

Through one of the big, picture windows out in the hall overlooking the snow-covered mountains with the groomed ski runs and the lifts dangling above in the moonlight, I watch Hawk open the front door of his official, sheriff department SUV and wait patiently while Abu climbs into the front seat. Then Alice slides into the rear and the unit pulls out of the lodge's parking lot and disappears into the distance.

HAWK

TERRA DIAZ TURNS ON HER HEEL AND WALKS away from me. Again.

As I watch her go, I think it's probably just as well. There's not a chance in hell I'd be able to hold her in my arms and spin her around the dance floor without pulling her in too close to me. Holding those sinful

Mountain Man's Need

curves of hers possessively and letting her feel what she does to me.

This isn't the time or place for that. It's a family event and even though I'm here in uniform.

When I accepted the post in this tiny, mountain community, I wasn't fully aware of just how much time I'd be putting in. Being the only law enforcement officer in town means being on duty twenty-four/seven, except for the few days a week when the sub-station in Keller's Ferry is on call.

My steps take me closer to Terra. It's not something I think about and it's sure as hell not something I do on purpose. The curvy little beauty has me under a spell and it's I'm drawn toward her. I'm one hundred percent obsessed and my obsession is one hundred percent wrong.

When I came up here a couple years back, Terra was just out of high school, barely even legal. That made it easier to ignore the way I noticed her presence any time she was around. Which is plenty, seeing as how her family has become like my own.

She's still too young for me. I'm fourteen years her senior and I've got no business looking at her the way I do. Not to mention the thoughts I have about her when I'm alone in my own home with my fist wrapped around my aching cock in the night.

I fought it at first. I tried not to notice the way her body has rounded into womanhood, the way her long, black hair sways above her ass with her confident strides-- usually away from me after making some smart-ass remark.

My girl's got a sassy mouth on her and rebellious streak a mile wide. She doesn't take well to being told what to do and her willfulness only makes me want to claim her more.

Every day I see her growing more beautiful, strong and confident like the other women in her family, and I've had to come to terms with the fact that this need for her is more than lust.

The hunger that gnaws at me more with every day that Terra isn't mine goes beyond obsession. I am smitten with the curvy little Latina rebel and I won't be sated till she's my wife.

From the edge of the room, my eyes follow Terra. Her eyes glance over at the bar where plastic wine glasses sit filled and lined up for the taking by the guests that are of age.

Technically, Terra could be drinking tonight and I'd have no say in the matter. When her eyes flick from the bar toward me, I know she's thinking the same thing. Sizing me up, deciding if she wants to push her luck-- or rather— my buttons.

When she veers in the other direction and heads for the table where her grandmother and Alice McAllister are huddled together with a line of small, plastic shot glasses between them-- no doubt filled with whiskey-- I'm not sure how I feel about it.

I want to praise her for making the better decision, but I'm also disappointed that she didn't give me an excuse to give her shit for not being twenty-one yet.

There are few things I enjoy more these days than catching Terra in the act of bucking the system. Just so

Mountain Man's Need

I can get a taste of her passion while she reminds me that I'm not the boss of her. Just so I can torture myself with thoughts of all the ways I want to hear her beg me to change that.

Alice leaves the table where Terra and Marcia continue to talk and my spine stiffens as I watch her head my way.

"My friend and I could use a ride home, officer." She doesn't even slur as she wraps her arm through mine flirtatiously.

"Alice, there are designated drivers here tonight for that." I pat the bony hand wrapped around my bicep and smile down at the old woman.

The green eyes staring up at me are not smiling back.

This woman is in her eighties for fuck's sake. How the hell is her hand so damn strong? I don't think I could pry her grip off my arm if I tried.

It's been like this since I got up to the Ridge. I still remember the night the Brick and Porter opened in town. When I agreed to give Vera Jones and Mable Hart a ride home, Current Jones warned me not to let his grandmother and her friend talk me into any detours-- but I didn't listen.

That was the night I got pulled into the seedy underbelly of Moonshine Ridge's local crime syndicate. The Infamous Four have been blackmailing me into aiding and abetting ever since.

We're talking real crime; trespassing, breaking and entering. Hell, Vera and Mable stole a whole herd of goats out of the Diaz barn last year-- with my help.

Alice is still looking up at me, waiting for my answer.

"Let's go then."

I do my level best to make it clear that I disapprove.

"Got us a ride!" Alice practically cackles with glee as she hails Marcia.

Marcia slugs the last shot of whiskey left on the table as she gets up. I see her shaking her head and tsking at whatever Terra says to her as she watches her grandmother head toward me and Alice.

A tinge of guilt stiffens my shoulders, after all, I'm the law here. It's my sworn duty to prevent the kind of goings-on that I'm about to be a party to.

I keep telling myself it's all fun and games, really. These four women have a lifetime of history together, their hi-jinks go back over sixty years now. I'm making sure no one gets hurt, that their feuding doesn't get out of hand.

The guilt passes quickly enough as I load the two women into the SUV and listen carefully to the plan that they begin to spell out as soon as we're on the road.

Truth of the matter is, this is fun as hell.

Chapter Two

Terra

Something's weird tonight. Everybody's here.

It's not weird that my entire family is at the homestead; my grandparents' property is the heart of our family. Or, I guess Abu and Papa are the heart of our family.

My parents or one of my brothers always seems to be around, but it's weird to see everyone's truck in the driveway in the middle of the week like this.

I pull up the back drive, the long stretch of two-track that leads directly to the back of the barn and the guest house next to it.

When I started my daycare, I moved in with my grandparents so I could be closer to the business. I didn't mind living in the house but Abu insisted that a young woman should have more privacy so I moved into to the little cottage.

My grandmother never got to live alone. She went straight from her parents' house to her husband's house and even when Papa was drafted to the war in

Vietnam, Abu already had Vale. She thinks it's an important experience to have before I get married and start a family of my own.

Not sure when that's likely to be.

I get that twenty is still young, it's not like I thought I'd be married with two kids by now like Hyacinth McAllister-- but I guess I did sort of think I'd be serious with someone by now. Someone I'd be planning a future with.

As the youngest of five kids, I've always wanted a big family too, but the pickins on the Ridge are slim and none when it comes to men my age and men my age have never been very interesting anyway.

Abu's been dropping a lot of not-so-subtle hints about Hawk. Like maybe he likes me and like maybe she'd be happy if I liked him back but...ugh.

The deputy is nice and all but, for a man with a bad-ass name like "Hawk," he's just-- boring. Too clean cut, too buttoned up. The epitome of a good-guy. The kind of guy that says "yes ma'am/no ma'am," calls my dad "sir..." drives drunk little old ladies home kind of good guy. Not the kind of guy I'm into *at all,* good guy.

Dropping the pile of stuff I carried inside on a chair as I close the door behind me, I hear voices outside. A lot of voices. All male.

I recognize the deep rumbles of the men of the family and I'm sure they're headed out to the barn for some guy time.

Before I have the lights on inside, I look back out the door to watch them. I'm about to call out a greeting to my brothers when my eyes catch on the new guy walking between Vale and my father.

"Daddy." It comes out of me in a throaty whisper, exactly the way I'd like to be saying it to him.

Seriously, the man is hot with a capital *"yes please."*

As the group of men make their way to the outside staircase leading up to the barn loft-- which is decked out in true man cave style-- I get a decent enough look at the stranger among them from the row of solar lights along the barn.

His hair is cropped short at the back but longer on top. I can't make out the exact color from here but it's lighter than my family's black tresses so I'm going to bet on brown.

A full beard shadows his face, shorter than any of my brothers' but definitely a mountain man-- someone who grew up in a place like Moonshine Ridge. A man with hands that are callused from swinging an ax into seasoned firewood all summer and shoveling snow off the walk during the winter.

A shiver works its way down my spine, all the way to my pussy where I'm feeling suddenly very hot and wet at the thought of what hands like that would feel like on my skin.

My eyes are pinned on the new guy as he climbs the stairs to the loft. He's wearing a dark t-shirt that stretches across a massive chest, and a fleece-lined flannel over it that doesn't hide the thick bulge of biceps that I am one hundred percent sure would have no trouble lifting me up and holding my curvy frame against a wall.

Tree trunk thighs, check.

Mouth-watering ass looking insanely hot in those jeans? Double check.

By the time they've all disappeared inside, it's confirmed. This is the man of my filthy, filthy dreams.

Now I just need to find out who he is.

HAWK

I'M A MAN OF HONOR. I LIKE TO DO THINGS ON the up and up-- my involvement with Marcia and her friends and their pranks on each other, notwithstanding-- I have a lot of respect for the Diaz family and I don't want to do anything that might damage our friendship.

That's why I'm here tonight, nervous in the barn's upper level that's been converted to a recreation room.

It's the first time I've stood in this room with a beer in my hand and felt nervous about facing the five men of the Diaz family.

Even at 85 years old, Alejandro stands over six foot. I'm not a small guy myself, but facing Terra's brothers, father, and grandfather— all holding pool cues in their hands, standing around the table that stands between me and the only easy exit— has me keenly aware that our friendship and my badge only go so far with men when they're protecting someone they love.

"So, you gonna tell us what's so important that you wanted to talk to us all together?"

With our shared background in the Corps, Vale and I bonded quickly when we met. The cautious tone of his voice now has me shaking my head quickly to dispel his concern-- there was an altercation awhile back when he was forced to discharge his pistol in self-defense.

That's the official story and I'll go to my grave before I give up a single detail that might cast a doubt on my friend's justification for his actions.

Tense shoulders around the room relax at the reassurance that my reasons for calling the men together tonight isn't an indication that an investigation has been reopened.

My own shoulders, however, stay tense.

"You know I've got a pregnant wife at home, right?" Glen jokes, leaning over the pool table to take the break.

"You know I'm trying to have a pregnant wife at home." Mesa grumbles in my general direction as he leans in for the next shot.

"Well, I'm trying for a pregnant wife at home too," Montana jokes. "So hurry up."

The room erupts in laughter, including myself, taking a bit of the edge off my nerves.

Terra's father is in his sixties and after raising five children already, I'm pretty sure he and Lark are beyond trying for any more.

"Me too," Alex pipes up, sipping his beer from the bottle to a new round of laughter and a few words of encouragement from his grandsons.

"Then what's up, Hawk?" Montana brings the

conversation back on track. "Why'd you want us all together?"

It's instinct to go for my hat, but I'm not in uniform tonight. Without my hat to hold onto, I'm at a loss of what to do with my hands.

"You all know how much I appreciate the way the Diaz family has taken me in since I came up to the Ridge, and you know I have the utmost respect for all of you. I wouldn't want to overstep myself by doing anything that might jeopardize our friendship--"

"Cut to the chase." Glen's impatient voice mirrors the look on all the men's faces.

The pool game has been forgotten, as all five men stand to eye my serious tone with some suspicion.

I clear my throat and take my shot.

"I'd like your permission to court Terra."

The men erupt in howls of laughter. The deep bass of their voices bouncing off the wood paneling and rattling the windows.

Mesa laughs so hard, he has to lean on his cane while Vale wipes an actual, fucking tear from the corner of his eye.

Alejandro drops his head forward, his entire body shaking in silent laughter, and Glen slaps his dad on the back when Montana starts coughing from his laughter.

I fidget with the loose change in my pocket, and wait while they compose themselves.

Finally, Montana manages to straighten his face and respond.

"What did Terra have to say about this?"

Dropping my gaze to the bottle I'm holding in my hand before looking back up to meet the amused, dark eyes of the man I hope will be my father-in-law someday, I humbly confess.

"I haven't spoken to Terra yet, sir. I wanted to speak with you first."

The guys howl again. Montana visibly bites the inside of his cheek, fighting the urge to join his sons in their amusement.

"Hawk!" Glen gasps out his words from laughing so hard, "What the hell are you thinking, man?"

"Are we talking about my baby sister? That's the Terra you want to date?" Vale's not at all mad, he's still laughing.

"You know Tee does not respond well to authority, right?" Mesa cautions through a smile, "She gives the delivery guy attitude when he asks her to sign for a package. There is no way you are getting near her with that Dudley Do-Right thing you have going on there."

"Your whiskers just barely came in, man," Glen adds-- they've been teasing me about the new beard since I arrived. "You are *not* ready for a Diaz woman."

"Hawkins," Montana manages to pull himself together and I appreciate hearing his voice take the stoic tone so I know he's taking my request seriously. "You know we like you. You are always welcome here and I'd be proud to welcome you into the family. But my boys are right... Neither of my girls are much for tradition--"

"Gets it from her abuela," Alex mutters with a combination of frustration and reverence.

"It's not my place to give permission to date my daughter, but I do wish you luck, son."

The laughter starts up again.

"You're a brave man, Hawkins. I'm gonna miss you when Tee buries your ass in the woods." Vale gets to his feet and pats me on the back as if he's genuinely concerned for my safety.

Business concluded; unfinished beers are poured out, bottles dropped into the bin, pool cues returned to their rack and the game forgotten.

These men all have wives and families that they're eager to get home to so I follow them back out into the night, laughing easily among them even though it's at my own expense.

My gut gnaws with the fear that they're right, but I feel lighter knowing I won't have to fight the men I hope to call kin in order to claim my woman.

Chapter Three

Terra

As soon as I hear the men laughing outside the back door, I jump off the kitchen stool I've been perched on while I watch Abu making cookies.

"Night, 'lita." I head for the door as grandmother shoots me a curious look at my sudden exit.

"You leaving, Mija?" Papa asks as he passes me outside the door.

"Yeah, I have to get up early to open the center." I give my grandfather a hug and let him kiss me on the cheek.

"Okay, Tee, you have a good night."

He gives me a weird look and a vague smile but he doesn't say anything else before disappearing into the house.

The sound of engines starting drowns out the murmur of men's voices and I hover just behind the garage, hoping to get a better view of the guy I saw earlier.

Lights go on and then the rumble of diesel

engines fades as trucks head out to the main road. Vale and his friend are the only ones left, standing beside Vale's truck which is running with the lights on, ready to go.

I don't want to be too obvious in front of my brother. He'll give me hell if he sees me flirting with one of his buddies. But if I wait till they part ways, I might miss a chance to meet his friend.

Straightening my back, I do my very best casual stroll back to my cottage-- being careful to take a route that goes directly by my brother and his sinfully hot friend, of course.

As I get a little closer to them, I'm able to make out a few more details about the guy. He's a couple inches shorter than Vale so he must be around six, three. His hair is definitely a dark brown. It's not as neat as before, as if he's run his hand through it to brush it away from his face. It's even longer on top than I'd thought it was, and I wonder what it would look like after my hands had been in it while he had his face between my legs.

The little fantasy hits me hard and I have to pause for a second and catch my breath. Because, hell yeah, I would definitely let this man scratch my thighs with his beard.

When he notices me coming toward them, my brother shoots me a grin that makes me feel like I'm the butt of a joke I didn't hear-- with three annoying older brothers, I know that grin well-- then he pushes off the side of his truck and slaps the other guy on the shoulder.

Mountain Man's Need

My steps slow down as I try to process the complete scene as it comes into full view.

"Hey, Tee!" Vale lifts his arm in a wave toward me but doesn't wait for me to approach.

"Check in with us later so we know you're still alive, right?" I hear Vale tell the other guy as he jumps in his truck, and takes off, leaving his friend standing alone in the semi-darkness.

Weird.

I'd expected my brother would stick around to at least introduce me to his friend. Maybe glower at the guy a little to warn him not to mess with me.

Guess I don't warrant the same protective big brother act that Meadow got.

The way Vale took off, it's like he thinks I already know this guy-- and definitely doesn't think the guy is going to do anything inappropriate.

Well, the joke's on my brother, because I plan on making sure his friend does all kinds of inappropriate things to me.

"Good evening, Terra."

Uh oh, I know that voice.

"I was hoping I'd get to see you here tonight."

The man closes the distance between us while my brain scrambles to make sense of how Deputy Hawkins' voice is possibly coming out of the man I've been drooling over for the last few hours.

How is this even possible? I feel like I've been catfished.

When did his voice get so low? I don't remember it ever having that deep, growly thing going on before.

"Let me walk you home," he offers, gesturing toward the door to the little house on the other side of the driveway.

"You grew a beard."

Man, I am all kinds of Captain Obvious right now. I use my free hand to stroke my own chin like he might not know what a beard is.

"I figured it was time to start fitting in with the locals...and, uh, your grandmother told me I looked like my nuts hadn't dropped."

He clears his throat and laughs nervously like he just cursed in front of a four-year-old or something, but I am busting up.

Hawk falls into step beside me as I head for my house. My brain is spinning, not sure at all what's going on. A few minutes ago I was naming the babies I was planning on having with this guy and now it turns out he's the same boring deputy that I've been avoiding for months.

This means that the jacked-up, classic Ford Bronco sitting in the driveway must belong to him too. No trace of the regulation SUV with the sheriff's logo all over it.

"What are you reading?" Hawk gestures toward the paperback in my hand which I quickly clutch close to my chest.

"Just some book I saw recommended online."

I do my level best to make it sound about as interesting as a math book. Thankfully, it's got a discreet cover on it and a vague title that doesn't give away the over-the-top level of smut on the pages inside.

HAWK

When she came out of the house, she headed straight toward me and Vale. There was a look of interest in her eyes, and I was certain they were set on me.

That changed as soon as I greeted her and now that we're alone, my little rebel's gone distant, but it's not the same cool distance she usually puts between us.

Something's different about her tonight, letting me fall into step beside her and making small conversation as I escort her to her door.

Maybe it's wishful thinking, knowing I've taken a step closer to courting her and claiming her. Desperately looking for signs that I'm on my way to making Terra mine.

As long as she'll have me, of course.

Her brothers' teasing rings in my ears and I know her family is right; Terra's a headstrong young woman that's determined to control her own destiny. Maybe that's what it is about her that has my body on fire at the thought of her.

All I know is that the curvy little thing climbing the steps to her front door beside me is the only woman that's going to be in my bed and definitely the only woman who will ever be in my heart.

This is my chance to say something that will make her see me as more than just the local badge, more than a friend of her family, more than some stammering old man with a crush on her.

It's my chance to make a connection with her. Show her that I'm a man. A man who can care for her in every way she'll ever need.

Instead, I stumble over myself, too intimidated by the beauty standing only a couple feet in front of me, looking like she's ready to bolt through the door and leave me out here in the cold all alone.

I ask about her book. Pathetic small talk but I've seen Terra with a book in her hand plenty of times. I know she reads romances and I'm curious what sort.

The thick paperback she's clinging to now looks innocent enough but when I ask about the book, a deep blush rises in her cheeks. Her breathing picks up a notch and she wets those tempting, pillow lips with the tip of her tongue. The sight makes me go hard instantly.

"Is it any good?" I ask, nodding toward the book, fighting to keep the conversation going and keep myself from overstepping the boundaries that still lie between me and that sassy mouth of hers.

"It's okay," she answers evasively, making me even more curious about what she's reading.

I make a mental note of the title, visible along the spine, with plans to look it up later to see what kind of book she might be reading that she doesn't want to talk about.

"So what were you guys doing tonight?" There's a familiar snark in Terra's tone that sounds more like the woman that has me hopelessly transfixed.

Shuffling my feet on the worn wooden boards of the porch, I drop my head and scrub the back of my neck with one hand.

"We had some business to discuss."

Terra snorts, her dark eyes lighting with mischief.

"'*Business*,' riiiight. Drinking beer and playing pool, just the guys, on a weeknight. Whatever you say, Deputy."

She looks toward the big farmhouse where Alex and Marcia live, her pretty features changing from laughter to curiosity.

"Would your little 'business' meeting with the boys tonight have anything to do with the new *pond* at Mable Hart's place?"

Suddenly I'm choking on my next breath, caught in a coughing fit at the unexpected mention of the latest prank in the ongoing feud between Terra's grandmother and three other women that make up the local historical society.

"You heard about that?"

"Zephyr's my bestie, remember? She says it's way too big for a couple of old ladies to have dug it overnight with shovels."

A tired sigh escapes me.

"I was told the Harts dug it. Had to go out and cite them for not getting a permit first." I explain the official story calmly, sticking to the legalities of the matter without letting myself think about the details.

Terra eyes me skeptically. She's suspicious, I can tell.

"But you know the Harts didn't dig a pond...in the

middle of the night...in January. Right? You know it was Abu and Alice. It happened the night of Mesa and Robin's wedding, they must have snuck back out after *you* took them home."

Those dark eyes narrow on me as she emphasizes the fact that I took them home that night. Like she's accusing me of not being a better babysitter.

"No, our business didn't have anything to do with your grandmother and her friends." I recover my senses and adopt my official voice to assure her that wasn't the subject of my meeting with the menfolk of her family this evening.

It earns me a cold glare and a firm jaw. All traces of that playful smile of hers wiped clean from her face.

"Well, it's cold out here, *Deputy*." To make her point, she rubs her arm with her free hand, "and I have to get up early for work. It's good to see that your nuts finally dropped."

Just like that, Terra disappears through the door in a blindingly quick motion that leaves me gaping after her, all alone on her porch.

The door locks behind her, letting me know she won't be coming back out to check on me. Silently, I take pride in her for having the smarts to keep her door locked-- even if I'd rather we were on the same side of the damn thing.

Chapter Four

Terra

SPARROW: "DID HE ASK YOU OUT YET?"

It's the second time my sister-in-law has texted to ask if Hawk has asked me out.

She thinks it sweet. Romantic, even, but when I found out that the real reason he'd been at the homestead the other night talking to the men in my family-- *just* the men, mind you— was to get their permission to date me, I came unhinged.

I've been grossed-out ever since; disgusted with myself for what I was thinking about while I got myself off in the shower after he left.

I can't believe I thought he was hot in his street clothes. With that beard growing in thick and dark, tricking me into thinking there could be something more interesting under his clean cut, old-fashioned fuddy-dud exterior.

For a second, I was even thinking maybe he's the one who's been helping Abuela and her friend play those tricks on Vera and Mable. They definitely aren't moving all that snow and dirt by themselves; someone is helping them. Someone with access to heavy equipment.

It would have taken a back-hoe to dig that hole on the Hart's property a few weeks ago. Not to mention, Alice and Abu were both pretty drunk when Hawk took them home that night.

My grandmother isn't any better at following rules than I am, but she wouldn't drive drunk.

Since Hawk was the one that took them home, I thought maybe he was in on it with them, but I should have known better. He's so straight-laced, he'd snap in half if he tried to bend a rule.

I'm surprised he hasn't found a reason to arrest them yet.

The idea that Hawk might have a bad boy streak hiding under his goody-two-shoes persona turns me on. Thinking of him prowling the town in the middle of the night, helping a couple of old ladies play pranks on each other makes him seem human-- and hella hot.

I've known the deputy is interested in me for a few months now, but he's always been so damn polite about it. Never once pushing his luck to stake his claim-- and now, really? Asking my dad and my brothers for *permission* to ask me out? Before he's even asked me if he can have my phone number or bought me a cup of coffee.

So *not* hot.

As if the universe hears me thinking about him, the official sheriff vehicle pulls up in front of April's cafe where I've been staring out the window while I grudge-sip my latte.

Of course, there's no way I can escape before he gets inside, either.

"Morning, Deputy!" April sings out from behind the counter.

She's already pulling shots for his drink and I don't like the way I feel when I see the way he smiles back at her as he leans on the counter between them and makes small talk with the cute new girl in town.

April moved to Moonshine Ridge last fall and opened up the coffee shop. Finally bringing decent coffee to the Ridge.

I've been getting along with her, making a habit of walking over from the center before opening up every day to enjoy a latte and do a little reading-- or just bullshitting with my new friend and filling her in on the local gossip.

Until I see the way Hawk smiles at her. The way she already knows exactly what his drink of choice is and starts making it before he orders.

It's enough to keep me from taking the opportunity to escape while Hawk is preoccupied. In fact, it's enough to make me forget that I wanted to escape at all.

"Thanks, April."

I hear that deep voice and press my thighs together. Not because his voice suddenly makes me go all sticky between my legs, mind you! It's just me tensing up because I'm so mad at him.

Right. I remember now. I'm pissed at the man

looming over me in that ugly, beige uniform, with that dumb hat pulled low over his forehead while he watches me ignore him with his espresso in one hand and a croissant that April had saved *just for him* in the other.

"Morning, Terra."

My thighs tighten under the small table...because I'm mad, not because I suddenly can't *not* notice that his voice is dark and rough with a touch of amusement in it that makes me want to hear him read all my favorite books to me-- especially the dirty parts.

"Mind if I sit with you?"

It takes a lot of effort to shrug this nonchalantly without looking up from my book.

The chair opposite me scrapes against the flooring and creaks slightly under his weight, reminding me he's a pretty big guy.

Thoughts of how easily he could hold me down and make me beg are suddenly all up in my head, totally unwelcome, making my thighs press harder together while my pussy clenches.

It's the book, I tell myself. This one's even smuttier than the last one and I've been on a dark romance binge lately.

Obviously, I can't keep reading while he's watching me. It's...weird.

I try to tell myself it's creepy, but that's not it. It's something else entirely and I don't like it.

"I read that book." Hawk says conversationally as he leans over the small table between us. That hint of amusement is still there, but it's over-ridden by something else. Something darker that sounds conspiratorial.

A shiver runs along my spine and settles between my legs where I'm already in denial of the heat that's building.

Then I realize what book he's referring to-- the one I had with me when he was out at the homestead.

Oh. *That* book. That is not the sort of book our prissy, uptight deputy should read.

Now it's my turn to be mildly amused, thinking of the lawman sitting across from me in his perfectly pressed uniform and how uncomfortable he must have been reading one of my filthy dark romance books.

Did it shock him, I wonder. Was he disgusted? Did it turn him on?

Now I'm just plain uncomfortable, squirming in my chair to relieve the pressure building between my legs while I envision the man sitting across from me with that book in one hand and his dick in the other.

Nope! Not going there. This is the guy who actually asked for permission to ask me out, remember? This is the sheriff's deputy. The guy who walks two blocks out of his way to use the crosswalk. The only crosswalk in Moonshine Ridge. The one that literally is only painted on the road because our main street is, technically, a state highway and it's required to have a crosswalk where it runs through town.

I never even noticed we *had* a crosswalk until I saw Hawkins going out of his way to use it.

This man doesn't have a rebellious bone in his body. He literally gave Cody Fell a citation for selling firewood without a business license two seasons ago.

Deputy Hawkins has probably never even considered using his handcuffs for any non-regulation purpose.

"How'd you like it?" I finally look up at him and give him my best innocent smile, knowing damn well there's no way he read the whole thing. He seems like the kind of guy who would have to take a shower and go to confession for even knowing that level of smut exists.

Proving my point, he blushes. A deep shade of pink colors his face all the way into the beard that has grown in thicker and longer in just the few days since I last saw him.

"Well, I read the book before it in the series," he mutters, eyes on his cooling coffee. "And then I read the two books after it."

My hand falls off the book I'm reading currently, allowing all the pages to fan shut and lose my place, since I refuse to break the spines on my paperbacks.

I look up at him and stare in open surprise.

"Wow, that's two more books than I made it through," I confess. I mean, the smut was hot, but the story was all over the place and it kinda stopped making sense halfway through book two.

He clears his throat and sips his coffee.

"I guess I just wanted to see how it was going to work out for them in the end," he admits.

Mountain Man's Need

HAWK

THOSE BOOKS WERE INDECENT. READING THE first one made me feel dirty-- not because the material was so outrageous, but because I felt like I was invading Terra's privacy in a way.

I knew she read romance and I knew she liked the ones with the sex scenes left in, but up until a few nights ago, I had no idea what a "dark" romance was, let alone just how dirty a dirty book can be and still get labeled "romance."

The thing had *flowers* on the cover for fuck's sake.

By the time I finished it, I had to read the rest of the series...and now I have a better appreciation for the woman sitting across from me now.

Terra's a rebel and she hates being told what to do-- so getting a look at what turns my little rebel on was downright enlightening.

I'd be lying if I said I'd never thought about how much I'd like to tie her to my bed and tease her till she begged me to let her come.

Now I know she'd like it.

The way the dark eyes staring at me are nearly black now with her pupils dilated and those thick lips made for sucking dick are parted like that's what's on her mind too, tells me that she's all too aware that I know her secret now.

My dick is uncomfortable in the starched uniform

trousers, rising up to fight my belt for space while the zipper threatens to leave a mark where it's cutting me in two.

The moment of tenseness between us passes after a beat or two of silence with our eyes locked. Then she drops her gaze and rifles through the pages of her book in search of the place that was lost.

I drink my coffee and finish the pastry that April saves for me every morning.

"Terra, I wanted to ask you if--"

Her hand raises as if to stop me, but she doesn't look up from her reading.

"Sparrow told me why you were at the house with the guys the other night," she says in a flat tone laced with cynicism. "Not interested."

Just like that, we've gone from one extreme to the other-- fire to ice-- making me wonder what the hell just happened.

One minute Terra was eye-fucking me. She practically had visible thought bubbles hovering over her head that said "Fuck me, Daddy," in them and now she's back to giving the me the same cold shoulder she's been turning on me for months.

"What did Sparrow tell you?" I ask, half wondering out loud and half asking in earnest. What could Vale's wife have said to Terra that has her shutting me out so completely?

This time, Terra carefully places the bookmark into the crease of the pages to keep her place before closing the book and looking up.

There's heat there, but not the same as before.

Pretty brown eyes narrow, glancing over me and hovering a beat on the badge pinned over my left breast above the tag with my last name embroidered on it, then rest back on my own eyes.

"You know it's not the eighteen hundreds anymore, right?"

She doesn't wait for me to respond.

"Women actually get to decide who we date these days. We get to decide who we date, who we marry, and who we fuck. If you want to ask my father for a date, date him. Same goes for my brothers."

I hadn't realized how loud her voice had gotten till I hear a couple men laughing from near the counter.

"Told ya so," Mesa's voice booms across the small cafe, followed by more laughter from both him and his brother-in-law, Ozzie, standing with him.

"Ugh! You guys are such *pigs!*" Terra grabs her book and her coffee from the table, shouting at her brothers and, I'm pretty sure, all men, as she stomps out of the cafe with steam billowing from her ears.

"What just happened?" April questions from behind the counter as she slides a couple to-go cups across the laminate toward Mesa and Oz.

"Oh nothing," Mesa answers, "just my baby sister handing the deputy his ass."

April looks like she's about to ask more questions when the bells on the front door ring and Raine Hart walks in, shaking off the snow from his coat.

Suddenly April's interest in our conversation is lost, her eyes only seeing the man that just walked in.

"Talk later, Hawk," Mesa mumbles as he passes me

on his way out while Oz stays behind to chat with Raine.

When I came to the Ridge, I learned quickly who the big family names are around here-- who has friends and who has enemies in this small town and where those bonds and feuds were formed.

The people of Moonshine Ridge either love or hate the Hart men. Mesa's on the hate side of the line, so I'm not surprised to see him make his hasty retreat.

After I've finished my coffee and made small-talk with the remaining occupants of the cafe, I zip up my jacket and adjust my hat while I stand under the porch awning outside April's cafe.

Across the way, Terra's outside, shoveling snow that's built up from this morning's flurries from the entrance of her daycare center so no one slips on their way in or out.

I ought to leave her be and go on with my day, but dammit, she's got a building full of little ones that need her attention, she doesn't need to be out there shoveling snow off the sidewalk.

Pulling up my collar, I make the short walk to her building, preparing myself for whatever she has to tell me and hoping she doesn't say it with that shovel to the side of my head.

"Let me do that." Reaching for the shovel, my hand brushes hers and feels that it's freezing cold from being out here without gloves on.

"I've got it," she yanks back on the handle but I've already got a firm grip so there's no way for her to win this fight.

"Your hands are freezing, Tee."

It doesn't take any effort at all to uncurl her frozen fingers but it does take a hell of a lot of effort not to hold them against my chest to warm them for her.

Settling for gently massaging her hands with mine, I notice the way her breathing kicks up at the casual contact and I can't help but take advantage of it.

Pulling her a little closer to me and kneading her small hands till they're a little less cold, I do my best to hide the pride I feel at the way she allows me to take care of her and the soft look in her eyes.

"I'll clear the sidewalk off. You get inside and get yourself warmed up. I don't want to see you back out here without some gloves on, hear me, Rebel?"

She casts a glance at the snow shovel leaning against my hip and quirks an eyebrow at me but doesn't argue.

The tip of her tongue swipes along her lip and she pulls the lower one between her teeth. I can tell she's considering whether or not she wants to fight me on this, but she's freezing and she's got a bunch of kids inside waiting for her to come back and start their day.

After a pause, she gives me a nod.

Before I drop her hand and let her get back inside, I lean down to whisper in her ear.

"Good girl."

A shiver that has nothing to do with the cold shakes her shoulders before she looks back at me with narrowed eyes. She doesn't get a chance to snark at me though, because her assistant is at the door asking for her help.

Terra disappears inside and I do my civic duty, pitching in to help the local businesses and keep the people under my jurisdiction safe.

Or maybe I'm just a hopelessly love-struck guy shoveling snow off the sidewalk for a pretty girl.

Chapter Five

Terra

Zeph: Are you sure you know what you're doing?

Me: They never even lock it. No one's going to see me. I just have to know.

Zeph: Don't get caught, I can't afford to bail you out.

Me: Pffff. As if. Hawk won't arrest me, he's too busy asking my dad if he can date me.

Zeph: 😂

Me: 🙈

Me: Think about it, there has to be a reason the grandmas are getting away with their shit. None of them have gotten arrested since Hawk took over after Eric. Someone is helping them.

Zeph: You think Hawk is in on it?

Rocklyn Ryder

> Me: Finding out. TTYL.

> Zeph: BE CAREFUL!

I made sure to park farther down the road where there's a wide turnout so it's not obvious that someone's snooping around the county equipment shed. Now, I have to get from here to the shed without being noticed.

It's really been bugging me, how my grandmother and Alice have managed some of the big capers they've pulled off in the last couple of years.

Of course, there's also the question of how Mabel and Vera are managing their retaliation pranks. Last year they stole all the goats right out of my grandparents' barn while we were all in the house. I just don't see how two old women in their eighties could have done that on their own.

Zephyr's brother, Cane, has game cameras set up around the Hart property and one of them caught a frame of the backhoe that dug the new "pond."

It's not a pond. It's a pretty sizable hole about three feet deep that appeared overnight near the private drive that leads up to Mable Hart's house.

When Zephyr texted me the picture that her brother's camera caught of the backhoe, I realized it looked a lot like the tractor the county houses here in the equipment shed.

Moonshine Ridge is a mountain town and mountain towns need heavy equipment for all kinds of things, from plowing snow to clearing the occasional dead cow off the road.

For one, although a lot of people do have private equipment, the county loader is the only one I know of on the Ridge that big, and two, it's blue. It was bought in an auction from the O'Leary ranch down in Slow River and all their equipment is the same trademark blue.

Thing is, the photo from the game camera isn't great. It only shows a little bit of the tractor and, even though the night vision mode is pretty good, it's hard to make out a lot of details.

There's a possibility that the tractor in the photo isn't actually the same blue color as the county's, but it does have a weird spot on it where a decal has been scraped off.

All I have to do is sneak into the equipment shed and check the loader against the photo and I'll know for sure if it's the same one.

I just have a hard time believing our deputy is actually involved. Hawkins just isn't the kind of guy who gets his hands dirty, you know?

I sneak up to the shed. The big, metal building is set off the road in a clearing along with big piles of gravel and sand that they truck in every summer for road maintenance. There's a giant roll-up door on the front of the building that is never locked.

Mesa showed me how to work it once when I came out with him to get the smaller tractor. Since he works for the fire department, he's one of the people who has access to the shed and he needed the Bobcat for a job he was on.

That's how I know the big door is never kept locked, and that's how I know the trick to get the big counter-weighted flywheels to move without much effort.

Cringing as the door rises enough for me to crawl under, I glance around nervously.

Very little effort, but lots of noise. Oops.

No lights go on, the mountains around me remain pitch black in the January night. It's not even ten o'clock yet, but the mountains are already asleep.

I only raise the big door by a couple of feet. Not enough to draw attention if anyone does pass by on the road. The shed is built at an angle to the road to allow space for moving the trucks and tractors around, so it's not likely that anyone will notice.

Getting down on my hands and knees, the concrete foundation is so cold it bites through my jeans and freezes my ass when I lay down to shimmy under the door. Once inside, I have to use the flashlight on my phone to avoid tripping over anything.

Out in the distance, I hear a car going down the road.

I quickly shut the flashlight off and wait till the engine noise passes by.

Then I open up that photo Zephyr sent me and hold it up while I let the flashlight illuminate the back of the big loader.

It's definitely the same one.

I'm so busy staring at the tractor and running through the implications, that I don't even notice that the car must have doubled back until headlights light up the inside of the shed.

Shit. Shit. Shit.

A car door opens and slams shut outside and heavy boot steps crunch over gravel and ice, making their way toward the roll up door.

I should have closed it once I was inside.

Ducking behind the tractor, I hold my breath and hope whoever it is figures someone just didn't close the door all the way.

"Hello?"

I should have known it wouldn't be just "someone." No way I could get lucky enough for it to just be some good Samaritan checking to make sure things are OK. Nope.

"This is the sheriff. If anyone's in here you need to come out with your hands up now."

Hawkins sounds grumpy tonight. His deep voice reverberating off the sheet metal walls with a warning tone that sounds downright menacing.

I've never heard his voice sound like this. He sounds dangerous.

Okay, I admit it-- it's hot. And a little scary. Which is also kinda hot.

I stay crouched behind the tractor and clench my thighs, holding my breath and willing my heart to stop racing.

The bright beam of a high-powered flashlight

sweeps across the space, throwing shadows up on the walls around me.

His boots land with heavy steps as he moves farther into the building and I tense up at the sound as he starts making his way along the wall toward the back.

The slightest movement in here echoes like a shotgun blast. If I try to hide from him, I'll just give myself away. My only hope is that he doesn't come all the way around to the back wall.

HAWK

IT WAS THE FLASH OF LIGHT INSIDE THE SHED that caught my attention as I was driving back to town.

When I circled back around to check it out, I noticed the door standing open about eighteen inches off the ground. Just enough for a bear to think it's found a safe place to nap and definitely plenty of room for a family of raccoons to make a home out of our local equipment shed.

But bears don't carry flashlights-- though you never know with raccoons-- so I don't kill the headlights on the SUV when I pull up directly in front of the big building. I also don't raise the door any higher-- I don't want to make it easier for an intruder to escape.

As soon as I'm under the door, I draw my gun and identify myself, hoping the light I saw was just a trick of the eye and I can close up the door and head home.

Mountain Man's Need

Seeing as how the only hardened criminals on the Ridge are the raccoons and the old women, and the latter have been accounted for today, drawing my weapon is an act of protocol more than necessity.

My eyes adjust to the shadows inside the shed and I pull my flashlight out of its place on my belt and sweep the high-powered beam around the building.

Nothing looks disturbed. Probably whoever last accessed the shed didn't make sure the door was completely down. It's got a tendency to jump back up if the chains that operate it don't catch just right.

It's been a long day, and while I'm rarely completely off duty up here, I do work a regular shift. One that technically ended hours ago. I'm eager to get home, peel off the damn uniform, and get in a hot shower.

My head hurts and I'm half crazy from the way Terra's been giving me the cold shoulder since telling me off at the cafe.

I see the way her eyes track my movements, watching me walk the main street every day as I make my rounds and check in with the local businesses after stopping by April's cafe for my coffee each morning, damn if my little rebel isn't doing her best to avoid actually talking to me.

As tempted as I am to just call it good here, close the big door and head home, I have a job to do and there's a right way to do it. Years of military service and then more years of law enforcement in the city taught me not to get complacent. Even in a place like Moonshine Ridge.

One sweep around the perimeter of the big shed ought to be plenty enough to reveal any sign of intruders-- human or vermin.

I start a clockwise loop, sweeping the flashlight across anything that might hide something in the shadows.

No one's hiding in the cabs of either tractor. The shelves along the walls are clear. I've just holstered my weapon when I come around the back of the big loader and see the figure huddled behind it.

Their features are completely obscured by the black hoodie but I'm guessing it's a teenager from the smaller stature.

Adrenaline rushes my veins and I reflexively spring into action. Acting on pure instinct and muscle memory, I've got the kid on his feet, with his hands cuffed behind him before I slow down enough to take in any more details.

Like the blood red nail polish on the fingertips of the ungloved right hand that's now struggling against the cuffs. And the tendrils of long, black hair that have escaped the hood of the sweatshirt.

"Goddammit, Hawk. It's just me."

Terra shakes her head side to side in a violent motion to knock the hood of her sweatshirt off so her face is revealed. Then she turns her head to look back at me over her shoulder and glares at me like I'm the one in the wrong here.

And I am.

Because my dick immediately springs to attention like a bloodhound catching a scent.

She's bent over in front of me with her wrists locked together just above the round ass that's pushed out toward my crotch.

Dammit. This isn't supposed to have my brain spinning out of control with thoughts about how badly I want this woman. My dick shouldn't be rock hard and dripping pre-cum with the need to make her mine right now.

This is damned inappropriate.

"What the fuck are you doing in here, Terra?"

My left hand presses between her shoulder blades, pushing her back down to the hard surface in front of her and maybe more forcefully than necessary. I'm far too wound-up to handle this professionally.

Fighting to keep control, I quickly pat her down, doing my damnedest to avoid noticing the curves I've been burning to touch for months.

Her cell phone, keys, and lip-gloss get set on the flat surface of the tool cart nearby.

I'm too fucking close to her. Trying to pin her body still with my hip and thigh so I don't give myself away but she's struggling against my hold. Pissed at me for not letting her go, and when she reaches her cuffed hands back to grab at me, she manages to do exactly that.

"I was--"

We both freeze instantly. The words she was about to say die in her throat and the shed goes silent except for the thud of my pulse and Terra's rough breathing.

She's only got one glove on, probably needed bare fingers for her phone. I should be worried about someone being here with her but all I can think about is the way her ungloved hand curls around the bulge in my pants.

Chapter Six

Terra

As soon as I heard him start walking around the big loader, I knew I was caught. All I could do was pull the hood of my sweatshirt around my face and shut my eyes tight while I prayed something would distract him before he found me.

Of course I couldn't get that lucky.

He didn't even give me a chance to say anything before he yanked me to my feet and cuffed my hands behind my back.

I thought he'd back off once he knew who I was. Unlock the damn handcuffs and let me talk my way out of this but it's like he's even more pissed that it's me.

He pins me to the cold steel tractor with his leg while he pats me down and empties my pockets and I can't stop myself from struggling against him.

Not because I want him to let me go, but because I want more of him pressed against me.

This is so fucked up. I am so fucked up.

Twisting in his grip I just want to feel more of his brute strength pinning me down. My fucking thong is so wet that my thighs are sticky and I'm more pissed off about how turned on I am right now than about getting caught.

When my hand manages to make contact, I don't honestly know what I was expecting. His waist maybe, his stomach, his arm...but not *that*.

Everything stops for a second. I totally forget whatever it was I was saying.

Hawk doesn't move. It's like he's frozen. He's still leaning into me with the side of his body, with one hand pressed between my shoulder blades.

He's so much bigger than me. How have I never noticed that before? The way he's got me pinned makes it clear that there's no chance I can overpower him. I'm not going anywhere unless he lets me.

Heat wells up between my legs and leaks out of my core in a new wave. My clit is throbbing and there's no way to relieve that ache with my hands in cuffs and my feet spread out by his.

My fingers curl around him. Exploring the length of him and gasping at how incredibly hard he is.

I've read a lot of spicy books but I'm not prepared for feeling the real thing when it's in my hand under the thick material of his uniform slacks.

It's not enough. I want to feel more of him. I need to hold him in my hand, I want the heat and the heft of him filling my palm...and other things.

Maybe it's me reaching for the zipper on his fly, or the way I push back to grind my ass against his hip, or

Mountain Man's Need

maybe it's the embarrassingly needy little whimper that I can't hold in, but the spell is broken.

Hawk jumps backward, putting empty air between us and leaving me feeling cold and empty where I was burning up a second ago.

"Terra."

His voice is a warning-- like he's scolding me for misbehaving. That just makes me more turned-on.

"Fine, whatever, Hawk." I grumble, spinning to face him and giving him a glare to show him how much I disapprove of him suddenly remembering the stupid rules.

I'm flustered and needy and if he's not going to get me off then I want to go home so I can do it myself.

"If you're not going to play, just let me go."

I pull my hands to one side to show him where they're still cuffed behind me.

For the first time since he found out it's me in here, I feel like I'm in real trouble.

The county sheriff's SUV idles just outside with the headlights pointing directly at the partially open door. Everything lower than two feet is lit up like Christmas in here, but it makes for harsh shadows that cling to every corner and contour around us-- including Hawk.

Tension draws tight between us as I watch the shadows darken his face, turning the congenial features I'm used to seeing into something dangerous.

A second ticks by and I steel myself for my first ride in the back of a cop car.

Then something happens. It's like an electrical current jumps between us and Hawk snaps. Suddenly

I'm spun around, facing away from him again but the grip he has on me is far from procedure.

One arm is wrapped around my torso, pinning me tightly against his chest with his hand gripping my chin to force my head back against his chest.

If my hands weren't still cuffed behind me, he'd have that massive ridge in his pants pressed between my ass cheeks. Instead, it lines up with my hands again. This time, when I curl my fingers around his girth, he doesn't move away. He presses closer, trapping my hands between us and making it difficult for me to explore the way I want to.

His other hand is dropping quickly from my stomach to the space between my legs where I'm on fire now.

"Play?" It's a whisper tickling my ear with his hot breath and making my nipples harden. There's a catch in his voice that makes it sound like he's about to break.

"You're going to be the fucking death of me, Rebel."

One strong hand keeps my head pulled back against his shoulder while the other slides between my legs over my jeans.

The pressure against my aching pussy is almost enough to make me come just like that.

My fingers squeeze tighter, my hands fighting to move along his shaft despite the thick material of his uniform and the awkwardness of the handcuffs.

When he reaches farther to run his fingers firmly along the seam of my pants I melt against his chest.

Mountain Man's Need

Dropping my head back on his shoulder voluntarily with a moan as I widen my stance to give him more room to touch me down there.

The hand on my jaw relaxes, sliding down my throat with a firm grip that's also weirdly tender before his arm moves lower and that hand cups my breast.

When his fingers pinch my nipple, it's enough to make me tremble even through the thick hoodie I'm wearing.

I always thought that when I started sexually experimenting with a real, live, man, that I'd be one of those vocal women that remember what words are so I could ask for what I want.

Turns out, I'm just a wet, needy, moaning glob of jelly. If Hawk lets go of me right now, I'll melt into a puddle on the floor, or maybe I'll dissipate into vapor and disappear in the air. Hawk's grip on me is the only thing making me real right now.

"Rebel, you're drenched, baby."

There's that deep, raspy voice in my ear again, making me crane my neck and lean into it.

If he thinks I'm wet outside my jeans, he should feel inside.

It's like he can read my mind.

HAWK

RULES GO OUT THE WINDOW WHEN MY LITTLE

Rebel is rubbing her ass up against my throbbing cock begging me to touch her.

I don't even know if she's aware of each little plea for more that makes its way past those sweet lips of hers, I only know that as soon as she pressed herself back against me with a throaty little moan, I'd give her anything she asks for.

She's fucking soaked through the denim of her jeans. I can feel her heat and the wetness on my fingertips when I run them between her thighs.

Her hands work their way between us, twisting in the cuffs till she's got my dick nested between her fingers. I can't let her keep her hands on me-- things are already out of control in here and if she keeps touching me, I'll lose my damn mind.

What the hell am I saying? I've already lost it. This situation is about as fucked up as it gets but with Terra's soft sighs and the way she arches into my touch, I don't have a chance in hell of thinking straight.

My only intention right now is to give her what she needs.

"Hawk." It's not even a whisper, it's more her lips making the shape of my name while she gasps. "Touch me, please."

Long, thick lashes flutter as if her eyelids are too heavy to lift. She turns her head up to look up at me and catches that puffy bottom lip between her teeth.

Any rational thought I had left blinks out along with my better judgment.

I catch her wrists together in my free hand,

pinning them to the small of her back so she can't torture my cock anymore. Pushing her forward, I trap her body between mine and the big tractor in front of her again before thrusting my other hand between her soft stomach and the blessedly stretchy fabric of those tight jeans she's got on.

My fingers get past the edge of the narrow little thong she's wearing, making my imagination light up with curiosity about what color the silky little panties are.

One brush of my fingertip against her bare flesh has both of us jumping like we've been shocked.

Her little pussy is even wetter at the source. It's so easy to slip my fingers between her folds and when I test pushing one finger inside her, she's so drenched that it slides in easily despite how fucking tight she is.

Just one finger is enough to set off a series of tiny convulsions as her inner walls try to pull me deeper.

"So needy," I choke out as I push farther in. "Your little pussy wants more than my hand, doesn't it, Rebel?"

For an answer, Terra's feet shuffle wider apart and she squirms to give me better access. Then she's fucking my hand in earnest, doing her best to find the friction her body is craving.

She's bent over in front of me, her head down with the side of her face resting against the cold steel of the tractor's fender but if it's uncomfortable, she doesn't look like she notices.

"Do you even know my name, Rebel?"

I bend down over her to growl in her ear, working

my hand to match the rhythm she's setting while I continue to squeeze her cuffed wrists together tightly against her back.

"Terra. Answer me. What's my first name?"

Her long black hair has mostly worked its way out of the sweatshirt where she had it stuffed down the collar under the hood. It falls in a tangled curtain across her pretty face as she pants and mewls but she opens her eyes and looks over her shoulder at me with a nod.

"Justice," she whispers, "Justice Wyatt Hawkins."

I love the way my name sounds coming out of those lips when she's half crazed like this. I like hearing that she knows who's here with her, whose hand is down her pants, and who's going to be making her come in just a few seconds.

"Good, now can you remember that name when you're coming for me, baby?"

I slip my finger against her clit, and smile at the way she grinds against me for more.

Her head bobs against the tractor emphatically.

"Justice."

It's downright fucking reverent and it nearly makes me come in my pants like a damn school boy.

"Good girl."

My pressure increases, her body picks up its pace, and then her voice lifts in a strangled cry as she does her best to keep from being too loud.

"Fuck, Hawk...God yes. Oh my God...*Hawk!*"

I'm not gripping her wrists anymore, somehow, she's managed to weave her fingers through mine so

Mountain Man's Need

she's squeezing my hand tight while her sweet pussy floods my other hand with cream that I'm dying to taste.

Still bent over her, I pepper the side of her face with soft kisses as she convulses and finally goes limp beneath me.

Neither of us say a word as I take my hands off of her and unlock the cuffs but the spell is broken.

What the fuck did I just do?

Reaching down to grab my hat off the floor, I straighten it back on properly. I don't even remember when it got knocked off.

How long have we been in here? The SUV is still idling out front.

Stepping back to give her some space, I'm all too aware of how fucking wrong my actions were. Terra stands just a few feet away, rubbing her wrists like they hurt. Did I have the cuffs too tight? Did I hurt her when I was holding her wrists? What is she thinking? Will she ever forgive me?

Her clothes are askew, her hair's a mess. Even in the shadows, I can see how flushed her skin is, her breaths still coming hard and heavy, making those magnificent breasts rise and fall hypnotically.

She doesn't say a word. Just stands there staring at me with her eyes narrowed and her jaw tight. Those pretty lips that were begging for me to make her come just a few minutes ago, now pressed together in a firm line as she glares at me accusingly.

"Shit, Terra--" I yank the hat back off my head,

raking a hand through my hair nervously. "There's no excuse for what just happened, Tee, I'm so--"

"I swear to *God*, Hawkins--"

She raises one hand in an open palm to cut me off. Her eyes narrow even further and the look on her face is about as serious as I've ever seen on a woman.

"If you fucking apologize to me for that I will never let you touch me again."

I stand dumbfounded as she gathers the things I pulled from her pockets and heads out of the building, sliding under the roll up door before I can get my wits about me again.

"Hold up, Rebel." I call after her once I'm outside, before she can walk away. "Where's your car?"

Terra's face has softened but she's still looking at me like she doesn't recognize me. Her hand gestures up the street.

"I'll follow you home."

"I don't need a police escort, Hawk. I know where I live."

"And I'm going to make sure you get there safely."

Terra rolls her eyes at me and turns on her heel, hiking back to her car at a fast clip.

I know better than to try to insist on giving her a ride.

After double checking that the shed is secure, I pull back out onto the street and wait while she pulls out in front of me so I can follow her home.

The Diaz homestead is dark when we pull up in front of her little cottage. She pulls into the space beside the house and I pull up alongside the porch and wait while she climbs the steps and unlocks the front door.

I lower the window, struggling for the right thing to say but as the door swings open and the light flicks on inside, Terra turns around to look back at me with a guarded expression.

"Goodnight, Justice," she says dryly, but I see the faintest hint of a smirk perking one corner of her mouth before she gives me her back and closes the door.

As I pull out of the long driveway, I lift my hand to my lips and taste the remnants of her sweetness still coating my fingers, thinking how she insisted on using the only name she ever calls me by while she screamed for me.

Of course she didn't do what I told her.

Chapter Seven

Terra

"So, it is the same backhoe then?" Zephyr plops down next to me on the couch and whispers so the kids don't overhear us talking.

It's getting late in the day and only a few kids are left waiting to get picked up. Hyacinth works across the street, helping to run the sporting goods store that she and her husband own. And Ginger owns the brewery next to the new cafe. They usually walk over and pick the kids up together but they're running late today.

"Mmm," I mumble absently.

"I really thought you got caught," Zephyr says-- again. "I mean, it took you so long to answer me, I was sure you were going to call me from the sheriff's station."

My co-worker slash bestie has been fishing for info all day.

I barely even remembered to text her back when I got home last night to let her know I was okay and I promised to tell her everything when we got to work this morning.

Except, I just haven't been able to bring myself to tell her *everything*. I don't know why, but I don't want her to know that Hawk caught me in the shed at all, and I sure as hell don't want to tell her what happened after he did.

"So do you think the deputy is the one that was operating the loader?"

"I don't know, I mean, Hawk's not the kind of guy that breaks rules, right?"

Memories of last night wash through me and I hope my friend doesn't notice if I'm blushing. He definitely broke some rules last night. I haven't been able to think about anything else since.

"What if he does ask you out, Tee? Are you going to go?"

"What?! No! I mean...I don't know. Why would you think I'd go out with him?"

Zephyr regards me curiously.

"Because he's *hot*, Tee. And he's *into* you. I mean, you already know each other, he's tight with your brothers, none of them tried to kill him when he asked if they were okay with him dating you-- even though he's like eighteen years older than you--"

"Fourteen."

Zeph gives me a *look*. It's a look that says she's onto me. I hate that look.

"Huh, I thought he was the same age as Vale."

"No, he's right between Vale and Mesa," I explain. "He only did eight years in the Marines before he retired and went into law enforcement back in Georgia."

The look deepens and I realize I just fell right into her trap.

"He knows you want a million kids, right? And he's got that big house and a good job and I bet he'd be the *best* dad."

Zephyr's eyes go all starry when she mentions Hawk as a dad.

I was just barely starting to think of him as a different kind of *daddy*...now she's got me picturing him taking three a.m. feedings and pushing strollers and teaching kids how to ride bikes.

And I don't like that Zephyr is thinking about him the same way, just like I don't like the way April saves croissants for him every morning.

I don't want Hawk raising anyone's kids but mine.

Zephyr catches me glaring at her and gives me a smile that says she knows exactly what's up.

"He even has a cute nickname for you-- *Rebel.* You should totally wife the deputy." She winks and giggles.

The fact that I'm laughing so hard with her makes it hard to pull off a believable disgusted look.

"What?" I ask when she stops laughing and gives me a pointed look.

"You like him."

"Eww. No." I wrinkle my nose in protest but I know I'm not convincing her. Hell, I'm not even convincing myself.

"I know you don't like the whole good guy scout's honor thing in a guy but Hawkins obviously has a bad boy streak in him if he's been helping the grandmas out with all the shit they've been pulling lately..."

Zeph leans close to make sure the kids playing in the rec room don't overhear and whispers in a conspiratorial tone, "I bet he's *fire* in bed."

"Ohmygod, I can't believe you said that!" I give her shoulder a hard shove.

"Man's got handcuffs, Tee-- just sayin'."

Speaking of fire, I can feel myself blushing so hard I'm worried I might burst into flame.

My bestie tilts her head when she sees me blushing then her eyes open wide.

"Oh. My. God. Terra-- What. *Happened?* You did get caught in the shed last night, didn't you?"

Shaking my head vigorously to the negative doesn't faze her.

"Hawkins caught you in the shed, that's why you got home so late. That's why you didn't answer my texts. Did something happen? *ohmygosh it did.*"

Zephyr and I have been friends since kindergarten, despite being on opposite sides of the grandmother rift. There weren't a lot of other girls our age on the Ridge when we were growing up and we both have too many brothers that are too much older than us.

Even if the Harts have a totally different family dynamic going on than we do-- Zephyr and I get each other.

She's only working for me till I get the daycare center established enough to hire someone, then she wants to go into floral design. She's been putting off a sweet apprenticeship opportunity in Slow River so she can help me out here.

"You have to tell me." Her whisper is accusatory and a little hurt and I feel bad for not filling her in but...

"*Are you still a virgin?*" The sound is completely out of her voice but it's easy to read her lips for that question.

"Yes! *For fuck's sake, of course I am.*" I mouth back at her, both of us slide our eyes over the three young ones that are continuing to play across the room.

Zephyr has about the same amount of sexual experience as I do-- *did*-- and we've always promised to tell each other about any new experiences right away. So I get why she's upset with me and all but it's different than I thought it would be.

I thought we'd have high school boyfriends and stumble through all our firsts around the same time. I pictured us laughing about how awkward and clueless boys were-- now I'm feeling kinda possessive about my experiences.

I'm feeling possessive about *Hawk*.

Thankfully, the door opens and both Ginger Jones and Hyacinth McAllister walk in together. It's obvious they were talking about something serious but as soon as they walk in, they both rush to scoop up toddlers while Hye's oldest, Rose, rushes to tell her mom about the day we had.

"I'm so sorry we're late," Ginger tells us, "Current had to go pick his grandmother up at the station and I had to wait till I had a break before I could leave the brewery. I should have texted, but I didn't know it was going to take this long."

"Yeah, Ash is picking Alice up at the station too," Hyacinth explains.

"Oh no! I have to go," Zephyr's phone chimes in her pocket and when she checks the message, she's gathering her things quickly, "Raine says Grandma needs to be picked up too."

"At the sheriff's station?"

"Yup," Zeph checks the new message she just received, "looks like they're all there."

"Ash said they got in a fight," Hyacinth offers.

"Apparently there was some property damage," Ginger mentions.

"And stabbing," Zephyr mumbles after her phone goes off again. "I have to go."

Following the women outside, I'm saying my goodbyes to babies and friends when I notice Mesa's truck parked by the tavern across the street.

The driver's seat is empty but Abu is sitting in the passenger seat looking tired. She sees me and waves.

"What happened to you, 'Lita?" As soon as I get across the street, she lowers the window and I get a look at a pretty serious bruise covering her right cheek.

"Psh." Her hand raises and drops, indicating it's nothing. "The old bitch clocked me when I was trying to pull Alice off of her. Last time I try to help."

"Vera hit you?"

I can't imagine Mable landing a punch that hard. Mable's barely even five feet tall.

Abu's shaking her head though. "Mable, she had a book."

"Mable hit you with a book?"

Abu's head bobs affirmatively.

"Have you been drinking?" I'd been about to lean in through the window to give her a hug when I got a whiff of whiskey. That probably explains some of it.

"We were playing Never Have I Ever over at Howard's." Abu's dark eyes sparkle with mischief, "Alice is snockered."

"Worse than Vera?" I laugh, thinking about my grandmother playing a drinking game like a sorority girl. My money would definitely have been on Vera Jones for being the most experienced of the four.

"Alice. Hands down," Abu says proudly, "that woman has done shit you've only read about."

Do not ask. Do not ask. Do not ask. I breathe deep and let it go.

"Did Justice arrest Mable?"

My grandmother is neither too drunk nor too upset about the fight to miss a beat. Her head swivels to eye me carefully, one gray eyebrow rising up her forehead.

"Justice?"

"Hawk. Did Deputy Hawkins arrest Mable for hitting you?"

"Oh, I know his name, Mija. I just didn't realize you were on a first name basis with the man you hate so much."

Great. Now I'm blushing again.

"I don't hate him, Abuelita," I mumble quietly.

"No. Nobody got arrested, sweetheart. No one's pressing charges."

"Hey kid." Mesa messes with my hair as he passes behind me, carrying a big bag of takeout in one hand.

"You should see the other guy." He quips, gesturing to Abu's shiner as he hands her the bag through the open window. "She stabbed Vera with a toothpick...We're doing dinner at the homestead, you on your way home? There's plenty for everyone."

"Nah," I answer my brother as he climbs behind the steering wheel, "I have some stuff to do in town.

"Stay out of trouble, 'lita."

Jumping up on the step rail, I lean through the window and kiss my grandmother carefully on the cheek, trying to avoid the darkening bruise.

Mesa slips the truck in gear and Abu raises her window, waving at me with a sly grin as they pull away from the curb.

HAWK

Today might have been the single worst day on the job since I took the post in Moonshine Ridge.

Despite jacking off twice after I got home last night, I didn't get any sleep. All I could think about was Terra's sweet moans while she was coming on my hand for me in that cold, musty shed. I'm never going to be able to go in there again without getting hard.

Mountain Man's Need

I never did find out why she was in there. And the reason I never found out just keeps reminding me that what happened was off the charts inappropriate. I should never have let things get so out of control.

Then I remember the dangerous flash in her eyes and the way she accused me of not wanting to *play*-- I never wanted to *play* so damn bad in my life-- and that just leads to another session of jerking myself off, thinking about a dozen other games I want to *play* with that woman.

On top of not getting any damn sleep last night, I didn't make it to the cafe this morning which meant not just missing out on the caffeine I could have used to get through the day, but I didn't get to see Terra either.

Too damn busy driving down to Keller's Ferry to help them out with some trouble they're having down there.

I was feeling pretty grateful to get back up on the Ridge where crime consists of consists of crossing outside the crosswalk when Ginny Sanderson called me out to the Smalls place with a very strong suggestion that I do a wellness check-- only to find the infamous four brawling in the yard like hellcats.

When I got there, it was obvious there'd been more than eighty-year-old fists flying. One side of Marcia Diaz's face was already purple, Vera Jones had half a toothpick jabbed in her arm, and it took genuine effort to pull Mable Hart off of Alice McAllister.

Of course, Howard wouldn't say a word about what happened. He's not going to press charges for the property damage and I know it. But dammit if those old women didn't clam up quiet as a fucking crypt rather than snitch on each other.

In the two years that I've served on the Ridge, I've seen those women pull all kinds of shit on each other. Hell-- I've helped them pull shit on each other-- but I never thought I'd see the day when Alice McAllister would sit in the back of my car with an ice pack against a bleeding bald spot where Mable ripped a chunk of hair clean out of her scalp, swearing up and down that it was an "accident" and of course she wouldn't be pressing charges against her "good friend."

I had to call Mesa to bring the fire station's small truck out so I could keep them separated while we transported all four of the women to the station.

On the ride back to the station, I listened to Mable and Vera drunkenly remind me of all the reasons I wasn't going to book them on any charges. I think Mable actually called me their "bitch."

It's actually funny now, looking back on it after all four of them have been picked up by family and I'm off the clock and free to go home.

The sub-station down in Keller's is on call for the next few days and I have a few real days off to look forward to.

I'm ready to get out of the uniform, take a long shower, and enjoy a cold beer. Or two.

I was hoping to see Terra today. Since I missed her this morning, I'd planned on stopping by the center before she closed up for the night. Of course, by the time I got out of the station, she was long gone and I think she's the only one of the Diazes that I don't have a personal phone number for.

In the shower I fist my cock again, thinking about the way she forbade me from apologizing while she rubbed the indentations the cuffs left in her wrists.

Fuck, I felt like an asshole for taking advantage of the situation like that. It was a straight up abuse of power and there's no excuse for my behavior... but when I reply the way she looked at me after--flushed and sated and staring at me like she was really seeing me for the first time, the dark promise in her words-- that there could be a next time, reminding me that last night only happened because she let it. *Wanted* it— it sends me over the edge, causing me to paint the tiled shower wall with another load of cum that was meant to get shot deep inside my little rebel's womb.

A few minutes later, I find myself wandering through the kitchen with an unopened beer in one and my phone in the other.

I could call one of the guys, or Marcia-- scratch that, I'm not ready to talk to Marcia after today-- but Vale would probably give me Tee's number. Or I could drive up to the homestead to see her in person.

I hate that I didn't get to see her today. It's not right to have done what we did last night and not talk to her today.

Deciding that maybe it'd be better to call her than show up uninvited, I pop the bottle cap off the beer and type out a quick text, hoping to get her number.

While I wait on the answer, I head back up the stairs to the master bedroom where I left the TV on, settle on the corner of the bed and start flipping through channels.

As soon as I saw Moonshine Ridge, I knew this was going to be my home for the long haul. I bought the house with money I'd been saving for just that reason and a GI loan.

It's way too much house for just me, but the plan was always to fill it with a family eventually. I just didn't know who I'd be having that family with or how long it would be.

Now I know I bought this house for Terra. Five bedrooms that we'll be filling with kids and might even have to add on-- I remember her saying she wants a big family like the one she comes from and I can't wait to give it to her.

In the meantime, the master suite is where I spend most of my evenings; sitting on the bed, watching TV to unwind, wishing Tee was snuggled up beside me.

After a few minutes, I realize I left the phone downstairs still waiting to hear back from Vale.

Downstairs, I find the phone on the kitchen counter where I left it. Draining the last swallow of the rich amber ale that I picked up from our local brewery, I grab another one from the fridge and pop the cap before checking Vale's reply and saving the digits in my contacts.

But before I can decide between texting and calling, there's a knock at my front door and when I check the window, I see the devil herself standing on my porch.

Chapter Eight

Terra

It's not a big secret which house is Hawk's. Pretty much everyone in Moonshine Ridge knows where everyone else lives and even though I've never been here, my brothers have plenty of times.

Moonshine Ridge doesn't have any gated communities but if we did, the Lakeshore Cabins would be one of them.

It's a small subdivision of newish construction that's only about ten or fifteen years old. Only fifteen houses that are all at least four bedrooms, sitting on wooded two-acre lots and every one of them has lake shore access.

It's a pretty big joke with the locals that they're called "cabins" because they're some of the biggest houses in town.

And this one belongs to Hawk.

It's not like I expected him to stop by today. Or time his coffee run this morning to bump into me. Or, I don't know, *text me* or something.

He'd probably call, though. He asked my dad and my brothers for permission to *court* me, for fuck's sake. He seems like the kind of guy who would *call*.

Justice Wyatt Hawkins seems like the kind of guy who would call a girl after something like...um... last night. But he hasn't, so I don't know if I'm intruding on his personal space or not by showing up at his house.

Maybe he got all guilt-ridden after he went home last night, just like I told him not to. Maybe he's never going to touch me again. Maybe he's chickened out of asking me out after that.

I climb the front porch steps and roll my shoulders to relax them. Trying to remind myself that that's not even why I'm here. I don't even care if he's still interested or not.

When was the last time I knocked on a door anyway? I usually just text to say I'm here, but I don't have Hawk's personal number and there's no way I'm asking for it from anyone I know has it. So I knock.

I kinda thought I'd see him around town today and get it from him but after seeing Abu's face-- I guess he was busy all afternoon.

I'm about to knock again when the door unlocks from inside and swings open.

My mouth goes dry and my panties go wet.

Off-duty Hawkins is definitely a sight I can get used to.

His hair is damp and mussed like he got out of the shower and didn't comb it after toweling off. The new beard is a definite keeper, it's longer and thicker than when I first saw it last week and it makes me wonder how often he was having to shave to keep his face so baby smooth all this time. I have to remember to thank Abu for beard-shaming him.

He's wearing a pair of dark gray sweatpants and I literally cannot help myself when my eyes drop down to check out the outline of his cock between his legs.

I mean, they're gray sweatpants, it's like, a thing--ok? And they are way hot on Hawk.

I like the way the plain blue t-shirt molds to his chest, stretching across his pecs and hanging looser over his waist, but I wish he wasn't wearing a shirt at all.

My curiosity has been killing me, wondering what he looks like. If he has hair on his chest, if it does that thing where it forms a trail all the way down, what's at the end of that trail...I feel myself swallow hard.

"I was texting you." His voice has that rich, dark thing going on again. The way he sounded when he asked if I knew his name.

The memory makes everything tingle.

"What does my grandmother have on you?"

It's the real reason I came here tonight. Well, mostly the reason anyway.

I swear my showing up on his doorstep has nothing to do with not being able to get him out of my brain, with the way I can still feel his fingers inside me or wanting to properly explore that hard length I had my hands wrapped around.

Seeing the smile slip off of his handsome face when I bring up my grandmother and her friends makes me want to come clean with my ulterior motives. I liked it better when he was looking at me like he was excited to see me.

I want Justice Hawkins to be excited to see me.

He steps aside and holds the door open wider, gesturing for me to come in.

"What do you mean?" He sighs heavily and leads me past a formal living room into a large kitchen.

"You want something to drink?" He asks, reaching into the fridge and holding out a can of soda, "I'd offer you a beer but--"

"But you're not my dad or my husband, so that would be illegal even though we're on private property and highly unlikely to get busted by the cops. Right?"

I take the soda, totally noticing the way he looks at me when I say *husband*. His nostrils flare and he jaw ticks, but he just rolls his eyes and shuts the fridge.

Three more months till I'm twenty-one but this is the hill the man wants to die on. Even though we both know the jig is up on his whole good boy routine.

"So, answer the question," I pop the soda open and hand it back to him so he can pour it into the cup he's just filled with ice. "How is it that Mable Hart hit my grandmother in the face with a book and didn't get arrested for assault today?"

Hawk runs his hand through his hair, messing it up even more and making it even harder to look at him without thinking about ways I want to be the one messing it up.

"Marcia never said anything about getting hit with

Mountain Man's Need

a book. She told me she hit her face on the side of the table when she fell."

"Mesa said Abu stabbed Vera with a toothpick, why didn't you arrest Abu?"

"Vera said it was an accident."

"You believed them?"

He turns to lean back against the counter, sipping beer from the bottle before answering with a short laugh.

"Hell no, I don't believe them. Your grandmother and her friends are insane. I don't even know why they were all together at Howard's place. It seems like a pretty obvious recipe for disaster to get all four of them in the same place at the same time, but there's nothing I can do if they all stick up for one another."

"They were playing Never Have I Ever," I tell him.

"What's that?"

"The drinking game? Like, someone says something they haven't done and anyone who has done it has to take a shot."

Hawk's mouth twitches under that sexy beard and he scrubs his hand down his face before looking up at the ceiling.

"Alice was *blitzed*."

He laughs as he considers the implications and my chest squeezes at the sight.

Getting used to sexy Hawk is one thing, admitting there might be more to my feelings than that is something else.

"I've got a movie queued up on the TV upstairs. Wanna watch it with me?"

"You didn't answer my question."

"I'll make popcorn."

HAWK

"Cane's been trying to pull the permit to put a pond on that spot for a year," I explain while I watch the microwave countdown. "But the county keeps stalling. This way, there's a citation that means the county has thirty days to issue a permit retroactively."

"So, Alice and Abu had you dig the hole to help the Harts out?"

I laugh, hitting the end button before the timer counts down. "Hell no! They thought it was great that Mable got hit with a ticket for a hole she didn't dig."

"But why?" Terra watches me open the popcorn bag carefully to avoid the steam before I dump it in a bowl. "Why are you helping them at all? Can't you get in trouble for it?"

"Is my little rebel worried about my reputation?"

Terra snorts. "No!"

But there's worry in her face still.

"You worried about my job?"

To that, I get a vague half shoulder shrug.

"Pretty sure stealing the goats was an actual crime," she mutters.

"I fucked up when I first took over the post up

here. The night Ginger and Current opened up the Brick & Porter, Vera and Mable had been drinking pretty heavily and I offered to take them both home. Current tried to warn me but I thought they were just sweet old ladies."

"Joke's on you," Tee scoffs, following me up the stairs.

"I spent the next day helping Alice swap out the flat tire on her Jeep when I realized Mable must have dumped those nails in the driveway when she was 'just dropping something off for her friend.'"

It's not until we get upstairs that I realize what I'm doing, leading Terra to my bedroom.

"We can watch the movie in the den if you'd rather." I clear my throat, aware that this might look like I'm expecting something more than a movie.

Terra's gaze sweeps around my bedroom. It's a big master suite, but there's nowhere to sit and watch TV other than the king size bed.

She rolls her eyes at me and heads straight for my bed, kicking off her shoes before crawling up and settling on one side.

I'm glad I threw on the t-shirt when I got out of the shower. I didn't bother with boxer briefs under the sweats and I've been half hard since she showed up on my doorstep. Seeing her making herself comfortable on my bed has my dick rising to full attention, so hopefully, the shirt's long enough to hide it.

"Then what happened?" She ignores the bowl of popcorn I'm careful to set between us, but she's picked up the handcuffs that I dropped on the nightstand when I got home.

"I made the mistake of telling Alice that I'd brought Mable and Vera by the night before. I hadn't put two and two together yet, I just wanted to make sure Alice found whatever it was that Mable had left for her. Next thing I knew, Alice and your grandmother were calling me for a *'favor.'*"

Terra laughs softly, but her eyes are fixed on the silver cuffs as she spins one through the one-way catch over and over. The clicking noise it makes has my balls tightening with the memory of the last time I used them.

"Doing a favor for those two is like doing a favor for the mafia," she says.

"So, you understand how I became indentured in the local crime syndicate."

It looks like Terra's satisfied with my confession because she doesn't ask any more questions. The TV is still paused on the other side of the room and I reach for the remote to start the movie when she moves the bowl from between us and sets it on the nightstand where she found the cuffs.

My hand freezes, holding off pushing the play button while I watch her.

She's fucking gorgeous. She's turned toward me, sitting on her knees in the middle of my bed, still fascinated with the cuffs.

There's a flush in her skin that tells me I'm not the only one who's never going to look at those things the same again.

Her black hair falls in a silky curtain down her back, one thick tendril having found its way over her shoulder where it drapes down and hangs off the tip of one ripe breast.

She's wearing a red sweater today. It's got a scooped neckline and a cropped hem that hangs shy of the bow tied in her drawstring pants. Cute ones that hug her curves but hang loose from her thick thighs, with oversized square pockets sewn on the outside and more drawstrings that gather the cuffs at her ankles.

She looks like a present waiting to be unwrapped.

"What are you thinking, Rebel?"

There's a look of mischief in her eyes that I'm starting to recognize. She fidgets with the cuffs again and shoots a look at my hand still holding the remote.

Her mouth curves in a slow smile that sends a tremor down my spine.

"I wanna try something." Her whisper is such a perfect combination of innocence and seduction that I almost don't even notice her locking the cuff around my wrist.

I'm distracted by her movements when she suddenly rises up and swings one leg over my thighs. She's straddling me, with those luscious tits grazing my face as she pulls my arms over my head and I hear the click.

Did I really just let her handcuff me to my own damn headboard?

I test this revelation with a firm tug, feeling the restraint as the cuffs clank against the open metalwork of the ornate bed frame.

This was not something that occurred to me when I bought the heavy piece of furniture, I swear, but Rebel's teaching me all kinds of new things.

"Take off your sweater." I'm in no position to issue an order but I'm hungry for those tits.

Terra moves farther down my legs, standing on her knees, and not giving me the pressure of her sweet pussy against my aching cock.

"You're not the boss of me."

Amusement dances in her eyes as she sits back over my knees and pulls the sweater over her head anyway.

The sight of her perfect breasts overflowing the lace-trimmed cups of a black bra have me groaning but she won't bring her body within reach of my mouth.

She leans forward just enough to touch me, running her small hands over my shoulders and down my chest, taking her time to feel every line of my tensed body. She drags her fingers down the center of my chest and runs them across my abs. My stomach flinches at the light touch. My breathing is hard and barely controlled.

Then she sits up again, positioning her hot little center right over my rock-hard cock and rocking against me. My hips buck under her, desperate for more.

I hold my breath when she reaches behind her, afraid that I might wake up any second and ruin the dream before the best part.

Her bra loosens and she lets the straps drop off her shoulders before revealing those full breasts that I've been imagining. My mouth waters and I pull against the fucking cuffs again, frustrated at not being able to touch them.

"Fuck, Rebel," I moan, rolling my hips under her and straining forward, so hungry for just a taste of one of those dark nipples. "What's your plan here, baby?"

"Told you, I just want to try something."

The loss of her heated core pains me but I'm quickly rewarded with the sight of her round ass raised high as she bends over me, pushing my shirt high over my chest while her lips press against my stomach like a test.

As she wiggles her way farther down, her fingers hook into the waistband of my sweatpants, dragging them down my hips and lower till they land on the floor at the foot of the bed with a soft rustle.

She takes her time crawling back up between my legs while I widen them to give her room but she doesn't look at me.

I'm afraid to breathe, afraid to break the spell. Still not sure what she has in mind here. If all she wants is to explore my body, it's hers. But when she gets to the point where she can't ignore the throbbing monster in front of her face anymore, I watch in awe as she slowly presses a kiss to the base of my dick, making it-- and me-- jerk violently.

Rebel grins at my reaction and then she wraps one hand around my shaft and slides her tongue over the head of my dick. I almost lose it just from watching the way her eyes close as she savors the pre-cum she laps from the weeping tip. Then she grasps my thigh with her other hand and stretches those fuck-me lips all the way around me.

Chapter Nine

Terra

This is both easier and harder than I imagined it would be.

His cock is so hard. Like, how is that even possible? It's like hanging onto a steel pipe but so much more fun. The skin stretched over it is so soft, with veins running along it and when I get the hang of opening my jaw right, I can feel the whole thing pulsing and throbbing in my hand and my mouth.

I mean, I've read a lot of books, but I guess I always thought "throbbing" was a metaphor.

Not only is Hawk's dick literally throbbing, but his whole body is vibrating. I wonder what he'd be doing if his hands were free right now.

I wasn't sure what I was going to do when I cuffed him to the headboard, then I thought I just wanted to test this, just try it out a little bit. Now I don't want to stop.

His dick is huge though. Like, bigger than I

thought the real thing would be. I can barely get my fingers all the way around it and the more I work to take him all the way down my throat, the more I'm drooling all over him.

Hawk's making a lot of noises that sound like he's dying and every time the handcuffs clang against his headboard like he's trying to pull free it sends a shock wave through me and my panties are fucking flooded.

This is a way bigger turn on than I expected it to be.

"Fuck, Rebel, what are you doing, baby..." I think it's a rhetorical question so I don't stop to answer.

When I hear his head hit the headboard, the whole bed shakes from the force. Hawk makes a guttural noise; his knees bend under me and he thrusts his hips and starts all-out fucking my mouth.

It's a rough motion and I have to fight to keep up with him but I'm determined not to let go.

"Rebel...baby...you don't want to keep doing that..."

I can't help smiling around his girth, which I've almost managed to take completely down my throat. I very much *do* want to keep doing this.

"You're going to make me come."

His voice has gone super dark and feral. He's not all groans and gasps anymore. I can tell he's staring down at me when he says it and there's a warning in his words that makes me think carefully about what he's saying.

I want to make him come. I want to feel him lose control and I want to be the reason it happens. Tightening my grip, I feel the blood surging through his thick cock. I want this, I love the powerful feel of having control over him like this, and I want to impress him.

One more deep stroke down his length with my mouth and I feel the head of his cock swell at the back of my throat. It makes me gag against him and maybe that's the trigger but suddenly I'm swallowing mouthfuls of hot, thick, liquid. Greedily sucking it down and cleaning off anything left over with my tongue before releasing him with a soft pop and gasping for breath.

When I look up at him, his hands have let go of the headboard and they're just dangling limply in the cuffs. His chest is rising and falling heavily and his eyes are closed like he's sleeping.

He looks even hotter this way. All worn out and relaxed, and all because of me.

"Good girl." His eyes open but the lids are heavy as he praises me with a smirk.

I know he's teasing me because he read that book I had, but-- I like it.

Praise kink is one of those things I always thought I'd hate in real life, like it'd make me feel like a dog doing a trick. Turns out...it makes me want to learn more tricks.

Reaching over to the nightstand, I pick up the keys to the cuffs and unlock him.

For a man who looked half dead three seconds ago, Hawk is suddenly full of energy again. His hands fly up and embrace the sides of my face, pulling me into a passionate kiss.

I kissed Samuel Miller at Gold Camp when we

were junior counselors during the summer of our sophomore year.

It was gross.

Kissing Hawk is not gross. It's not gross in a way that makes me wonder why I haven't kissed him before. Why have I wasted so much time not kissing this man?

Hawk's not my first kiss, but he's going to be my first everything else...and hopefully my last.

Still kissing, he rolls us over so he's on top of me.

He's still got his shirt on and I still have my pants on and this seems all wrong to me. It feels like we've done enough at this point that we shouldn't still have clothes keeping us apart.

"What did I do to deserve that?" He asks, pinning my arms above my head while I wrap my legs around his waist.

"Nothing. That was payback."

I squeeze my thighs around him, tilting my hips and pushing my pussy up against him.

Hawk stares down at me with the corner of his mouth lifted in a smirk.

"So that was a revenge blowjob?"

"Um-- maybe? Was it...okay?"

I wasn't nervous till just now. The way he's looking at me right now, I don't know what he's thinking and I'm suddenly very aware that the years between us represent more than just time-- Hawk has lived experiences that I've only read about. What if I don't live up to his expectations?

"Yeah." The weird look he was giving me goes soft

and his lips press against mine again. "It was fucking perfect, Terra."

That's better than another *good girl*. Warmth washes over my entire body as he whispers those words into my ear.

His hands slide down my arms to the sides of my body and I frantically pull his shirt off, desperate to finally feel his skin against mine.

He's moved down. I'm still pinned under him but he's got his face between my breasts. His large hands wrapped in my squishy flesh, pushing and kneading them together and kissing one and then the other like he can't make up his mind.

"Give me half an hour, Rebel," he mumbles with his mouth full of one of my nipples, "and I'm going to get revenge on you with my cock."

HAWK

HER TITS ARE SO FUCKING PERFECT. LARGE enough to overflow my palms and perfect for wrapping around my dick while I titty fuck her. The thought of watching my cock slide between these soft mounds has me surging back to life already and I mentally add that to the growing list of things I plan to do with her.

The only thing left between us now are the soft cotton pants she's wearing. The ones with all the drawstrings that have been begging to get untied since she got here.

Terra arches her back, giving me more of the breast I'm currently working on. Her fingers are clasped around my neck and head, but when I reach between us to pull at that tempting little bow keeping her pants cinched to her waist, I get a tap on my shoulder instead of the needy whimper I was expecting.

"Hawk..." It's a timid whisper. "Justice, stop."

Immediately, I do what she asks. Taking my hands off her and giving her space as she pushes herself up with her elbows bent behind her.

"Maybe we should talk for a minute."

Talk. Yeah. Sure. With me naked and my cock so hard I could hammer nails with it and those perfect tits swaying in front of me. Talking should be easy, sure.

But my rebel is a lot more important than my erection. I can't remember ever hearing this soft, shy tone in her voice and I'll do anything to make sure she feels safe with me.

When I move to roll off of her, however, she catches me between her knees, not letting me go.

It fills me with pride, knowing that she's comfortable enough to ask for the time she needs but still wants me close.

"What is it, Rebel? If you don't want to do thi--"

"I want to." She cuts me off quickly and her enthusiastic reassurance has me sliding back up her body, repositioning to pull her on to my lap with her legs wrapped around me.

When I squeeze her ass cheeks hard and pull her tight so she can feel my hard cock straining at the covered space between her legs, her eyes roll up and then settle back on mine.

She presses her lips to mine for a kiss that's not nearly enough and fixes me in a hooded gaze.

"I *really* want to," she repeats. Then that sweet blush darkens her cheeks, "But I've never done it before so I figured you should know that?"

"Are you telling me you're a virgin, Rebel?"

My cock jumps, even more desperate to claim what's mine.

Last night, when she was coming on my fingers, I noticed how tight she was but it hadn't occurred to me that might be why.

Terra's a wild child, I know she's spent summer nights up at the river drinking around campfires with the other kids on the ridge. I'm not delusional enough to think legal age limits would keep her from going after whatever experiences she was interested in having.

"Don't be gross about it, okay? I hate when men put a premium on a woman's value just because her '*virtue*' is still intact--" she pauses to make a gagging expression and it's about the cutest thing I've ever seen. "I wasn't saving myself for you or anything, I just never wanted to do this with anyone else so get that look off your face."

I could not wipe this look off my face if my life depended on it right now. I get what she's saying and I'd be in love with this woman no matter how much experience she had but, fuck me, if the primal beast inside me isn't roaring in triumph.

"Gotta admit, Rebel, there's a caveman inside me beating his chest right now," I confess. "But I don't care as much about being your first as I do about being your last."

"Last?"

Terra leans back, letting her hands slide down my bare chest where her fingertips blaze small trails of electricity while she traces the space where the hair grows over my pecs. She tilts her head, her thick hair falling between us as she turns the single word into a question that needs a proper answer.

"Last, Terra." I run my hands up her torso, loving the way she shivers under my touch. "I didn't want your family's blessing to date you-- I want to marry you."

Her breath hitches as I move one hand between us to cover her stomach. "I want you to be the mother of my children. I'll fill you up with babies and we'll fill this house with love."

She just stares at me, unreadable.

"You still want to do this?" I manage to ask, terrified that it's more than she's willing to give me. "With me?"

"Holy shit," she murmurs softly. "Yeah."

Terra's pretty throat works in a hard swallow, her eyes locked on mine as her head starts to nod.

"Yeah, Hawk, That's-- that's exactly what I want."

"With me?"

Mountain Man's Need

Now she laughs, moving against me again, letting me know she's ready to pick up where we left off.

"Of course, with you."

Then she leans close and whispers against my ear so softly it's like a confession so secret that not even the furniture is allowed to hear.

"I kinda love you."

Chapter Ten

Terra

It's the deepest secret I've ever kept but it's time I let him in on it.

When he lets me up for air again, I feel his cock digging into my crotch, hard and insistent like it'll bust right through the fabric of my pants.

"I thought you said you needed half an hour?"

"I do." His voice that sexy, dark purr again while he pulls the string that unties the bow keeping my pants on. "But not to get hard again for you."

When he tugs my remaining clothes over my hips, I do my best to help him out. Seems to me I've been wearing too many clothes for a while now.

"I figure half an hour is plenty of time to make you come on my tongue at least twice."

Hawk settles between my legs and I spread my thighs wide to make room for him.

"Fuckin' perfect." I hear him say to no one in particular before he slides his tongue against me.

It doesn't take much for him to prove his point. I'm

a quivering mess under him in no time. Who knew having your pussy licked felt that good?

Okay-- I'd heard rumors, maybe I should have been prepared.

I'm still high on the first post orgasmic endorphin rush when Hawk starts priming me for the next one.

His fingertip draws lightly along my seam till I'm squirming and begging him to give me more. Then his mouth is on me again, hot, wet, and hungry, he licks along every crease and fold, finding the places that make me shiver, the places that make me jump, the places that make me scream with my fists in his hair while I lose myself a second time.

I'm still panting heavily when I feel his lips making their way up my body.

"Was that half an hour?" I joke with him when we're face to face again.

"You want another one, Rebel?"

His fingers slide back down between my legs, stroking just firmly enough against my over-sensitized clit to make me jump.

"I want to make sure you're good and relaxed. I need this tight little virgin pussy to take my whole cock."

His dirty words have my core clenching as new need builds inside me.

Hawk notices. "Damn, that made you wet. Do you like thinking about having me balls deep inside you?"

I'd answer him but I am too busy rolling my eyes into the back of my head and moaning at that very thought. Also, he's doing that thing with his fingers again that we're both quickly learning turns me into a sopping, begging mess.

"I'm not putting anything between us, understand? I want to make sure you feel everything when I'm fucking you."

Shit, I swear I almost come again right then.

"I'm on the pill anyway."

"Why?" Hawk's fingers stop their little tap dance at my entrance and he looks down at me so sternly I have to stifle a laugh.

"Period stuff," I assure him. His features soften but he still looks unhappy about it.

"We'll talk about it later," he grumbles and I know we'll be rushing this wedding date or my sister won't be the only Diaz girl doing things out of order.

"Fuck me now, Justice. I need you inside me."

He doesn't make me beg.

"I can't promise this won't hurt," he tells me as he lines himself up against me.

I'll be surprised if it does, to be honest. He's had more than one of those thick fingers inside me more than once now and there hasn't been any blood and definitely no pain, but his fingers aren't as big as his cock so I nod in understanding, not quite sure what to expect for my first time.

Between my own desire spilling out of me in anticipation and the pre-cum coating the wide head of Hawk's dick, he slides into me easily at first.

"Relax, Rebel," he coos against my ear when I tense up, "let me in. It'll feel good once you relax."

He smiles down at me when I let out the breath I was holding.

"Good girl."

Something feels like it opens up inside me, letting him slide so deep there's nothing left of him to give me when I moan at the way he fills me up.

"Terra." The way he says it makes it sound more like *Terrahh* and it sounds so sexy I can't help but move under him, making him growl as he grips my hips in both hands like he wants me to be still. But I can't.

"I need to move," I whine, forcing my hips against his grip till he relents.

"Fuck baby, I can't take this. You feel too fucking good."

Hawk pulls back, so far that he almost leaves me completely. I can't describe the empty feeling he leaves behind, like I don't remember how to breathe without him inside me. Clawing at his back, desperate to be filled again, I try to follow his retreat before he pins my hips again.

"That what you wanted, Rebel?"

He slams forward in a hard thrust that makes the whole bed rock. All I can do is cry out at the force of it while shamelessly begging him to do it again.

HAWK

Mountain Man's Need

It's good that Terra's on birth control but I hate that this won't be the time my seed takes.

I've never known this side of myself before, the primal part that has me rutting hard and deep, determined to breed her despite the pills-- mark her so everyone knows I've claimed her, then watch her swell while my children grow inside her.

As soon as Terra's body relaxes and accepts me inside her, she's on fire to be fucked properly. Scratching at my back and thrusting her hips in search of friction in a frantic way that has me crazed with the need to provide it.

I don't know why I'm surprised when she begs me to pound into her harder and rougher, I've always known she'd be a demanding little tigress in the sack.

I fucking love it. I love it when I feel her fingernails gouging into my shoulder blades, I love it when her tight little channel clenches down on my shaft so hard that I can't keep thrusting, and when my bedroom walls echo with the sweet sound of her screaming my name, I'm powerless to do anything but release deep inside her, painting her womb with my cum.

"You're not even going to give me another *'good girl?'*"

After several long minutes lying with her wrapped in my arms, Terra gives me a playful swat against the arm that I have around her.

"Good girl." I'm so spent, I can barely form words.

"Do you even know what you're praising me for?" She's teasing, but I have a list.

"For coming on my cock," I murmur against her ear as I pull her closer to me.

"Mmm, I did do that."

"For agreeing to be my wife."

"Mm hmm, did that too."

"For screaming my first name so loud that my prowess in the bedroom is going to become part of Moonshine Ridge legend for generations to follow."

That one. I can tell that's the one she meant when she giggles self-consciously and curls closer. I smile against the smooth skin of my rebel's shoulder as she makes a satisfied little noise and mumbles something that sounds suspiciously like "and *you're a good boy*" as we both drift into sleep.

I think I understand the appeal of this praise thing.

Epilogue
Eighteen Months Later

TERRA

"I can't believe you're married and pregnant and I'm still a virgin."

Zephyr folds her legs up under her on the oversized patio chair and plays with the straw in her drink.

My bestie looks miserable.

"If it's any consolation, it's not as great as it looks." I poker-face the *hell* out of that lie. Married and knocked-up is awesome. Although, the excitement of being pregnant with twins has lost some of its initial charm.

When Hawk warned me that twins run in his family-- he has a twin sister himself-- I was really excited about it. I just didn't think we'd get twins on our first try. Now I'm pushing seven months, I'm already big as a house, it's summer, my feet hurt, I'm hornier than ever and there is almost no comfortable position for taking care of that.

And it's still the most awesome thing in the world.

"I appreciate the love behind your blatant lie," Zeph deadpans back at me.

"It'll happen, Zeph, give it time. You're down in Slow River now, there are way more guys down there, why don't you snatch up a hot cowboy?"

Hawk and I did rush the wedding, we gave everyone a two week heads up and tied the knot on Valentine's Day, just to be cheesy about it, since everyone was already giving us so much shit about hooking up at all.

When I told the family, there was a lot of money that changed hands. Apparently, everyone had taken bets. Abuela made out big time-- she was the only one who bet on us making it all the way to the altar.

Hawk was all about flushing my birth control right away but I was so close to turning twenty-one and I wanted to enjoy it— we waited six months and it took another six months before it happened.

"Meh." Zephyr dismisses my suggestion easily. She's chewing on the straw in her strawberry-lemonade while she zones out on something across the street. "Who's that?"

Following her line of sight, I see a man leaving the general store with a box of groceries.

"Augustus Damiani," I answer.

After I found full time help with the daycare center, Zephyr moved down to Slow River so she can work for one of the big florist shops in the valley. She's been off the ridge for a year now, and with her making a name for herself in floral design and me doing the whole domestic thing, we just don't get to see each other much these days.

She drove up today to keep me company on my day off while Hawk does the small-town sheriff thing.

We're sitting at one of the bistro sets that April puts out on the cafe patio during the summer, watching the Ridge move by in slow motion.

"Italian?" Zephyr's voice picks up with interest. "Is he mafia?" She whisper-screams at me.

"NO!" I laugh so hard one of the babies kicks, setting of the other one. We're having a boy and a girl and I full on expect them to come out fighting already. "Oh my God, no. He's just some guy that moved up here to work at the hydro plant.

"You read too much smut."

"Hmph, I wonder who recommends all my smut to me?"

Zephyr sags back in the faux wicker patio chair and chases a crushed strawberry in the bottom of her glass with her straw, giving me a pointed glare.

A truck comes blazing into the parking area, pulling in front of the cafe at an angle fast enough to scare the shit out of the tourists seated around the outdoor fire pit at the brewery that's located a few storefronts down the boardwalk from us.

The engine dies before it comes to a complete stop and it jerks still with the sound of an emergency brake being applied.

Neither Zephyr nor I so much as blink at her brother's dramatic entrance. It's all part of the scenery these days.

Raine jumps out of the driver's side, slamming the door behind him and heading to the cafe door at a dead run.

"You better not have been in the greenhouse!" Zephyr yells after the blur of blue jeans and wildflowers that doesn't stop to acknowledge her.

Good thing there's no one in the cafe right now, although, I'm not sure it would matter. Zeph and I watch through the window as her brother jumps the counter in a practiced motion, sliding over to the employee side and catching April around the waist before his feet even hit the floor.

"Gross." Zephyr grumps across from me.

I watch Raine pressing the bouquet of flowers-- that were definitely pilfered from my bestie's greenhouse-- into April's hand, his lips on hers as he pushes them both through the door into the back room.

"What? He's happy." I point out to Zephyr. "You like April, don't you?"

"I adore April," she assures me. "All my brothers deserve to be happy. I'm glad Raine found her. Don't mind me, I'm just jealous."

"You ever hear from Hayle?"

It's a sore subject. Zephyr's oldest brother disappeared a few years back after starting a pretty gruesome bar fight that didn't end well for him. No one's heard from him since.

Zephyr shakes her head sadly.

"I send him email sometimes, but I never hear back. I don't even know if he still checks that account."

"But he's alive, right?"

"Grandma says he keeps in touch. I guess she's the only one he still cares about-- Speaking of grandmothers, have they started up again?"

"Not yet," I answer.

Our grandmothers have been on good behavior since their big knock down, drag out fight right before Hawk and I got together for good.

"That can't be good," Zephyr notes.

All I can do is shake my head. Our grandmothers have been at war since before either of us were born. I can't remember them ever going this long without some sort of mischief. It feels creepy.

Heavy boot steps on the boardwalk interrupt us and when I turn, I see my sexy hubby heading toward us.

"He's lucky his grandmother owns this building," Hawk glowers at the cattywampus truck in front of the building taking up a good three parking spaces. "I ought to ticket him for that." He grumbles before turning his attention toward us instead.

"Hello, ladies."

The town sheriff doffs his hat, holds it to his chest and gives Zephyr a polite little head bow. Then my husband holds that hat up to block Zephyr's view while he drops a searing kiss on my lips and brushes a thumb over one of my nipples so casually, he could almost convince me it was accidental-- but I know him better than that.

"Could you guys go be gross in love somewhere else, please?"

"As a matter of fact, I was just coming to see if my

wife was about ready to do exactly that." Hawk's eyes on me and my swollen belly, his look full of pride and hunger.

"Does that mean you're off-duty Deputy Hawkins?" I tease.

That uniform is still ugly as hell, but he does look damn good in it.

"The law is never off-duty in these parts, Mrs. Hawkins." He winks down at me, giving his hat a low-key tip with just a touch to the brim.

"Oh my God, you two...Go!" Zephyr shoos me with both hands, "I have to stop by and see Mom and Grams before I go home anyway."

"Love you." I blow her a kiss from my side of the table and hold up my hands for Hawk to pull me out of the chair. I don't make it easy on him, making him show off the muscles that can still lift me like I weigh nothing, even with the two extra people I'm carrying around now.

Zephyr jumps up to give me a hug before gathering her things and heading for her car, glaring toward her brother's truck and shaking her head with a scowl before driving off in the direction of Hart's Gulch.

Hawk keeps his arm wrapped around me as he guides me down the steps like I'm blind but I've learned not to argue with him about his protectiveness. And maybe I don't actually mind if everyone in town sees that he's mine.

Besides, with him hanging on to me this way, it's easy to grab his ass.

"Did you just assault an officer of the law?"

He smirks as he holds open the door of the car and helps me maneuver into the seat.

"You gonna arrest me?" I hold my wrists out together for him like I'm waiting for him to cuff me, and look up at him through my lashes.

Hawk growls at me, stepping close so the open door of the SUV hides him as he draws one of my hands toward him and presses it over the bulge in his pants.

"No way, Rebel-- I'm definitely not giving you the right to remain silent."

Thanks for Reading
Mountain Man's Need

I hope you enjoyed following Hawk and Terra to their happily ever after.

I swear I did not know that the new deputy sheriff assigned to the Ridge was going to end up as one of our primary heroes back when I introduced him in Driven to the Mountain (Current Jones and Ginger.)

Much like Osprey "Ozzie" Lancaster of Mountain Man's Treasure, Hawk was just a side character— until Robin and Mesa's wedding reception when I saw him mooning over Terra like an obsessed puppy dog.

Which is totally not Terra's type, of course!

I can't even tell you how much fun it was to discover the smoldering bad boy vibes under Hawk's good two shoes, good boy exterior...and loved the way Terra discovered them too.

Terra and Hawk have been one of my favorite couples ever and it was hard to leave them.

Rocklyn Ryder

Are you curious to know how a bunch of old ladies playing Never Have I Ever ends up in a brawl?

The Never Have I Ever companion short is available to my newsletter subscribers.
Sign up at rocklynwrites.net

Next from the Moonshine Ridge Mountain Men

The Hart family:

Meet the Hart family, beginning with
Promises on the Mountain
Raine Hart

I could give a rat's ass about fancy coffee, but what I do like about having the new cafe open on the mountain is the curvy little thing brewing it.

The first time I set eyes on April Holloway, she looks like she could use a month of good meals and a good night's sleep.

I tell myself I'm just trying to help her out-- make sure her business takes hold here in a small mountain town where bearded men in flannel can't tell the difference between light and dark espresso roasts and don't care.

Or maybe it's the haunted look about her that I know all too well that has me wasting six dollars on a cup of coffee every morning.

All I know is that she stirs up something inside me that I never thought I'd get for myself and now I'll do anything to keep it. No matter how hard April pushes me away, I'll keep pulling her back.

Because now I know what it feels like to want to be alive.

April's fighting demons even darker than my own and I'll slay every one of them to claim my girl.

About the Author

Rocklyn prefers her romance reads to be short, cute, and dirty; low drama and a little over-the-top: extra points for growly, alpha heroes with beards.
Originally from the farms and ranches of Central California, Rocklyn grew up in the lap of the Sierra Nevada mountains. Those small towns will always be home, but Rocklyn was born to roam.
These days she spends her days exploring America's back roads in her camper trailer, writing steamy happily-ever-afters while looking for internet.
Keep in touch when you join her (mostly) weekly newsletter and never miss updates on what she has in the works-- and what's working and not in a life full of adventure and shenanigans.
Sign up by visiting Rocklyn online at https://www.rocklynwrites.net

Printed in Dunstable, United Kingdom